PENGUIN BOOKS

THE SNOW IN KUALA LUMPUR

Daryl Lim was born in Kuala Lumpur in 1984. He migrated to Sydney as a young child and grew up surreptitiously imbibing stories of his parents' homeland. His writing has appeared in *Peril* Magazine, been short-listed for a Varuna House Fellowship and is a recipient of a Writing NSW Mentorship. He loves all kinds of fiction but novels like *The Quiet American*, *On the Beach*, *The Sheltering Sky*, or anything by Kazuo Ishiguro, Cormac McCarthy and Annie Proulx (among others) seem to be the ones that linger in his psyche. *The Snow in Kuala Lumpur* is his first novel.

He currently lives in Sydney with his wife and son (in an apartment run by two sleepy cats).

T0096233

The Snow in Kuala Lumpur

Daryl Lim

PENGUIN BOOKS
An imprint of Penguin Random House

PENGUIN BOOKS

USA | Canada | UK | Ireland | Australia
New Zealand | India | South Africa | China | Southeast Asia

Penguin Books is part of the Penguin Random House group of companies
whose addresses can be found at global.penguinrandomhouse.com

Published by Penguin Random House SEA Pte Ltd
9, Changi South Street 3, Level 08-01,
Singapore 486361

First published in Penguin Books by Penguin Random House SEA 2023

Copyright © Daryl Lim 2023

ISBN 9789815058840

Typeset in Adobe Calson Pro by MAP Systems, Bangalore, India

www.penguin.sg

For Aleah & CJ

'The complexion of his mind turned from human to political. He thought no longer, "can I get on with people?" but "are they stronger than I?"'

A Passage to India

Contents

1959

One

When I was twelve, my aunt fell into one of the wells in our *kampong*.

We were down by the river when it happened, Kin Chew and I, whiling away the afternoon the way children do. I seem to recall wading through the waterweeds, trousers rolled up to the knee, flinging pebbles at the birds that lived by the water's edge when, out of nowhere, the sleepy kampong rhythm of the day was interrupted by an alarming sight. One of the village boys was racing along the opposite bank, shouting and signalling frantically in our direction. By the time he had reached us he was doubled over, out of breath.

'Your mother,' he panted.

Kin Chew and I exchanged looks.

'Whose mother?'

'Your mother lah, yours,' he wheezed, gesturing wildly at KC. 'Come quickly, come. She fell down the well.'

Sprinting back along the river, we could see a small crowd beginning to form in the distance as we made our approach. Thankfully, a group of men from the village had already managed to haul my aunt out with a rope by the time we arrived. She was crouched over in a little ball as we crashed into the scene, trembling on the wet concrete slab, surrounded by a dozen jostling, overly-solicitous legs; her thin shift was completely soaked through—clinging to her body—so that it felt almost indecent to look at her and Kin Chew was forced to avert his eyes until somebody snatched a bedsheet from a nearby clothesline to wrap his mother up.

'What happened? What happened?' our neighbours kept asking each other.

She did not appear to have been severely injured—a few scratches and an ugly graze on her shin seemed the extent of it.

'I am so careless,' my aunt replied in a small, shocked voice. 'I was drawing the bucket and slipped. I am so careless. So careless.'

I must admit I found the whole thing thrilling. Nothing as exciting had ever happened to me or anyone else in our family before, and for many days after the incident, it was all the people of the village could talk about. Prying neighbours kept asking me about the particulars of what had occurred, as if I had taken a tumble into the well myself, and for a while I enjoyed all the extra attention and gossip that attached itself to me. It was only after one of the nosier kampong ladies made a curious remark that I started thinking more about the circumstances surrounding the accident.

'There must be more to it than that,' the lady said to me. 'She just slipped? End of story? Come now, boy, you must not be so stingy with details. We all know what your aunt is like. Nothing is ever so simple with that woman.'

The comment did not bother me much at first, but the more I thought about it, the more the words began to fester in my mind. What did she mean, 'We all know what your aunt is like?' I had to admit I had never given my aunt much consideration before. What indeed was she like?

Sam Ji—that is what I called her, as she was the wife of my father's younger brother—was certainly rattled in the days immediately following her accident. Out of embarrassment or some lingering fright, she behaved as though the entire episode never occurred, which did not, to my mind, seem especially unusual; even a child knows that falling into a well is bound to be a traumatic experience. Nevertheless, I could not escape the nagging sense that there was some snide implication hidden in my neighbour's comment.

Equally puzzling to me was the way my family reacted to all this. The adults, my parents and oldest sister, seemed cagey about the incident, giving evasive or abrupt replies whenever I tried to broach the subject. Something in the way they ignored my questions set my small child's intuition on fire and I soon became determined to get to the heart of the matter for myself. I recall one night, not long after that day at the well.

I was sitting down to dinner and my sister had just finished setting the table with plates of blanched greens and preserved fried dace. Outside, the sun had dropped low beyond the river so that the kitchen was striped with the elongated shadows of the lime trees and stilted kampong houses that surrounded us. My father lit a kerosene lantern and set it on a stack of old newspapers as he came in to eat.

'Tinned fish again, is it?' he sighed.

'Don't complain in front of the children,' my mother snapped while transferring the lantern from the stacked newspapers to a hook on the wall. 'And stop leaving the lamp anywhere you like. Burn the house down one day, then you will know.'

My sister brought over a large clay pot of herbal soup wrapped in a tea towel and then started handing out bowls of rice soaked in hot lard. When the rest of us had been given a bowl, Siew Mooi prepared one for herself and sat beside the stove, fishing out leftover leaves of *gai-lan* from the wok with her chopsticks. Everybody was chattering away in Cantonese, several conversations going on at the same time when I said:

'The whole kampong is talking about how Sam Ji fell into the well.'

All at once, the table fell silent. My parents both looked up and stopped eating, their chopsticks half raised to their mouths. Sam Ji herself had just come to the low table, sitting cross-legged on the floor with everyone else. Her right leg was bandaged in a ream of stained gauze. For a moment, everyone turned to look at her, waiting to see how she would respond, but my aunt simply smiled and said:

'And what has everyone in the kampong been saying?'

I shrugged. 'Just that you were silly to fall in.'

'It was silly of me, wasn't it? I must be more careful next time.'

'Lucky you didn't hurt yourself too much,' I went on, peering at the dressing taped to her shin. 'Only a cut on your leg. Does it hurt very bad, Sam Ji?'

'No, Ah Tat. It does not hurt at all.'

'Everybody in the kampong thinks it is a great laugh. A grown adult falling into the well. Isn't it funny?'

Sam Ji smiled thinly and stroked the top of my head.

'Yes, Ah Tat. Your aunt was very silly, wasn't she? I will have to get you or Kin Chew to draw the water for me from now on. I am sure neither one of you would have been so careless.'

I don't know if it was my imagination or not, but the rest of the family seemed to be observing our exchange in a strangely intent way, sitting very still and pausing over their dinners, as if holding a collective breath.

Kin Chew, for his part, remained silent throughout the conversation, hunched next to his mother, and barely glancing up from his bowl.

'Everybody in the kampong is asking what happened,' I went on.

My parents looked at one another. Siew Mooi immediately jumped up from her spot by the stove and went around drawing all the curtains in the big room, remarking irritably, 'Why must you be such a pest, little brother? Can't you see, Sam Ji doesn't want to talk about it? Stop asking so many questions and eat your dinner.'

I turned to my aunt. 'Is that true, Sam Ji? Do you want me to stop asking questions?'

'I suppose I don't mind,' she said after a moment. 'But there isn't much to tell.'

'You see? Sam Ji doesn't mind talking about it. After all, everyone wants to know what happened. Why shouldn't she tell?'

'I'm afraid there's nothing much to tell, Ah Tat,' she said gently. 'I was silly, that's all. Simply very careless.'

'Did you slip?'

'That's right. I slipped.'

'But how did you slip?'

Kin Chew refused to look up from his bowl. I remember thinking to myself that he, of everyone at the table, should be most curious of all about precisely what had occurred that day at the well. He should have been pestering his mother for more details, right alongside me. Yet my cousin remained silent, staring impassively at his food. Sam Ji glanced down at her son for a moment and then turned her thin smile on me.

'I don't remember exactly.'

I laughed. 'You don't remember? But how can that be?'

'It all happened very fast, Ah Tat. A lot of water gets splashed around when you haul that bucket up. The concrete around the well can become quite slippery. I suppose I was leaning over a little too far and lost my footing.'

Sam Ji paused, and a faraway look came over her, as if she was recalling the event in her mind's eye.

'Next thing I knew, I'd toppled straight in.'

'You could have drowned, isn't that right, Sam Ji?'

'Yes,' she smiled. 'I was very lucky.'

'Were you scared?'

'Yes. Very scared.'

I nodded, thinking about her explanation for a while. Then I said:

'There's something I still don't understand, Sam Ji. The hole in the well is so small. I looked at it myself afterwards. Maybe a little boy or girl could have slipped inside somehow, like me or Kin Chew, but not a grown person. Everyone in the kampong is saying the same thing.'

It was at that point my mother intervened. We were always quiet whenever Ma Ma decided to speak. She raised her voice at me:

'I've heard enough, boy. If you don't learn to mind your own business, I am going to rub so much chilli in your mouth that you'll never dare move your lips again. Stop making a nuisance of yourself. I am sick of hearing about wells.'

That night, I lay awake on my bamboo mat, cocooned in mosquito netting and staring up at the dark thatches of *attap* in the ceiling. Something was awry, but I couldn't quite put my finger on what it was. In the end, I put everyone's tight-lipped furtiveness down to the fact that Sam Ji was still a little shaken by the whole experience and didn't wish to relive it. In fact, I would not have thought any further about the matter but for the odd encounter I had with Kin Chew the following day.

We were walking home along Batu Road after school and a group of our friends had just turned into one of the side-streets, leaving the two of us alone for the first time that afternoon. Kin Chew had not been laughing and joking with the rest of the group in his usual manner and when the other boys were gone, he stopped and pulled me aside. He seemed upset.

'Why were you asking all those questions?' he said.

'What questions?'

'About the well. Why did you *kacau* my mother about it last night?'

'I don't know,' I shrugged. 'I was just curious. After all, everybody in the kampong wants to know more about it.'

'Well, it's none of their business. And none of yours either.'

He turned away and set off at a brisk pace, heading down Batu Road towards the kampong. I chased after him.

'It's nothing to be upset about, KC. After all, your mother is safe now. She didn't hurt herself. It was just an accident.'

'An accident?' Kin Chew looked at me.

'Sure. Could've happened to anyone. The main thing is she is alright now, and we can all laugh about it. Isn't that so?'

'You think it was an accident.'

I frowned. 'What do you mean? Of course it was.'

'Are you stupid, Ah Tat? Don't you see? It was no accident.'

Kin Chew continued marching down the road and I found myself slowing for a moment, falling behind as I puzzled over what he meant. Cars and trucks were burring past us towards town, churning the dust into big mustard-coloured clouds. I hurried to catch up.

'Slow down, KC. What do you mean, no accident?'

He did not reply.

'What are you saying then?' I went on. 'You think your mother fell into the well on purpose?'

Still, Kin Chew refused to respond, maintaining his aggressive pace. I did my best to keep up.

'I never heard anything so ridiculous in my life,' I panted. 'She jumped down the well to cool off or something, is it? There's a whole river just outside the house for swimming, you think she prefers the well instead, har? How funny.'

'Forget it. Forget I mentioned anything. You're right, she just slipped.'

'Well of course she slipped,' I laughed, shaking my head. 'She said so herself. Sometimes lah, I don't think you got any common sense. I mean, what a thought. Jumping down a well. What for?'

When we reached the familiar clearing that marked the edge of our kampong, Kin Chew paused and shrugged off his backpack. It was dusty and hot and so he began to unbutton his white school shirt, peeling it off entirely. He wiped the sweat from his face with the shirt, leaving yellow-brown streaks all over the material, and then stuffed the shirt into his bag. I watched him, frowning.

'You shouldn't treat your uniform like that, you know. You need to take more pride in our colours.'

He strode away from me, bare-chested, the tail end of his school shirt hanging from his backpack.

'Why are you walking so fast?' I called after him. 'Slow down, Kin Chew! What's the matter with you? You're kicking up so much dust, it's getting all over my uniform lah! Kin Chew!'

Two

That was back when we all lived together off Batu Road. I can still picture it now, my childhood home. It stood on the banks of the Klang River, raised four feet off the muddy ground on wooden stilts cut from *changi* trees, the roof fashioned out of thatched attap. It had tall floor-to-ceiling shutters that could be folded on particularly humid days, and I often lay out on the balcony staring up at the empty wire birdcage that, even now, twists in the wind of my memory. The stoop out back is what I recall most fondly when I think of that house. I can picture my sister Siew Mooi as a sixteen-year-old girl, squatting on the bottommost step, pounding chillies in the mortar, or scrubbing the laundry on a washboard. The rest of the houses in the kampong were built in a similar fashion, each with an outhouse in the yard—little more than a hole in the ground with tin siding erected around it—and a common rainwater well shared between a few neighbours. The house itself was of no complicated design: two large rooms, side-by-side, separated by a narrow corridor.

My uncle lived across from us in a house that was almost identical. Growing up, members of both our families could often be found in one another's places, moving between the dwellings. Whenever my father became worn down by my mother's incessant nagging, he would escape to Sook Sook's house and the two brothers would sit on the back steps, smoking cigarettes and sipping brandy. The pair had fled China when they were scarcely more than boys and came to Malaya through Siam, drifting down the archipelago together, stopping in Kedah and Penang for short spells before finally settling in Kuala Lumpur. It was here that they found work in the tin mines. In time, they each got married and raised families. My father proved the more fruitful of the pair, siring five of us all told: Siew Mooi and the twins, followed by myself then much later, little Di Di. Sook Sook and Sam Ji were fated to have only one child. My cousin, Kin Chew, arrived the same year that I did, albeit on the other side of the Chinese New Year. This made him a rat: clever, dissolute, opportunistic, and possessor of a secret charisma. It was in stark contrast to my own sign, the boar: reliable, avaricious, and alas, immovably obstinate.

When Kin Chew and I were still quite young, my uncle was forced to flee KL under the most mysterious of circumstances. I was to discover much later that he'd run into some trouble with one of the secret societies that controlled the tin mines and I've since been told it had something to do with a large gambling debt. Almost overnight Kin Chew's father disappeared from the kampong, setting off to find work in a rubber plantation all the way over in distant Carey Island. None of us knew when, or even if, he would ever return. It was a time of great uncertainty for us all.

I remember that on the day we saw Sook Sook off at the Pasarama Kota bus depot, Kin Chew had not seemed unduly distressed. Certainly he was quiet, as we all were, milling about under that long rusty shelter on Sultan Street and mumbling our farewells, but when the bus to Port Klang finally pulled away in a hot blast of exhaust fumes, my cousin remained remarkably composed, his face unmoving, like a stone.

Over the next few years, my uncle would return to Kuala Lumpur no more than a handful of times, staying a few short days to pass on his paltry earnings before going back to Carey Island. While Kin Chew took his father's absence in his stride, Sam Ji had not coped nearly as well. The whole family noticed the changes in her. Sook Sook's wife had always been a beautiful woman, but over time her looks began to turn like a bad apple collapsing from the inside out. She ate less and slept more, emerging from long hibernations in her dark quiet house, face all flabby and grey with unrest. She seemed to simply surrender to her circumstances—something for which my mother was always witheringly contemptuous—until finally, not long after Sook Sook's flight, Sam Ji and Kin Chew were left with no alternative but to sell up their house and squeeze into ours. From that point on, nine of us lived in that tiny two-room attap dwelling, forced to renegotiate our carefully calibrated living arrangements.

My parents had believed that having Sam Ji come live with us would somehow buoy her spirits, that she might find some distraction in a house full of children or occupy herself with the thousand myriad chores that always needed attending to. It soon became apparent that this would not be the case. If anything, moving into our house seemed to make matters worse for her, and we all got to see the effects of Sam Ji's abandonment first-hand. She stopped bathing and had weeping spells, and her once lustrous hair began falling out. My sisters would find great tufts of it still attached to bits of her scalp whenever they cleaned the house as if she'd been pulling them right out of her head. My mother was the only one on our side who remained unmoved by her predicament and looking back, I suppose she had compounded Sam Ji's misery in many ways. Ma Ma would complain about the lack of space, making sure my aunt was always within earshot:

'The woman doesn't contribute. Never offers to cook or clean up or even bathe herself. Just lies in that room all day, crying over that louse of a husband.'

Once, I overheard Ma Ma trying to persuade my father into shipping Sam Ji and KC off to some distant relatives in Ipoh.

'She's my brother's wife,' Ba Ba hissed back at her in the dark. 'If I do not look after her, who will? I won't simply send the poor woman away. Where is your sympathy? And what of the boy? You know she's not capable of caring for Kin Chew by herself.'

My mother, it seemed, had little tolerance for Kin Chew either.

'The boy? Don't talk to me about that boy. We would be well rid of him too if you ask me. He's a devious little fellow, that one. You can see it in his eyes. Just like his father.'

* * *

A couple of weeks after my aunt's accident, I was up early carrying out my chores in the yard. It was quite dark, the sun still about an hour away from breaking over the kampong, and I was bringing back two pails of water from the well to help my mother with the washing. Ordinarily, she would've had her long copper basin waiting—the first batch of dirty laundry already sitting inside it, ready to be filled with water—but on this occasion she was instead sitting on the stoop, observing me closely as I came back across the yard in the dim early light. The rest of the family was still asleep inside the house and so it was just the two of us there that morning.

'Where were you yesterday?' she said.

'Yesterday? I was at school yesterday, Ma Ma.'

'I know you were at school. I mean after. After school.'

I set the pails of water down and went over to her hesitantly.

'I was down at the river watching Amin and Muhammad S. fly their kites.'

'Was Kin Chew with you?'

'KC? No.'

'You didn't see him at all? After school, I mean.'

'No, Ma Ma. He wasn't with me.'

She watched me for a moment, eyes narrowed and rubbing her hands together slowly. I stood before her and waited, arms stiffly by my sides. It took a long time for her to continue.

'It's very odd,' she said finally. 'All of yesterday I could not find Kin Chew anywhere. He's been disappearing altogether lately, have you noticed? Nobody seems to know where he goes.'

I shifted on my feet and looked around the yard uneasily. The rest of the kampong was still draped in the gloomy early light. My mother went on:

'I know how much time you spend with Kin Chew. You would know better than anyone else what he gets up to. Have you noticed anything strange with him these last few weeks?'

'Strange? I don't think so.'

'He's been acting very suspiciously. You haven't noticed anything out of the ordinary?'

'No.'

She peered at me. 'You are sure? Nothing?'

I frowned.

'Speak up, boy,' she snapped. 'I'm trying to talk to you. Are you sure there's nothing you want to tell me?'

'No, Ma Ma,' I said quickly. 'Nothing. I haven't noticed anything strange.'

She sighed and abruptly got up off the stoop, marching over to the outhouse and signalling for me to follow. She dragged the long copper basin out into the yard and together we began filling it with fresh water, going to and from the well several times. When the basin was full, she set her little footstool before it and squatted down, scrubbing the dirty laundry against the washboard with soap. She looked up at me as she was working.

'I want you to listen carefully to what I am going to tell you,' she said through gritted teeth. 'Your cousin is up to no good. I can feel it. I don't know what exactly, but I know he cannot be trusted. You are to watch him. Understood? If you notice anything unusual, no matter how trivial it seems, you are to come and tell me immediately. Do you understand what I am saying to you, Ah Tat? Anything at all.'

I nodded.

'Speak up for heaven's sake. Don't make me repeat myself.'

'Yes, Ma Ma. I understand. I will watch Kin Chew.'

'If we're not careful, that boy will bring his black fortune down on all our heads one day. You see if I am wrong. It's your father's side, all of them, degenerates and layabouts, all bringing their troubles to hatch here.'

My mother was soon muttering to herself, carried off on the long tangent of her irritation, and I watched her in silence, thrashing at the laundry as if it too had strayed onto her bad side.

'Your father is a fool if he thinks Kin Chew will turn out any different. He says I have no sympathy, no decency. Well, I say, what decency is there in allowing our family to be poisoned by the misfortunes of another? My concern is us. Our family, our children are what matter—I sweep the snow from my own doorstep, I don't concern myself with the frost on my brother's roof.'

At the time I remember thinking that it was rather strange of Ma Ma to talk of snow. After all, we lived in Malaya and nobody I knew had ever seen the stuff. It never occurred to me that snow could be a nuisance, or that it needed to be swept away. Of course, now I understand it was simply one of her aphorisms—the Chinese are fond of their sayings—but the imagery has stayed with me ever since.

'Your father's side—your Sook Sook and Sam Ji, Kin Chew even—they can all go to hell for all I care. What is it to do with us? Are you listening to me, boy?'

'Yes, Ma Ma. I am listening.'

'This is important,' she said, glaring at me. 'I want you to be wary of Kin Chew. He will bring you down with him if you get too close. Do you know what I mean when I say he will bring you down?'

'Yes, Ma Ma.'

'And what have I always told you, Ah Tat?'

'I must go up. I must make something of myself. Always, we must go up.'

She watched me for another moment, eyeing me sternly.

'Correct. We must always go up.'

Just then the sun started to come through the lime trees and Ma Ma looked across the kampong into the slowly ripening light. She returned to her scrubbing.

'Good. That's all I have to say. Go inside and help your sister with the stove. Quickly now, get to it. I don't have time for your dawdling. And don't forget what I said about your cousin. You watch him carefully, Ah Tat.'

* * *

My mother's firm admonition must have taken hold somewhere in the back of my mind because almost immediately I began noticing that Kin Chew was indeed behaving suspiciously.

Back then there was a little shophouse on Batu Road that specialized in fashioning old oriental-style clogs and every so often, KC and I were given the task of going into town to collect the wooden shavings left over on the workshop floor once the shoes had been chiselled and shaped. The proprietor was happy to oblige as it saved her the hassle of disposing of the offcuts herself. And for us, it meant a free and reliable source of kindling for the household. Whenever Kin Chew and I went down there we would sweep the blonde wooden curls and wedges into a hessian gunnysack before hauling the massive sack all the way home. On the way back we often stopped by Old Hong's sundry store for a cold drink, sweaty and covered in sawdust grit as we were, but on this occasion, Kin Chew had decided he wanted something extra for his troubles. Striding over to the counter and standing up on his toes, he called the shopkeeper over.

'Players Gold Leaf,' he demanded, slapping several twenty cent pieces on the counter. 'And don't forget the matchbook, uncle.'

Old man Hong narrowed his eyes and frowned, exchanging looks with one of his customers, another elderly gentleman who was seated opposite him. Between the two men lay a tissue-paper-thin chessboard, spotted with big wooden checks. Reluctantly, the shopkeeper placed the pack of cigarettes on the counter.

'That aunt of yours catches you smoking, you got these over at Chow Kit shops,' he said, sweeping up the pile of change. As Kin Chew reached for the Players, the old man suddenly barked, 'Wait a minute, boy. What's this?'

Picking out one of the twenty cent pieces, Ah Hong lowered his spectacles and held the coin up to the dingy light. The countenance of Queen Elizabeth had been blacked out with permanent ink.

'I'm not accepting these. Look! They're all defaced.'

Indeed, the faces on every one of the coins had been coloured over with black ink.

'It's still money, isn't it?' KC said, rolling his eyes. 'Clean them off with a rag if it's so important to you.'

'Don't get smart with me, you little rat.'

The shopkeeper's companion peered over at the half-black twenty cent pieces. He chuckled to himself:

'Let them be, Ah Hong. They're only being patriotic. *Merdeka Malaya*, isn't that right, boys?'

I recall this kind of thing happening all the time in those days. It had, after all, only been a couple of years since the country had declared its independence from the British, and little token displays of nationalism—like coins circulating with the Queen's face blacked out—were still everywhere in evidence: Robinsons Department store had started flying a giant flag over Mountbatten Road, and in all the eateries, taxicabs and barbershops of KL, radio-sets forever seemed to be playing snippets of *Negaraku* like the latest soda-pop jingle. For a time, you couldn't shop at the wet market or wait for a bus without overhearing some clever uncle's opinion on the latest newspaper editorial about the country's future. All the talk was of self-determination and destiny; of 'Malaya, reborn'. I didn't always grasp what was being discussed at the time but that didn't disqualify me from being wholly caught up in the popular mood. In many ways, it tended to be us children in fact, who were among the most enthusiastic supporters of Independence. We'd been taught songs about our new nation in class and been given the day off school for Merdeka. What wasn't to like?

In any event, it must be said that Kin Chew had never been one of those children who was stirred by the idea of Independence. Standing in Ah Hong's shop, arguing over the change, it was immediately apparent to me that KC had not vandalized those coins himself. He couldn't have cared less about Merdeka.

Outside the store, we dragged the sack of wooden shavings into the shade of a nearby lime tree and KC sat down heavily on the gunnysack, lighting a cigarette, and contemplating the burning tip.

'Since when do you smoke cigarettes?' I said.

'Since always.'

'Ma Ma is going to be mad as hell when she finds out.'

'Your mother doesn't need to know everything I get up to,' he said, sending a long thin stream of smoke my way.

Waving away the smoke, I crossed my arms and looked down at Kin Chew. He squatted on the gunnysack, puffing languidly, and I could see the smudge marks that had come off the twenty cent pieces, leaving his fingertips purple with ink. His upper lip was soon marked too, as he moved the cigarette back and forth over his mouth. I glanced up at the sun descending through the treetops.

'It's getting dark. Ma Ma warned us not to take all day.'

'Your mother doesn't scare me,' he said. 'I am not afraid of her, you know.'

'Come, Kin Chew. Hurry up. She is waiting for the wood to start the stove.'

KC shook his head and got up. He turned to me with a condescending smile.

'Go on then,' he said, giving the sack a dismissive kick. 'Pick it up and run off to your Ma Ma. Your turn to be the obedient little donkey.'

* * *

Kuala Lumpur was a place of great optimism back then. Those first few years after the inaugural Merdeka Day celebrations, all the townspeople and kampong folk were swept up in the fanfare and my father, like everyone else, had been carried away on that initial wave of excitement. Having seen for himself the great crowds pouring through the gates of the Bukit Bintang amusement park, he decided it was high time to capitalize on all that fervent enthusiasm. He took the money he had saved from years in the tin mines and purchased a pair of very expensive coin-operated machines: one was called the Strike-Bowler—with its blinking scoreboard and polished Formica platform made to imitate ten-pin bowling lanes—and the other was a Jukebox. He claimed they were all the rage in America and arranged for the machines to be placed in one of the arcades off BB Park's main thoroughfare.

The gamble did not, unfortunately, work out very well for him. After the jubilation of that first year of Merdeka died away, visitors to the amusement park started to dwindle and his machines sat in the darkened arcade, unused and ignored. Most people were still very poor at that time and Independence had not, it seemed, put any more money in their pockets.

Sometimes I would stay up late to help my father tally up the paltry returns from his gaming machines. I suspected he counted his takings late at night while the rest of the family slept to hide his embarrassment. We used to sit cross-legged on the floor before the low table, rings of light from the carbide lamp glimmering discreetly in the corner of the big room, counting out the coins. He would have his ledger and counting frame out, together with a large cloth sack from which rolls of change spilled out. On just such an occasion I remember he had been carefully scrutinizing a column of figures in his ledger when, suddenly, he shoved the book away and sat back on his hands.

'What is it, Ba Ba?'

'I must be tired,' he sighed, running a hand over his mouth. 'The numbers make no sense anymore.'

I positioned the ledger in front of me and started looking down the page. Turning to my father, I said:

'Maybe I can make sense of it. Can I try tallying up?'

Ba Ba grunted. 'Try if you like.'

I proceeded to run my finger down the column, adding up the totals and filling in my calculations with a pencil as I went along. After a few moments, the page was complete. My father was watching me and when I was done, he took the ledger and studied it for a long time.

'How did you do that so quickly?' he said.

I shrugged.

'You sure these are all correct?'

'I think so, Ba Ba.'

He continued to look at me for another moment before reaching over for the counting-frame. He adjusted his reading glasses and fiddled with the abacus, snapping the little beads across the wire rows, and jotting his own calculations down in the ledger margins. It took him a considerable amount of time but when he had finally confirmed all my answers, he removed his spectacles and sat back.

'You didn't use the counting-frame,' he said.

'No.'

'And you worked all that out in your head just now.'

I nodded.

He lit a cigarette and grunted, the thin tendrils of smoke drifting slowly across his face:

'I suppose they are teaching you well enough at that Methodist school. Your mother tells me you are doing well.'

'I think so, Ba Ba.'

'That's good, Ah Tat. You must keep up the effort. But always remember, classwork is not the answer to everything.' He considered something for a moment before going on, 'Come, Ah Tat. Let me show you what I mean. Here, take a look at this.'

He indicated one of the piles of coins on the table.

'That is last week's earnings from the Ten-Strike machine. And the pile next to it is from the Jukebox. Count it for me.'

I did what I was told and again, my father seemed impressed.

'Did you notice anything?' he said.

'The takings don't match up with the counters on the machines.'

'That's right, Ah Tat. The machines have been coming up short lately. Every week now for the last month, the totals have been incorrect. Today's count is the worst yet. There's not even eleven dollars here when there should be more than sixteen. Do you see?'

'Yes, I see.'

'Not only this machine but the Jukebox as well. Every week, short three or four dollars. Why do you think that is, Ah Tat?'

I shrugged. 'Maybe the counter on the machine is broken.'

'A broken counter? On both machines? No, boy, I don't think so. You must use your head properly. Think. Why do you think the totals are not matching up to the counters?'

I thought for a moment.

'I don't know, Ba Ba.'

'They don't match up because someone is stealing from my machines.'

I looked back down at the ledger. 'Stealing?'

'That's right, boy. Stealing. Like I said before, schoolwork is not the answer to everything. No matter how good your arithmetic, it won't help me find the culprit, will it?'

'I guess not.'

My father then reached across the table and picked out a roll of twenty cent pieces from the cloth bag. He tore open the paper sleeve and spilled the coins out onto the table. I watched him.

'Pay attention now,' he said. 'I will show you what you cannot learn from all your schoolbooks,'

He started blacking out the face of Queen Elizabeth on each of the coins, one after another, with a permanent marker.

'What are you doing?'

'What do you think? A thief can catch himself, is it? We will put these coins back into the machine and follow the trail. See whose hands come up dirty.'

I stared at the half-black coins. My father looked at me and shook his head, smiling to himself.

'It's as I said. They don't teach you everything over at that Methodist school.'

* * *

When my mother found out Kin Chew had been stealing from the BB Park machines, she reacted by giving him the most ferocious beating any of us had ever witnessed. Unable to draw tears from Kin Chew with the thin rattan cane she reserved for punishment, Ma Ma lost all control and took up a wooden clog instead. She forced Kin Chew's hand onto the table and repeatedly hammered the heel of the clog against his knuckles. Still, KC had refused to cry out. I remember Sam Ji sitting on her heels in the corner of the house as the whole thing unfolded. She was rocking back and forth with her hands clamped over her mouth, eyes screwed shut. Eventually, my father was forced to intervene.

'Enough! That's enough. The boy's learned his lesson.'

My mother backed away shaking, looking down at Kin Chew with an almost dazed expression. Everybody in the house had gone silent, stunned by her sudden vehemence, and Ma Ma too finally seemed to recall herself, dropping the clog onto the floor where it landed with a dull flat thud. Far from being creased up in agony, I saw the briefest flash of something unexpected on Kin Chew's face. It was a look close to triumph.

It was later that night, or even in the very early hours of the following day that I remember waking up with a jolt to the sound of an eerie scratching coming faintly from somewhere within the house. I sat up on my bamboo mat, its thin slats damp with sweat, and looked about the room. On one side of me drowsed my baby brother, belly down in his cot, sucking on an old rag, and in the other corner lay Sam Ji. Kin Chew was wrapped in her arms. My cousin had fallen asleep on the floor with his hand resting in a kitchen pan filled with water and menthol. There was no movement in the room and yet I could still hear a strange scratching noise coming from somewhere inside the house. I got up and crept out to the corridor. There, by the back stoop, crouched before the iron stove in utter darkness was my mother, feverishly scrubbing away at the inside of its soot-blackened hatch door.

* * *

The next day I came across Kin Chew sitting on his own on the edge of the riverbank. He was squatting by the shallow water with his palm buried in

the cool muddy slop, absently watching the stream run over his wrist. I slid
down the bank to the water's edge to join him.

'Does it still hurt?' I said.

He pulled his hand out of the mud, rinsing it off in the slow-moving
water, and then held it up to his face.

'No. Doesn't hurt.'

'Are you sure? It looks all swollen. Maybe it's broken.'

Kin Chew flexed his fingers tentatively and grimaced before pushing
his hand back under the muddy soil. He shook his head.

'No. Doesn't hurt at all.'

I got down on the ground and removed my shoes, sitting beside him
to stretch my legs. I put my feet in the rivulet, amongst the shoots and
small pools of water, letting the thin stream riffle over my toes. I frowned,
looking across at KC.

'Ma Ma told me to tell you that Siew Mooi will take you the medical
hall in town later today. She said you better get the yee-sung to have a
proper look.'

Kin Chew frowned. 'I'm not going to the medical hall.'

'But Ma Ma said you better go.'

'I am not going lah, I don't care what your mother got to say about it.'

I was taken aback by the manner of his reply and simply nodded,
turning away to look down the bank. After a while, I smiled half-heartedly
at Kin Chew.

'She really blew her top, didn't she? I never seen her get so mad before.
I was afraid for you.'

'I wasn't.'

'I wonder how she found out. That you were stealing from the
machines, I mean.'

KC looked at me.

'Well, somebody must have told her,' he said.

'Right.' I nodded slowly to myself. 'Somebody must have told her.
I wonder who.'

On the opposite bank, an elderly woman appeared between the trees
and tossed a basket of rotting vegetables out into the river. A stray dog
padded along after to investigate. Refuse was strewn all along the bank
and the air around the litter was shivering with black flies. Kin Chew was
looking at me.

'Yeah,' he said quietly. 'I wonder who.'

1960

Three

The monsoons were late the following year. As March shaded into April, the downpours that so reliably flashed through hot KL afternoons in previous years had, even by Ching Ming, failed to materialize with any kind of regularity. Days passed without relief and soon everyone was commenting on the humidity. The odd weather did mean however that the children of the kampong continued to take their kites down to the river. I often sat under the lime trees to watch the village boys race knee-deep through those tracts of wild grass, the tails of their fighting *patang* trailing after them. A giddy thrill would always rise inside of me whenever I saw one of their kites rapidly ascend into the sky, circling on its invisible tether in the overcast evening light, hovering and swooping unpredictably so that it looked from afar like some fantastical predator bird stalking the tiny shouting figures below.

We used to watch them together, Kin Chew and I, but lately he seemed to have lost all interest in kite-flying. I had noticed, in fact, that he had lost interest in many of his favourite pastimes: playing cards and swimming in the river, or stick-fighting on the outskirts of the kampong. My cousin claimed to have simply outgrown such childish games, but I soon formed the impression that KC was deliberately avoiding me for some reason. To make matters worse, his sudden coldness toward me occurred around the same time that I was becoming aware of just how deep the distrust between the two sides of our family truly ran. I was to learn the extent of it when Sam Ji approached me one day, on an afternoon when everyone else was out of the house.

23

'What are you doing there, Ah Tat?' she said. 'Playing mechanic?'

I was in the big room dismantling some old parts of my father's Ten-Strike bowling machine, trying to figure out how the contraption worked, and looked up at my aunt as she came into the room.

'I am fixing these old fuses,' I replied. 'Ba Ba thinks they're broken but I think they only need some new wire.'

'How clever of you, Ah Tat. Who taught you to do that?'

'Nobody. I taught myself.'

She watched as I tinkered with the fuses for a moment before shuffling closer to me. There seemed to be something tentative in her manner.

'Ah Tat, I thought we could have a little talk before the others get home. Just a little talk, between the two of us. What do you say to that? Will you put away your toys and spare a moment for your Sam Ji? It's very important.'

'They're not toys,' I frowned. 'They're fuses.'

'Oh yes, of course. I'm sorry, darling. Will you put away your fuses?'

I unwound some copper wire from a new spool and continued working.

'It's very important, Ah Tat. A matter for adults. Do you think you are old enough to discuss important adult matters with your Sam Ji?'

'Adult matters?' I looked up at her. 'Of course I'm old enough. What is it, Sam Ji? Tell me.'

I put the fuses to one side and waited for my aunt to continue but having started, she suddenly appeared at a loss as to how to proceed. She kept glancing out the window onto the pathway leading up to the house as if afraid someone would interrupt us at any moment. Finally, she went on:

'I need you to keep something for me. It's very precious, so you must make sure you take good care of it. Would you do that for Sam Ji?'

'What is it?'

'It's very precious to me,' she said, withdrawing a little bundle that had been concealed in the waistband of her trousers. It was wrapped in a red silk handkerchief. 'You must promise to keep it safe, Ah Tat. Here, look.'

Before handing it over she cast another furtive glance out the window. Then, kneeling beside me, she carefully laid the bundle between us and unfolded the silk handkerchief. Inside there were two pieces of jade: one bangle and the other a hairpiece, together with a thin gold wristwatch and some other trinkets.

'Your Sook Sook gave these to me for our wedding,' she smiled. 'I've kept them all these years.'

I picked up the watch and studied it, tapping the face and then holding it up to my ear. It no longer worked and immediately, something inside of me yearned to repair it. I stared at the rest of the jewellery.

'You want me to keep these for you?'

'That's right, Ah Tat. But you must hide them, that's the most important thing. Only you can know where they're kept. Nobody else.'

'Me?' I looked up at my aunt. 'Why me?'

'Because I trust you.'

'You want me to hide your jewellery? Who are you hiding it from? I don't understand.'

She paused for a moment before proceeding. 'You're almost an adult now, aren't you? We can discuss adult matters, can't we, Ah Tat?'

'Yes, Sam Ji.'

'Yes?'

'Yes, yes. We can discuss. I am old enough. What is it?'

'Well,' she sighed. 'As you know, your Sook Sook has been over in Carey Island for many years now. And every month he sends the family a little money, so we can all get by. That money is very important. We all rely on that money, you understand? But recently there has been a problem on the plantation, and it seems your uncle won't be able to send anything home this month. Maybe not for many months. I am afraid things will become very difficult for the family soon. The grocery bill at Ah Hong's shop is getting bigger all the time and the old man won't give us credit forever. Your mother's already gone down there a couple of times to try and reason with him.'

I frowned worriedly. 'Sook Sook didn't send any money? Ma Ma won't be happy.'

'That's exactly right, Ah Tat. Your mother will be very upset.'

'But what does that have to do with this jewellery?'

'Well, your Ma Ma will be expecting to get some money from me this week. She's counting on it. And that's only fair, I suppose, but you see Ah Tat, I don't have any money. Sook Sook has nothing to send me. In fact, this jewellery is all I have in the world. Do you understand now, why it must be hidden?'

I thought for a moment, staring at the gold wristwatch and pieces of jade.

'Because Ma Ma will sell your jewellery if she finds it,' I said.

Sam Ji smiled sadly at me.

'You understand adult things after all. I've kept these little trinkets a secret for as long as I could but your mother searches my little corner of the room whenever she cleans the house. It will only be a matter of time before she finds them. That's why you must keep them safe for me.'

I nodded quietly.

'You mustn't think me selfish, Ah Tat,' she continued. 'I don't want to keep this jewellery for myself. It's Kin Chew that I am thinking of. When he leaves home one day, I want to make sure I can give him something to start his life with. I have so little to offer but I'm afraid your Ma Ma wouldn't understand a thing like that. Do you see what I'm saying?'

'I think so.'

'You do?'

'Yes, Sam Ji. I understand.'

'Oh, Ah Tat, I am so relieved. I was hoping you would hide the jewellery with the rest of your belongings. If you keep it all neatly packed away, your Ma Ma will have no reason to go through any of your things.'

Once again, Sam Ji glanced quickly out the window.

'But we must hurry. Your mother will be home any minute now.'

I folded the red handkerchief over the wristwatch and jade pieces and then tucked the bundle away with my set of screwdrivers. Sam Ji watched as I did this, and when I looked up at her again, I thought I could see little tears starting to form in her eyes. She quickly blinked them away and said:

'You're a good boy, Ah Tat. But remember, you mustn't tell anyone. That's the most important thing. Your mother especially.'

'I know.'

'Not even Kin Chew can know.'

I shook my head. 'No, I wouldn't tell Kin Chew. If he found your jewellery, he might try and sell it all himself. For cigarettes, or something stupid like that.'

'I am afraid that's quite possible,' she sighed. 'He's been so difficult lately. I mean, imagine. Stealing from your father's arcade machines. I have no idea what's gotten into him.'

She looked down at her lap, staring at her pale delicate hands. Now that her red silk bundle was safely tucked away, she seemed to relax, though there still appeared to be something troubling her. She turned to me after a moment.

'The two of you spend so much time together. You might be able to give me a better idea of what's going on.'

'Going on?'

'Well, I suppose I want to know why Kin Chew has been acting so,' and she paused for a moment. 'So strangely.'

'Strangely? How do you mean, strangely?'

'He just hasn't been the same lately. I can't put my finger on what it is. Your sisters have noticed it as well. The way he acts sometimes. It makes me worry.'

I remember waiting for her to continue. From the look on her face, it appeared as though she was going to say something further but instead fell silent, lost in her own thoughts. Suddenly, she snapped back to attention and stared at me as though realizing I was still sitting there before her. She smiled and patted the back of my head affectionately.

'Don't pay any attention to me, Ah Tat. It is a mother's duty to worry. That is all this is.'

'He doesn't like to play with me anymore,' I said quickly.

'He doesn't?'

I shook my head. 'He stopped coming down to the river to watch the kites. And he doesn't even eat with me at school now. He used to like to fence—I pretended to be Hang Tuah and he would be Hang Jebat, leading the rebels—but now he says he's too old for any of that.'

'So what does he do?'

'Nothing. Just sits on his own all day.'

I picked up the set of fuses and began fiddling with the parts once more. My aunt became quiet, vacantly observing me at work. When she eventually spoke again, her voice was low and grave.

'Tell me, Ah Tat. Do you ever get frightened around him?'

'Frightened? Of Kin Chew?'

'Has he ever done anything to scare you? Anything to make you feel afraid?'

I stared back at my aunt.

'I know the two of you get into fistfights sometimes. All boys do, I know. But he's never really hurt you before, has he, Ah Tat? I mean really tried to hurt you?'

'Hurt me?'

I was about to say something further when she hastily waved the question away as if regretting having asked it in the first place. She got up and went over to the stove and brought me a tea towel to rub the machine oil from my hands.

'No, of course not,' she said. 'Forget I mentioned anything. He would never hurt you. He's still a good boy. A good boy, just like you.'

'A good boy? He's not a good boy. He's bad all the time.'

'Oh no, you must not say things like that, Ah Tat. That's your mother talking. He's a good boy, he really is. In his own way.'

I shrugged. 'If you say so,'

'Try to understand. When your Sook Sook left, I thought that coming here to live with the rest of the family would help him. I thought your mother's discipline might straighten him out. Now I am starting to see it's only made things worse.'

She paused and looked at me for a moment.

'You must watch over him, Ah Tat. Make sure he doesn't stray too far from the correct path.'

I nodded silently, preoccupied once more with my fuses.

'His father is all the way over in Carey Island now and well, after you boys turn a certain age, a mother can only do so much. You will watch over him, won't you? For his own good. He has nobody else to show him the way.'

'Yes, yes, Sam Ji. I will look after him. Don't worry lah.'

My aunt watched as I continued tinkering away, unwinding the old, singed wires and clipping lengths from a new spool. She stopped me abruptly, gripping my hands so tightly that it was almost painful.

'You two are practically brothers. Don't ever forget that. You must always look out for one another. Nothing could be more important.'

She had spoken in an uncharacteristically firm way, as I'd never heard before or since.

'Promise me now,' she said.

I nodded quietly, returning her serious expression.

'Don't worry, Sam Ji.'

'Promise me. I want to hear you say it.'

'I will. I'll look after him. I promise.'

* * *

I suppose I did not heed my aunt's words as carefully as I should have. Despite my promise, I failed to watch over Kin Chew closely enough and looking back, I now realize it was in those early years that the first signs had started to appear. What was to take place in the following months would show me just how far KC and I had drifted apart by then, and the increasingly dark thoughts he must have been having; thoughts of which I had only the faintest inkling. Perhaps if I had intervened back then, when we were still very young, things could have been different.

In any case, it was precisely because Kin Chew and I were spending less time together that I was, in a way, fated to meet someone who would prove to have an inexplicably tenacious influence on me in the years to come. Had I been playing with KC like we used to, then it is highly likely I would simply have ignored the lonely Malay boy who was wandering around the outskirts of the kampong that day.

I remember I was out by the river, gazing up at the kites circling the pink evening light when one by one, the village children started reeling in their patang to go home. In the distance, the evening call-to-prayer could be heard echoing from the mosque, and I had decided to head home myself when, on the opposite bank, I spotted a lone figure scurrying about the half-light in an aimless, panicked fashion.

Making my way closer, I realized it just so happened to be one of the Malay boys who had recently joined our class at the Methodist Boys School. There were only a handful of Muslims who were enrolled in MBS at that time, and they tended to stand out amongst the Chinese cohort like sore brown thumbs, and so, though we'd never actually spoken before, I had recognized him immediately. I stood on my side of the river and continued to observe his odd behaviour. He was frantically running up and down the bank, pausing every so often to peer into the distance, before scurrying about once again. It was like watching a twitchy field mouse. Finally, I called out to him:

'You there! What's the matter?'

The boy stopped and squinted across the distance at me. I waved at him and indicated the makeshift bridge that was located slightly downstream. It was the upturned hull of an old *sampan* that spanned the narrowest part of the river, its planks weather-rotted and grown into the terrain over many years of use. The small dark figure trotted over to the old bridge, thumping hurriedly across it.

'I know your face,' he said as he reached me. 'You go to my school.'

'Yeah lah, we got Civics together with Reverend Healey. What's the matter? You look lost.'

The boy grinned sheepishly at me.

'It is true. I'm lost.'

'Not from around here, are you?'

'No, I am not from here. I only just moved to Kuala Lumpur at the beginning of the year.' He looked around, scratching the top of his head. 'Problem is lah, I forgot the way to Kampong Baru.'

'Kampong Baru?' I pointed to the silhouette of the minaret on the horizon. 'Just follow the mosque. It's the next kampong over.'

'That way?'

'Just follow the mosque. When you come to Batu Road, cross over at the bicycle shop and keep going. Kampong Baru is on the other side. Cannot miss it.'

He frowned and looked up at the sky.

'It's getting dark,' he said. 'You think I can make it back before nighttime?'

'If you hurry.'

The boy stared in the direction in which I had pointed but made no move to leave. I noticed every now and then he would glance anxiously over his shoulder. After a moment, he said:

'I was out here watching the kites.'

I smiled. 'Me too. I like to watch them as well.'

'I must have lost track of time,' he murmured. 'I only just now realized how late it is, after I heard the call-to-prayer.' He looked into the evening sky once again with a miserable expression. 'It's so late now.'

A thick grove of banana trees was just behind him, sprouting from the side of the dirt track, and he kept glancing over his shoulder at the ragged shadowy shapes formed by the plants. Still, he made no move to go.

'What is it?' I said.

'Nothing. It is just that it's so dark already. I will not make it back to Kampong Baru before night.'

'There is still some sun left. You can if you hurry.'

The boy frowned.

'What about ghosts?' he said. 'Do ghosts live here?'

'What?'

'Ghosts. You are local, you must know. Like I said, I am new to town so I got no idea if this is a ghost area or not.'

'Ghosts?' I said, smiling. 'You mean like *pontianak*?'

He looked at me, eyes widening slightly. 'You seen them before, have you? Pontianak? Here?'

'Are you joking or what?'

'They like to hide in the banana trees,' he said, spinning around and eyeing the dark grove. 'Got to have eyes in the back of your head. Are you sure you never seen ghosts around here?'

I laughed. 'No.'

'No, of course not. Ghosts don't live in big towns like Kuala Lumpur. There are too many people around for them to show themselves.'

'There's no such thing as ghosts.'

He furrowed his brow. 'You townsfolk always say that. But there was a ghost where I used to live, in my old village. She was always looking for young boys. I saw her once.'

'You saw a ghost.'

'I saw.'

'With your own eyes?'

'Not my own eyes exactly. But a friend of mine saw. He told me he was fishing in the river, the Langat River behind my old village, when out of nowhere she came flying out the jungle. Flying lah! Her toes never even touching the *lalang*. She chased him all the way back to his house.'

'There's no such thing as ghosts, my friend. Don't worry.'

'There's too many people in KL for them to show themselves,' he repeated quietly to himself. 'All the traffic and streetlights from town would scare them away. Isn't that so?'

I nodded, smiling. 'Sure.'

'Wait, where are you going? You're not heading home now, are you? Right now?'

'Yeah lah, I'm off.'

'Can we walk together?'

I thumbed back in the opposite direction. 'My kampong is that way.'

The boy's face dropped.

'Don't look so scared,' I laughed. 'Just follow this track out to Batu Road and then cross over and keep going. You will reach Kampong Baru in no time.'

We stood around the riverbank for a while longer and eventually I made another move to leave, but as I stepped away, this strange dark boy began following me. I walked a little way off and still the boy hovered nearby, keeping me within sight.

'What are you doing?' I said. 'Planning to come all the way back to my house, are you?'

'I don't know. Maybe.'

I looked out over the kampong. The sun had disappeared behind the attap houses, and a warm wind started to sweep down past the river. The banana trees along the bank were beginning to whisper and sway ponderously and I could see him watching the sinister shapes with barely concealed dread. He hadn't brought a flashlight with him.

'Ayah,' I sighed. 'Alright. I will walk back with you. But only up until Batu Road.'

He looked at me. 'Batu Road?'

'Only until Batu Road. There are streetlights on Batu Road. But then I got to get home. My mother will get mad as hell if I'm not back in time to help with dinner.'

The boy nodded and fell in behind me.

We walked together through the kampong with the *limau* trees releasing their delicate white petals across our path, like cigarette ash drifting in the breeze. Warm light was glowing in the windows of the attap houses as people turned up their kerosene lamps. I could hear the garbled sounds of radio programs floating from their doorways.

'I am Kin Tat, by the way. Lim Kin Tat. Everyone just calls me Ah Tat.'

'I'm Hasan.'

I nodded. 'Yes, I know.'

The boy had been distractedly checking over his shoulder but paused to look at me.

'You know my name?'

'Everybody at Methodist Boys knows your name.'

'They do?'

'You're new, right? Hard not to notice when someone new shows up to class. Plus, you're the only Malay in our form. The rest of us is Chinese, in case you're blind.'

He nodded slowly, continuing in silence. After a long pause, he turned to me with a questioning look, as if a thought had just occurred to him.

'Do they talk about me, the other boys?'

I shrugged. 'A little, I guess.'

'What do they say?'

'They say you're a real *jakun*,' I grinned. 'A jungle boy from some faraway place nobody ever heard of. Never even seen a traffic light until you shifted over to town recently. Is it true?'

He frowned. 'I am no jakun.'

'But it's true you're from far away.'

'I suppose it is true. My family's in Mimpi. They all live there. Everyone except me, that is. I got a scholarship to a proper English school so that's how come they sent me here. To study at MBS.'

'Mimpi? Never heard of it. Out near Kajang, is it?'

'Past Kajang even. Closer to Seramban.'

I gave a low whistle. '*Alamak*, that sure sounds like you're a jakun to me.'

We walked across the grounds until we had left the smell of cooking behind us; the everyday domestic noises of the village, along with its gentle reassuring lamplight, soon faded with it. The sun had set completely by this time, and we continued in near total darkness. I knew the well-worn tracks of the kampong in my bones and had not needed a flashlight or lantern for many years, but I could sense Hasan had become more agitated than ever, blindly peering into the black line of twisted raintrees that attended our path, shrinking at the slightest sound or movement from within. At the darkest point along the way he clung to my hand like a small child.

Finally, as we were climbing the steep bank that marked the edge of the kampong, the sounds of light traffic began to fill the air. Hasan visibly relaxed. We came out through a clearing in the trees and walked towards Batu Road. A steady stream of cars and lorries rumbled across our view, heading in and out of town. Old men were squatting by roadside tea stalls, smoking cigarettes, and fanning themselves in the last of the day's heat. The sooty orange sodium lamps started to flicker on above them. I pointed across the main street to a row of dilapidated shophouses.

'You know the way from here, right? Just go down the road until you get to the bicycle shop. Do you see it? Then turn off and keep going. You will get to Kampong Baru in no time.'

'You're not coming with me?'

'I told you, I've got to get home. Just turn off at the bicycle shop and keep going.'

He looked at me uncertainly.

'Hurry up,' I laughed. 'Go on lah, it is only going to get darker. There is no such thing as ghosts anyway.'

I watched as Hasan made his way across Batu Road. Once he reached the bicycle shop, he stopped to look back at me. There were no longer any streetlights beyond that point, and he stood in the last dim circle of lamplight for a long time. Finally, just as I thought he would lose his nerve and come skulking back across the road toward me, the boy made a sudden dash into the dark. Shaking my head, I turned to walk home. I couldn't help but smile to myself, picturing him sprinting all the way back to Kampong Baru, as fast as his short legs would carry him.

Four

It was around this time we received a letter from Carey Island with some thrilling—and altogether unexpected—news. Kin Chew's father had written to tell us that the rubber estate had promoted him to assistant foreman. He would now spend much of his time in the office helping with the tappers' paperwork and company book-keeping, or overseeing the women in the processing sheds, the upshot of which was an end to years of backbreaking labour in the rubber-tree fields. More importantly, the new position had come with a significant raise. Sook Sook was aware of the family's money troubles and went on to assure us that his backpay would be more than sufficient to settle the bill at the provisions shop. In fact, he didn't anticipate having to worry about grocery bills ever again. He was coming back to KL to celebrate, his first visit in more than two years, and we were to expect him early the following month on the late bus from Port Klang.

And so, on the morning of the first of November my father chose our plumpest chicken and went to see Uncle Teng, a particularly helpful neighbour of ours who had all the equipment for butchering in his yard. Kin Chew and I went along to assist, stacking the firepit with kindling and filling the heavy black iron cauldron with fresh water from the well. When it came time to slaughter the chicken, my father bound its feet together tightly in his fist and flipped it upside down in one smooth motion. A large conical funnel was bolted to the edge of a workbench, and he lowered the bird headfirst through the metal cone, exposing its head at the narrow end, before slitting its throat in an assured practiced way. From the open neck, blood pooled into an empty drum positioned underneath, and for a moment it appeared as though the bird would quietly surrender to its fate, but then the sound of its claws scraping against the metal siding became increasingly desperate, and the animal proceeded to kick and thrash about for what seemed longer than possible. I started to cry. Uncle Teng came and put his arm around me.

'Don't worry, child,' he laughed. 'Don't worry. It's all over.'

'She's still alive!'

'No, it is dead now. It's gone. You have to be brave, Ah Tat. Like your cousin, see how brave he is.'

Looking up, I saw that KC was breathlessly watching the last protracted flutter of the animal, his eyes wide and bright with excitement. He looked almost giddy.

Afterwards, the carcass was put into the boiling cauldron to loosen up its feathers and then fished out and slapped onto the bench, steaming off the wooden block. My father stripped the quills with a short, curved blade so that by the end, the bird was pale and pink-white, responding flabbily in a disturbing way when touched, as though the flesh had come from something quite human. He opened the chicken up the middle, yanking out the gizzard and the guts and the heart and all the small purple organs. Then he dumped the innards into the drum together with the drained blood and gave them to Ah Teng.

'Your wife makes better black curd than mine,' he said. 'But I'll keep the feet.'

When we got home, the twins were in the big room scrubbing the floorboards on their hands and knees. The yard had been swept and Siew Mooi was sent to the bakery on Batu Road for sweets and a tin of biscuits. Sticks of incense were lit and placed on the mantel in the big room and my mother went about preparing the chicken, cleaving it up and frying the portions in sesame oil and garlic and then steaming it all in a large clay pot with rice wine and ginger and black wood ear fungus.

In the afternoon, Kin Chew and I followed my father out to the truck. We piled into the back seat and drove into town, to the Pasarama Kota transport depot on Sultan Street, and waited for the bus from Port Klang to arrive.

* * *

I hardly recognized Sook Sook when he stepped off the bus. He looked darker than I remembered, much older and worn down. He had with him surprisingly little: a limp, half-empty duffel which he lay across his lap on the drive home, and a paper bag containing two bottles of brandy that clinked constantly at his feet as the truck trundled up Batu Road. He chain-smoked clove cigarettes, and the pungent odour filled the cabin of the truck; they had the same sweetly acrid odour that seemed to leech out of his very skin.

'The boys are tall suddenly,' he said.

My father nodded. 'They're at that age. How is the plantation?'

'The plantation? Ah, not so good. Merdeka's changed everything. The rumour going around the estate is the company wants out of Malaya.'

Kin Chew and I sat quietly in the back, letting the men talk.

'They're thinking of packing up? That bad, is it?'

'Could be. The workers aren't helping the situation. Last month, a group of tappers went to the foreman and demanded we all demonstrate together. It's only a few agitators now, but every week more and more get bolder.'

My father frowned. 'Will you still have work?'

'Things have settled for now. The whites are anxious to keep the peace.'

My uncle turned around and grinned at the two of us in the back seat. He said to Kin Chew:

'What's the matter, boy? Got nothing to say to your own father after all this time?'

Kin Chew shrugged, looking out the window of the truck.

'What's to say?' he mumbled.

'You've grown tall.'

KC continued to stare silently out the window, refusing to make eye contact. Sook Sook turned to the driver's side and frowned at my father.

'What's the matter with him?'

'Nothing's the matter.' I could see my father's knotted brow in the reflection of the rear-view mirror looking back at us. 'He's just too excited to talk. Isn't that right, Kin Chew?'

When we got home, Sam Ji was waiting outside the house. We pulled over in the truck and Sook Sook got out and nodded to her and handed her his bags.

'Everybody's waiting for you inside,' she said. 'Where should I put your things?'

My uncle looked at his wife.

'I'll put them in my room then,' she said. 'Are you hungry? There's chicken.'

* * *

That first night, my father took Sook Sook to Ah Teng's place, and the two brothers did not return until dawn of the following day. They stumbled up the stoop together, their conversation musical and nostalgic, reeking of tobacco and cherry brandy. In the afternoon, my uncle crawled out of bed and went to lie in the hammock outside the house, sobering up in the sun. That was the pattern for much of his stay with us. Most nights he would head into town to gamble and get drunk, followed by a day spent dozing under the lime trees.

Occasionally though, Sook Sook was obliged to forgo the mahjong table to catch up on some of the work he'd brought back with him from the plantation. On those nights he would seek me out to help with his company's book-keeping. My father had told him how well I was doing in school, with mathematics and elementary accounting, so every now and then we would sit together in the dirty light of the carbide lamp with his work papers spread out on the low table before us. Sook Sook would open his ledger and have me calculate the rubber tappers' EPF payments, which I would then pencil into the margins.

'I wish I could take you back to the plantation with me,' he would smile, giving my ear a playful twist. 'Imagine the time you'd save.'

As it turned out, not everyone was so pleased that I was spending so much time with my uncle. About a week into Sook Sook's stay with us, my father had to take me aside for a stern dressing down.

'Why are you so greedy with your Sook Sook's time? He's only in town a short while. What are you doing?'

'Ba Ba?'

'Stop being so selfish, Ah Tat. It's very important for a boy to be close with his father. You must not get in the way all the time.'

What Ba Ba did not understand was that KC wasn't interested in bonding with his father. Kin Chew himself had told me as much, going as far as to instruct me to deflect as much of Sook Sook's attention away from him as possible. He said he was done with the old man. The comment might have surprised me but for the conversation I'd overheard take place between them the night before. As I recall, it was the middle of the night and I had been awakened by low voices coming from the back stoop, just outside the house.

'It's late,' Sook Sook was whispering. 'What are you doing up, Kin Chew?'

'I smelled cigarettes. I came to smoke.'

'I didn't know you smoked,' came a chuckle. 'Here, try one of mine. All the tappers in the plantation smoke these. Gudam Garang, clove cigarettes. What do you think?'

After a pause, KC's voice came back, 'Not bad. I used to smoke Players before. But now I switched to Viceroy. Steve McQueen smokes Viceroy brand. *Thinking man's filter, smoking man's taste.*'

'Say what?'

'Steve McQueen lah. The cowboy.'

The soft glow of a kerosene lantern was filtering into the house from outside. Stirring on my bamboo mat, I sat up and peered through a gap in the wooden planks of the room. Sook Sook was squatting on the back steps underneath the sooty light of the lantern.

'Sounds like your English is getting good,' he said. 'What is that you said just now? Cow? Boy?'

'Never mind. I'll just talk Chinese.'

Watching from the room, I couldn't quite make out where KC was standing, with only the occasional puff of smoke hinting at his place in the shadows. Sook Sook was staring at his son. He said:

'When I saw you last, you were only just past my waist. Now look at you. Tall enough to look me in the eye and smoking cigarettes. Remind me again, how old are you now?'

'Thirteen, almost.'

'I was thirteen when I came to Malaya with Dai Bak. All the way from China in a rickety old junk. Did you know that?'

'I know.'

'Dai Bak is good to us. He is good to you.'

'I know.'

'Bak Neung as well. She feeds you and washes your clothes. It's not easy for your aunt to take care of so many. Don't forget, she has her own children to worry about. You should show her more respect.'

Kin Chew remained hidden in the creaking, chirping night.

'She tells me you've been causing her a lot of trouble lately. Skipping classes and quarrelling with the other boys. She told me the headmaster caned you in front of the entire assembly not long ago.'

There was no reply.

'She told me you stole money from your uncle's machines. Is it true?'

By the chicken coop, I could see a tiny orange coal flaring briefly in the dark before skipping off in a scatter of sparks.

'Don't flick your butts everywhere, boy. You don't know how hard your aunt works to keep the place clean. And listen, I shouldn't have to tell you not to steal from the family. It's like taking food out of your own mouth. If you must steal, then steal from one of the boys at school. That way you're really getting something for your trouble. True?'

'True.'

Sook Sook cleared his throat, watching his son. 'Will you last long in that Methodist school?'

'They're very strict. The headmaster doesn't like me.'

'You should quit then. Go to work and start bringing home some money instead. Your aunt has been complaining she can't keep up with the bills. She thinks I should take you back to Carey Island with me. Learn to tap rubber. What do you say to that?'

'No, I want to stay in school.'

'School isn't for everyone, Kin Chew. It's not likely you'll become an accountant one day, is it? Or a doctor?'

'I guess not.'

'Think of the years you will waste in class. You're almost a grown man now, it's time to ask yourself some hard questions. Thirteen is no longer a child.'

I watched my uncle through a slit in the wall. He was looking down at his own hands in the muted yellow lamplight, scrutinizing the thickly callused palms and turning his mangled fingers over to consider all the knobs and scars and angry protuberances.

'I was barely thirteen when I started working tin,' he went on. 'At least you don't have to be on the dredge. Be thankful for that much.'

Kin Chew emerged from the dark, stepping directly into the light for the first time. He said:

'You want I should have hands like yours one day, is it?'

Sook Sook gave a little chuckle.

'Listen,' he said. 'People like you and me, we never rise so high up in this world. Better you learn it now from your old man than lie to yourself your whole life. Know your place. Believe me, boy, it is not so painful this way.'

'What if I'm not?'

'Not what?'

'Not like you.'

My uncle sighed. 'You're more like me than you'll ever know, Kin Chew.'

* * *

It was during one of those nights I was helping my uncle with his book-keeping that I first noticed the peculiar trend in the list of names he kept in the ledger from the rubber estate.

'Sook Sook,' I said. 'What is P?'

'P?'

I pointed to several annotations in the book. 'There. P.'

'P is for piece-rate.' He used the English word. 'It's the low rate of pay.'

I ran my finger down the column and repeated the names of the rubber tappers who'd had the letter marked out next to them in red.

'Krishnasamy. Chandrasekhar. Pillai.' I looked at my uncle. 'How come only Indians get piece-rate?'

'What do you mean, how come? They are Indians.'

I nodded slowly and then returned to the ledger, continuing to scan the lines of the book.

'What about Malays?' I said.

'What about them?'

'I don't see any Muslim names in here. How come there are no Malays at the rubber estate?'

He laughed. 'Malays? The *gwai los* in the company office know better than to hire Malays.'

'How come they don't like to hire Malays?'

'They're lazy. Everybody knows.' Sook Sook paused. 'Anyway, what do you care about Malays?'

At that point, my father came into the big room and poured warm water from the kettle into a glass of leftover tea leaves. He brought the glass over and sat down with us, inclining his head at me:

'Ah Tat's friends, they're all Malay. Isn't that so, boy? There's Muhammad Syahmi and that Amin boy you always go kite-flying with. And now there's that new one that keeps showing up at the house. What's his name again? The fellow that's still afraid of ghosts. Hasan, is it?'

Sook Sook turned and looked at me. 'Malays? Your friends are all Malay, are they?'

I looked at Sook Sook and then at my father.

'No.'

The two men exchanged a look, their faces wreathed in shadow.

Five

The next time I saw Hasan, it was on one of my long meandering walks through the kampong. He was wading through the Klang River, the front of his T-shirt hooked up over his neck, walking waist-deep through the murky water. Watching him, I soon realized he was searching for something, probing the river bottom with his feet, one yard at a time. Suddenly, he reached down and hauled an odd-looking contraption out of the water. It looked like a birdcage with an open bottom: two bulbous chambers woven from thin cane weave, separated by a fluted valve. He dragged it dripping out of the water and set it on the bank. I called down to him.

'Ai, Hasan!'

He looked up at the sound of my voice.

'Ah Tat,' he said.

'What's that you got there?'

'It's a fish-trap,' he called back. 'You never seen a fish-trap before?'

There was a wet ream of bubble-wrap plastered to the outside of the cane weaves and Hasan peeled it off with two fingers, a faint look of revulsion on his features. He flung the bubble-wrap back into the river.

'Fish-trap?' I laughed, shaking my head. 'Trust me, you won't catch any fish here.'

'Why not? I used to catch big ones all the time, back in the Langat.'

I leapt over the embankment and skipped down to where Hasan was squatting over his trap.

'The Langat River?' I guffawed. 'This is not the Langat, my friend. This is the Klang. Can't you see the big power station up there? And on top of that, you got the kelings from the Indian kampong, pissing and shitting in the water every day. What fish can you expect to catch in a river like this?'

'Where there's a river, there's fish.'

'Not this river,' I grinned. 'You really are a jakun, aren't you?'

I watched as Hasan pulled the trap upright and turned it over, carefully inspecting it from all angles to ensure it hadn't been damaged. When he was satisfied, he waded back into the river and reset the trap underwater, weighing it down with a large rock.

'You don't believe me? I am telling you lah, you won't catch anything.'

'I won't if I don't even try.'

Hasan scrabbled back onto dry land, wringing the water out of his shorts. He stood on the bank and peered into the leaden sky.

'The water is so low,' he sighed. 'Shouldn't we have more rain here by now?'

Looking along the path of the river, we stared at the run of the dissipated Klang winding its way into the distance. It was the colour of thin milky coffee. Farther downstream, there were patches where the current barely moved, seeping into great stagnant pools that merely bled over the terrain.

'It will come down sooner or later,' I said, looking to the horizon. 'Bucketloads. But it won't bring the fish, if that's what you're thinking.'

Hasan sat on the ground, hugging his legs forlornly and resting his chin atop his knees. He watched the motionless surface where he had just set the trap.

'Why so long-faced?' I said, hunkering down beside him.

'It's so boring here. No fish. No nice birds to watch. Got nothing much to do in KL.'

'Nothing to do?' I laughed. 'What do you mean, nothing to do? There's plenty to do. You just need someone to show you around. Come with me, come. I will show you, nothing to do.'

I took him back through the kampong, past rows of stilted attap houses lining both sides of the wide dusty street. It was a quiet Sunday afternoon and kampong folk were leisurely going about their business. Aunty Rozimah was on her porch, lounging in a daybed and listening to Malay love songs on the radio. Between two nearby houses a pair of

children were playing badminton across a washing line pegged with white
singlets and undergarments. As we walked past Ah Teng's house, I spotted
Amin and Muhammad S. up on our neighbour's roof, hopping deftly
about the gables, surefooted as little monkeys. The two boys were helping
to dismantle the old, thatched roof and replace it with flashy new zinc
sheeting. I waved to them as we went past.

Eventually we emerged from the kampong onto Batu Road and Hasan
followed as I led the way into town. As we walked, the trees overhead
started giving way to rows of double-storey shophouses with power lines
running above them, and peeling sunfaded billboards for F&N Cola and
Guinness Stout could be seen on the sides on the taller buildings. Traffic
was trundling noisily up and down both carriageways of the main street.

'You want something to do?' I shouted at Hasan over the din. 'Then
you got to go into town. This is where everything happens in KL.'

I took him to a dark musty arcade located right in the middle of Batu
Road. On one side of the gallery was the optical store and druggist; the
other, the pewter-smith and barber, but hidden in the back of the arcade
was my favourite shop in all of town. The Indian variety store had giant
wicker baskets out front, brimful of all types of assorted wares: calendars,
incense, flip-flops and flyswats, with coiled garlands of plastic jasmine and
marigold sagging in loops from the eaves. But it was the huge kite display
that I had brought Hasan to see. All manner of kites hung from the ceiling
and an entire wall of the store was adorned with the beautiful, intricately
patterned patang, pinned up like enormous butterflies. I smiled to myself
as Hasan gave a little gasp upon seeing it.

Afterwards, we went to visit one of the street hawkers outside the
Federal Cinema who was an old friend of my father's. He sold iced lollies
to patrons going in and out of the movie-house and though I never had any
money, the man always seemed happy to stand me a treat.

'Ah, young Ah Tat. What flavour today?'

'Sarsaparilla please, uncle. Can my friend Hasan have one too? He's
too shy to ask. Sour lime flavour for him.'

The man smiled and rinsed the sawdust off a massive block of ice.
He shaved and shaped two balls of ice and put them in paper cones for
us, adding colour with a spoonful of syrup. We sat on the kerb sucking
the ice lollies, watching townsfolk bustle up and down the street. The
Sunday matinee was showing in the cinema behind us, and I noticed the
ticket collector was dozing in his booth, so we snuck in to catch the last

half of *Tales of Scheherazade*. By the time we came out, it was already quite dark.

'How come all the actors were talking Chinese?' Hasan said. 'I couldn't understand a thing.'

'They make voice-overs for the Chinese crowd. But you're right, it's funny to hear Sinbad hollering in Cantonese.'

'I never knew there are so many Chinese in KL,' he mused. 'More than Malays even.'

We walked back through town as the streetlights came flickering on overhead. Most shops were closing for the day, the shopkeepers yanking shut their scissor-gates or overturning buckets of water on grimy tiles, but there were other places like the open-air eateries and drink sellers that just seemed to be starting up. Old men gathered to throw dice and smoke cigarettes, and by the roadside, a small crowd was being sold durians off the back of a lorry. Nearby, a beggar with no legs was playing an erhu for spare change. Hasan gazed at all the activity going on around him.

'It's so busy here. So many lights and sounds everywhere. So much happening. I never seen anything like it before.'

'I told you. Nothing to do, my foot. Better than chasing birds and fish around, isn't it? You got to know where to go, that's all.'

'I wish my mother and father could see it.'

'Your parents haven't been into town yet?'

'No,' he sighed. 'My parents don't live here with me. They're back in Mimpi still.'

I looked at Hasan. 'Your parents didn't come to KL with you?'

He shook his head, frowning.

'My uncle takes care of me here,' he said. 'But even though he's my uncle, it doesn't really feel like it sometimes. He's more like my big brother. I call him *abang*.'

'So it's just you and your abang at home?'

'Most of the time. Sometimes he brings girlfriends back. But they only stay a night or two before he sends them away.'

'He sends them away?'

'I don't think he likes any of them very much. He never keeps the same girlfriend.'

'Wah, must be a real Casanova to do that.'

We continued walking side by side, kicking a flattened aluminium can between us until it spun off the cracked pavement and into the roadside gutter.

'There was this one time,' Hasan went on. 'He brought this girl home, she looked about sixteen or seventeen years old. After only a day or two, he got sick of her, as usual lah, and told her to leave. But this girl, she wouldn't leave, no matter what my uncle tried. He chased her around the house, and they had this noisy argument in the kitchen, throwing things and screaming, but still, she wouldn't leave. And then, I tell you, the strangest thing happened. That night, she came into my room when I was falling asleep and got undressed and crawled into my bed.'

I stopped walking and looked at Hasan. 'She got undressed?'

'I know. She took off everything.'

'Everything? You're joking.'

'I'm not. She had hair, you know. Down there.'

'No kidding?'

'No, no kidding. But listen. She told me she was finished with my uncle and was free to be my girlfriend instead if I wanted. If I let her stay in the house for a bit longer, that is.'

'What did you do?'

'I didn't know what to do. I wanted her to get out of my bed because I was scared my uncle would walk in on us. But I didn't want to hurt her feelings, you know. So I just lay there next to her, trying not to move. Sure enough, you can guess what happened next.'

'Your uncle.'

'He walked right in on us. And there she was, lying naked next to me. Didn't even bother to cover up.'

'Ayah, shit. He must have been mad as hell, your uncle. Was he mad?'

Hasan frowned. 'That's the thing, Ah Tat. He wasn't mad at all. He even laughed, like he was happy or thought it was funny or something like that. Anyway, after a couple of nights of sleeping in my bed, the girl, her name was Min Hui, finally left the house. And my uncle, he came to me smiling, saying did she teach me anything.'

'Teach you anything?' I looked at Hasan. 'What's that supposed to mean, teach you anything?'

'That's what I said. My uncle wanted to know if she did anything in bed and I told him she just slept, that's all, but he kept asking what else she did, what else? And I said nothing. That's all. She slept. It was only then that my uncle got mad. I mean he really got mad. He kept telling me I wasted her and that she made fools out of us, or something like that.'

I scratched my head, unsure of what to make of it all.

'Your uncle sounds like a strange fellow.'

We continued walking up Batu Road and eventually Hasan became quiet. At the bicycle shop, where we would ordinarily have parted ways, he decided instead to follow me back to the river to check on his fish-trap. We walked through the darkened woods behind the kampong, slapping the mosquitoes from the back of our legs. At one point, he turned to me and said:

'My uncle gets like that. Whenever he goes out drinking Guinness. Afterwards, he comes home happy but also a little bit angry. I can't tell which sometimes.'

'You can't tell between happy and angry?'

'Not with him. He will tell a joke, or poke fun at me or something, but then I get scared to laugh. It doesn't feel right to laugh when he makes a joke.'

'Doesn't sound like a joke to me.'

Hasan seemed to think about this for a moment before nodding quietly to himself.

'Anyway,' he said. 'Thanks for showing me the kites today. And for taking me to see the picture show, even though I couldn't understand any of it.'

'It's nothing.'

'And for the iced lolly.'

'It is nothing lah. Don't mention it.'

'I had a good day.'

'What are friends for?'

'Can I ask you something, Ah Tat?' he said, turning to me. 'Do you ever get that strange feeling, when you have a good day but somehow it makes you feel even more sad?'

I looked at him in the dark. 'I don't think so.'

He nodded silently as we continued to walk. When we got to the river, Hasan rolled his shorts high up on his thighs and carefully waded out into the chilly waters. He wandered about the same spot for several moments before finally hauling the fish-trap out and bringing it onto the bank. He cleared the muck from its chambers and we both stood over the trap, peering at its contents. There was a wet mat of leaves and dirt plastered to the side of the cane weaves and lodged in the valve was a glass bottle of Coca-Cola. He worked the bottle free and flung it angrily into the woods.

'Didn't I say? There's no fish to catch here.'

He sighed and looked around dejectedly. The Maghrib call-to-prayer could be heard coming faintly from the distant mosque, signalling the setting of the sun.

'It's late,' he said. 'I better get home.'

'Do you want me to walk back to Kampong Baru with you? I got time.'

'It's alright, Ah Tat. I learned the way back already.'

'But what about the ghosts?' I grinned.

'It's okay,' he said, climbing back up over the bank. 'I know now. No such thing as ghosts in KL.'

Six

It was towards the end of Sook Sook's stay with us that year that we received some unwelcome visitors.

As I recall, my uncle had spent the day doing some banking at the OCBC in Old Market Square and had come home that afternoon looking irritated and worn out. As soon as he got back, he went straight for the hammock, cradling the radio and a bottle of brandy, and before long he was fast asleep, swaying gently in the sun. The rest of the family went about their business around him: Siew Mooi trimming the twins' hair one at a time, on a fold-out chair in the yard, while my mother haggled with the old hawker who occasionally passed through the kampong selling fermented tofu. Kin Chew and I were doing nothing, sitting on the back stoop and gazing out on the rest of the kampong.

Across our chicken-wire fence, a cluster of our neighbour's houses faced a grove of banana trees. Right at the end of that tree line, there was an old bus shelter where kampong folk often left junk they no longer had any use for: bicycle parts, crockery, secondhand clothes, and books and magazines. At present, there was a pile of zinc sheeting left over from the construction of Ah Teng's new roof. People from the kampong often visited that thatched shelter to see if they might find anything useful there, and it was not unusual for even strangers passing through the village to stop by and indulge their curiosity. I was therefore not particularly surprised to spot a group of boys I didn't recognize loitering beneath the attap bus-stop that afternoon. It was Kin Chew rather, who seemed unsettled by their presence.

'You see those fellows over there?' he said to me. 'Three of them. Hanging about under the rubbish shelter?'

I looked across the kampong, beyond the grove of banana trees.

'What about them? Probably just looking through all the junk.'

Kin Chew sat up, shaking his head. 'No, they're not looking through the junk. They're just pretending to. They've been hanging around for fifteen minutes now. Just hanging around, watching.'

It soon became clear that indeed, the three figures had no interest in any of the discarded articles but were instead observing the house from afar. They paced about the bus stop restively, glancing over in our direction every so often.

'What are they looking at?' I said. 'Are they looking at us?'

Kin Chew nodded.

'I know one of them,' he said, without taking his eyes from the group. 'You see the short fellow? In the dirty singlet? I've seen him in town from time to time. Piggy, they call him.'

Piggy was easily the youngest, around our age, while the other pair looked much older, closer to sixteen or seventeen years old. They were all smoking cigarettes.

'What kind of name is that?' I said. 'Piggy.'

'They're from the Hokkien Association on Foch Avenue. Rough types, Ah Tat. Triads.'

'Triads?' I looked at KC. 'What are they doing hanging around our house?'

Kin Chew frowned.

'What are they doing here, Kin Chew? Don't tell me you're in trouble. What did you do?'

'I didn't do anything,' he snapped. 'They're not looking for me.'

'They're not?'

'No, not me.' KC glanced over at Sook Sook, who was snoozing drunkenly in the hammock. 'They're after the old man.'

'What do they want with your father?'

'He's been playing mah-jong again is my guess,' KC sighed. 'Probably owes money to the wrong people. It must be bad, if they got Hokkien Society Boys following him all the way home. And I know that Piggy fellow. He is bad news.'

I stared at the shelter in the distance. The two older boys, large as fully grown men, were becoming restless and started kicking at some of the discarded articles piled around the bus stop. One of them rummaged through the junk and picked up an old radio set. He studied it for a moment, rattling it next to his ear, and then suddenly hurled the object into the ground with all his strength. The two large boys then proceeded to stamp on the shattered plastic casing repeatedly, for no apparent reason. The one known as Piggy ignored them and continued pacing about, smoking his cigarette, looking over at the house. Kin Chew and I watched them warily.

'What do we do?' I said.

'Nothing. There's nothing you can do.'

'Are they going to come over here and make trouble?'

'Not today,' KC murmured. 'They just want to find out where Ba Ba lives first. There are too many people around the kampong for them to start trouble.'

I looked about; my sisters were still getting their hair cut in the yard and a small group of our neighbours had just come out of their houses to trade with the tofu hawker. The Piggy boy smoked one cigarette, then another, observing the goings-on around the house.

Finally, the three boys decided to leave.

Kin Chew and I stood on the back steps, watching them disappear down the dusty track.

'Will they be back?' I said.

'They'll be back. For sure they'll be back.'

KC hurried down the stoop and went over to his father. Sook Sook was still asleep, and Kin Chew tried to rouse the old man, squeezing his shoulder and shaking him several times. Groaning irritably, he slapped his son's hand away and turned onto his side. The hammock swayed for a moment before settling back down. Kin Chew stared at him.

'Look at the stupid bastard. Lying there with not a care in the world. Got no idea what's coming for him.' KC made an abrupt about-face and marched back towards the house. 'Come, Ah Tat. Let's go. We got things to do.'

'What things?'

'We got to help Ba Ba pack.'

'Pack? Pack for what?'

'He's going back to Carey Island tomorrow.'

'He is?' I said, pausing to the look at my uncle. 'Nobody told me.'

'I am telling you lah.'

* * *

By the time Kin Chew and I returned from school the following day, Sook Sook had already gone. He'd managed to slip away sometime in the afternoon, spooked by KC's warning the previous night, and none of the family had seen him leave. He left no money or farewell message and all that remained beside his rumpled sleeping mat was an empty bottle of Cusenier cherry brandy. When Siew Mooi went down to the provisions shop later that evening, she discovered that my uncle had failed to settle our bill with old man Hong as he'd promised. My mother was incensed.

'How are we supposed to carry on? Every day I raise this family up bit by bit, *failing to sleep, forgetting to eat*. Must I drag you all out of this kampong myself? Will nobody help me?'

For several weeks afterwards, my father was forced to listen as she repeatedly threatened to expel Sam Ji and Kin Chew from the house.

'Why must we look after them? Your own brother can't provide for them, why must we? Haven't we enough mouths to feed? I say send them away. Send them away and be done with it.'

As it turned out, Kin Chew would save her the trouble. Barely a week after his thirteenth birthday, my cousin performed his own disappearing act, vanishing from the house without a trace. At first, we all assumed he was merely acting out in some way; that it wouldn't be long before he would show up for dinner, hungry and dirty and penitent. But then I discovered the jewellery Sam Ji had entrusted to me for safe keeping had gone missing. I realized then that Kin Chew would not be coming home.

Sam Ji's reaction to all of this was bizarre. Far from spiralling into despair, she instead made the peculiar decision to become a Catholic. After her Baptism at the church on Bukit Nanas, she set up an altar in the big room—much to my mother's ongoing chagrin—and took to visiting our kampong neighbours in a white mantilla, bringing them religious portraits that she claimed to have witnessed weeping. With time, she gradually gave up hope of discovering Kin Chew's whereabouts, clinging instead to the notion that he would one day return to her of his own volition, and as those days turned into months, and the months years, became increasingly pedantic about her elaborate prayer-time observances, always with invocations on behalf of all lost children and runaways.

Despite all this, none of us would have imagined it would be another four years before we'd so much as lay eyes on Kin Chew again. As it so happened, it turned out to be me who would finally discover what had become of him, late in 1964, when I met a secretive young woman claiming to have knowledge of his closely guarded whereabouts.

1964

Seven

Back then, I had a friend by the name of Sonny Tong. When we were growing up, Kin Chew and I used to play with him all the time, forming a little trio at *makan* breaks in our private nook behind the elementary school canteen and catching the bus home together every afternoon. Though we were ostensibly a threesome, I always had the feeling that were I not there, Sonny would just as soon have spent all his time with Kin Chew. The two of them shared a mischievous streak that I simply never understood, and my constant reproves were often a source of irritation to the pair. So, when KC ran away from home and suddenly stopped showing up to class, Sonny took his absence as hard as I did.

It was only later, during our adolescent years, that Sonny and I started bonding in our own right. At first, the only thing we ever had to discuss were our shared recollections of KC; how he somehow made us feel taller when we walked through the schoolyard with him, or how he'd been rumoured to be the one responsible for setting off a ream of fireworks in the headmaster's Fiat, scorching its fine upholstery and—according to those who'd witnessed the schoolmaster's reaction—provoking a wail of pure unguarded wretchedness from the otherwise implacably dignified old man. But as Sonny and I progressed up the forms of Methodist Boys together, we found reasons other than Kin Chew to remain friends. As it turned out, Sonny too would prove to be a dedicated member of the Boys' Brigade. We each harboured a secret fascination with drills and military etiquette, the badges and bronze pins and jargon and, especially I think, with the notion of attaining rank over one another. It was to my great satisfaction that by the end of high school I was Staff Sergeant to his Corporal in the Brigade.

When Sonny turned seventeen, he was given the keys to his father's sports car, a beautiful olive-green Alfa Romeo Giulietta, and after classes he would often take me into Petaling Street or the Cathay cinema to look at, or be looked at by, the night session girls. My mother loved Sonny. Whenever he picked me up in the Giulietta—looking like some Hong Kong film star in his dark glasses and slicked hair, Brylcreemed to an inky blue in the sunlight—Ma Ma would connive of a way to get him to take one of my twin sisters out on the town. I remember asking him once, at the behest of my mother, if he was interested.

'Not my type,' he'd said.

'Which one? Yin Fook or Yin Wei?'

'What do you mean, which one? They're identical, what. Both lah, flatter than chapati.'

Sonny possessed the kind of pedigree my mother looked for in all our associations: his father was the owner of the Tong Hing Soon & Son grocery chain and had stores in Chinatown and Pudu Road at the time. The Tongs lived, not in a wooden attap dwelling by the scummy Klang River like the rest of us, but in a proper brick-and-mortar house, double-storey mind you, in the cool hills slightly out of town. While Ma Ma frequently objected to my visiting Hasan in Kampong Baru, *to waste time with Malays,* as she put it, she never had anything to say whenever Sonny Tong came by to whisk me away in his sports car. I remember spending a lot of time over at Sonny's house in my final year of school. He would regularly have me over for dinner and then afterwards make a special point of escorting me into his garage, which doubled as a kind of storage bunker for his father's business. The sturdy metal shelves were always crammed full of the stores' excess stock: cans of condensed milk and fried dace, quail eggs, pickled radish; crates of 7-Up and F&N stacked right up to the ceiling; there were trays of chewing gum and Darlie toothpaste, herbal jelly, dried mushroom, woks and camphor blocks, Milo, instant noodles and brown bottles of calamine and tincture of iodine. I would often bring home a tub full of groceries that Sonny had casually unloaded onto me, which did little to hurt him in my mother's eyes.

'He speaks Hokkien too,' Ma Ma would say. 'And so handsome. Bring that boy home more often. One of your sisters will do for him.'

It was Sonny, in fact, who would give me my first clue as to Kin Chew's whereabouts. It had been almost four years since I'd last seen my cousin and I had given up hope long ago of ever finding him. If he still lingered somewhere in the back of my mind, then it was only because Sam Ji persisted in conducting her bizarre little rituals around the house. Throughout the years of KC's absence, she not only prayed twice a day for his return but maintained the spot where he used to sleep beside her, laying out his old bamboo mat every night, and then rolling it back up in the mornings, as though some phantom spectre of her son still ghosted home for bed at the end of each day. She even kept a pack of Viceroys on the altar shelf in case he showed up unannounced, wanting a smoke. No one else touched KC's pack of reserve Viceroys. It was the least we could do for Sam Ji. Apart from these occasional reminders I had all but forgotten my cousin even existed by the end of my school years.

It came, then, as quite a shock when Kin Chew was mentioned unexpectedly one sunny afternoon. Sonny Tong, Hasan and I had gone down, as usual, to our favourite coffeeshop on Petaling Street after school that day. As I recall, we were sitting outside at one of the plastic table-sets that spilled out onto the sidewalk, discussing what we planned to do after graduation.

'I applied for a scholarship at UM,' I said.

My friends turned to me, looking surprised.

'University?'

'That's right.'

'I don't know, Ah Tat,' Sonny said, pursing his lips. 'That might be a bit too ambitious. Even for you.'

Sonny himself was planning to go to university, but in the UK, once he'd finished school. Though he was the least capable student of the three of us, we all understood his father's money would assure him of a place abroad. To merit a place at the local university, however, was an altogether different matter. Hasan smiled at me:

'I think you will do it, Ah Tat.'

'There, you see? Hasan thinks I can do it.'

'What does Hasan know?' Sonny scoffed. 'He's only telling you what you want to hear.'

'I got as good a chance as anybody. Those Victoria Institute boys are not the only ones that make it to the U. I'm as clever as any of them.'

'Nobody's saying you're not clever, Ah Tat. It's just better to have low expectations.'

Sonny glanced into the coffeeshop, waving at one of the waitresses.

'Speaking of low expectations,' he grinned. 'What about our little friend over here? What plans when you finish, Hasan? Conquering the world, no doubt.'

'Actually, I was thinking of going home to Mimpi.'

This time, it was my turn to look surprised.

'Back to Mimpi? Are you sure?'

Hasan shrugged, continuing quietly, 'I was considering it. Kuala Lumpur does not suit me. And my mother always promised, when I finally get my high school diploma, she will let me come home.'

Sonny laughed aloud. 'Go back home? Look at this jakun, Ah Tat, can you believe him? As soon as he finishes school, the only thing he can think to do is run back to the jungle. You can do anything you like, Hasan. You got options now. You want to go back to being a kampong boy, is it?'

'I told you,' Hasan said through gritted teeth. 'KL is not for me.'

'Let me tell you something, Hasan. Your family do not want you to go home, not really. Why do you think they sent you to KL in the first place, my friend? Your mother got enough sense to know there is nothing for you back in Mimpi.'

Hasan turned away, looking off into the distance.

'What are you getting so upset for? Tell him, Ah Tat. Tell him how the real-world works.'

'Leave him alone, will you? Call the *aneh* over again, I am dying of thirst over here.'

The eatery was nestled in the ground floor space of the corner shophouse above it, with two sides that opened out onto the street. Inside, noodle and fried bread stalls formed a ring around a space crowded with sweaty patrons, the vendors' food carts seething and hissing hot oil that smoked out fully one side of the street. Waitresses sat across from each other at the spare tables, fanning themselves and chattering away blithely. One of them finally came out to our table on the street corner and wiped down the tabletop with a soiled rag.

'Makan?'

Sonny waved her away. 'No lah. Too bloody hot to eat. Send the aneh over with the drinks.'

When the sodas and cold milk tea arrived, Sonny sat back and loosened the knot of his necktie. He undid his top button and looked at us, sighing heavily.

'Whatever happens, at least one thing is for sure. Soon we won't have to wear these ugly uniforms anymore.'

I shrugged. 'Actually, I don't mind the uniform. Girls like being seen with Methodist Boys.'

'I suppose that's true.' He eyed a group of middle school girls in their turquoise-blue skirts crossing the distant intersection. 'In fact, I was thinking of taking the convertible past Foch Avenue tonight. See if any of those girls from Bukit Nanas Convent will go to the pictures with me. *Paris When It Sizzles* is showing at the Odeon.'

Hasan laughed as he took a swill from his drink, spraying the icy soda all over himself.

'The Bukit Nanas girls?' he smirked, drawing the back of his hand over his mouth. 'None of them will go anywhere with you, Sonny. Believe me.'

'Why not?'

'Gracie Chia told all her friends to stay away from you. She's been telling anyone with ears you're a cad.'

'A what?'

'She says you're a cad. She told me she seen your type before.'

Sonny shook his Rolex nonchalantly and leaned back with his hands behind his head. He sat there for a moment, making a sour face, before finally leaning forward and muttering to himself:

'No wonder those girls won't let me take them out anymore. That Gracie's been spreading rumours about me, the lousy *pundek*.'

Hasan and I shared a chuckle.

'I bet she's been talking all sorts of rubbish,' he went on. 'Just my luck, too. She knows practically everybody in town. Ah Tat, did I mention? She even knows your cousin.'

'Ping Ping? Or do you mean Elaine?'

'No, not them. She knows Kin Chew.'

'Kin Chew?' I paused, the cold milk tea halfway to my lips. 'She knows Kin Chew?'

'Sure, she knows him. I saw them together just the other day. A whole group of them, hanging around Foch Avenue after FEC classes.'

'You saw him? You actually saw Kin Chew?'

Sonny shrugged. 'I saw him. I waved to him, but the bastard pretended like he didn't recognize me. Can you believe that? I know it's been a few years, but we used to play together after school every day. Now he thinks he's too good to know me. Can't even say hello.'

Sonny and Hasan sucked down their sodas and called the waiter over for another round. The two of them then proceeded to get into an argument over who would pay. Sonny waved a five-dollar bill at the man, sending him away for the change.

'I can afford my own,' Hasan said, digging a few cents out of his pocket.

'Never mind,' Sonny said. 'It's only soda.'

'No,' Hasan insisted, pushing the coins across the table. 'You take it. I can afford my own. You don't pay for me. Take it.'

'Jesus Christ Hasan, fine. I'll take your twenty cents if it means so damn much to you.'

'I never asked you for anything.'

'What do you think? I got a secret ledger and every day I go home and mark down how many sodas you owe me. One day hand you a bill for what, three dollars? I lose three dollars every night in the laundry. Stop being so proud.'

'Always got to be the big man, isn't it, Sonny? Always.'

I looked out on the traffic crawling past the coffeeshop, preoccupied with my own thoughts. A lorry was unloading its wares in the middle of the street and a couple of people were shouting at the driver from their cars. All around us, the warm humid air stank of day-old produce wafting over from Old Market Square.

'What did he say?'

Sonny and Hasan stopped their bickering for a moment and looked at me.

'What did who say?'

'Kin Chew. What did he say when you saw him?'

Sonny frowned. 'I told you, he pretended like he didn't recognize me. Anyway, he was only there for a minute. He stopped outside the Hokkien Association building to chat to Gracie and a few of the other night session girls. After that, he disappeared.'

'Didn't you follow him?'

'Follow him?' Sonny looked at me. 'Why would I follow him?'

'You could have followed to find out where he's been hiding. As a favour to me. You know I haven't laid eyes on him for four years now. He is still my cousin, after all.'

'Ah Tat, you always told me, even if KC was standing on the other side of the street, you yourself wouldn't bother to cross over and say hello.'

'Did I?'

'You told me he could go fly a kite for all you care.'

I frowned and sat back.

'Yeah lah, but still.'

* * *

By then, many of our classes at MBS had become mere formalities as we waited for our final exam results to come in. On the days we wanted to bunk off, Sonny arrived at my house in the early morning, blasting the horn of his green convertible and creating a minor stir amongst my kampong neighbours. I must admit, I always liked being seen running out to the Giulietta.

'What's the plan today?' I said.

'Not school.'

'What then?'

'It's hot. Let's just cool off in the tank.'

'Fine by me. But let me drive this time.'

'Walao, get your own car first. Then can bloody drive all you like.'

I remember the kampong had started to become a noisy place in those days. On most mornings excavators appeared at the edge of the village grounds, digging up trenches for pipework to be laid down, their thunderous presence shaking the surrounding lime trees and causing them to drop all their hard unripe fruit. As we drove out of the kampong that day, leathery-skinned workers could be seen shouting across the machinery, pouring water down one another's backs.

Leaving Chow Kit behind, we turned towards the hills as the sun came out. Sonny put on his dark glasses.

'What a day,' he said, the wind in his hair.

The road rose steeply as we entered Kenny Hills, the car taking slow meandering turns, dipping, and rising in pleasing undulations. Off the side of the hill, slashes of red clay roof could be glimpsed intermittently through the thick foliage, the vale falling away below us in an enormous valley bowl, uncleared jungle wild with all manner of *penaga* and *tualang* and *kapok* trees. The air became cooler the higher we climbed.

'See there?' Sonny gestured at a fork in the road. 'The Prime Minister's house is up on that hill. Bukit Tunku Abdul he calls it.'

'Ayah, I know already. You mention it every time.'

We drove by the entrances of several villas and lavish bungalows. Sonny dropped the car into low gear and solemnly pushed the car up the next hill.

'Word around town is that you been looking for Kin Chew,' he said.

'Ever since you told me you spotted him the other day, I can't stop thinking about it. Still no luck yet.'

'If I was you, I would stop asking around.'

'What? Why?'

'Just leave it be, Ah Tat. Trust me.'

Turning into his home, we passed through a pair of tall black wrought iron gates and at the end of the driveway, a two-storey European-style colonial bungalow sat beautifully white against the forested backdrop, with large windows and wide verandas that led out into the gardens. Sonny parked the car in the double garage, next to a flashy brown-gold Mercedes-Benz.

'Is that new?' I said, getting out.

'Brand new, out of the dealership. My father bought it just the other day. You like?'

'I'll say. What happened to the other car?'

'We still got it. My mother drives that one now. But the old man always wanted a Mercedes in gold. Looks damn ugly if you ask me.'

'No,' I said quietly. 'No, it's beautiful.'

Crossing the lawn, we startled the Malay gardener as he was coming round the corner of the house. The man had been picking green papayas from the little coppice out back and he steadied the large basket of fruit balanced on his head, saying in his broken English, 'Sorry, young sir. Sorry, sorry,' before waving us in ahead of him.

That afternoon, Sonny and I stripped off and climbed into the large rainwater tank at the back of his house. We waded about for a half hour, hanging off the tin siding of the tank, the metallic din of our conversation repeating on us as our voices echoed round the circle of the corrugated drum, shimmering in our ears.

'When do you leave for London?' I said.

'October.'

'So soon.'

'Yeah. It's soon.'

'It's decided then? For sure you are going?'

Tilting his head back into the water, he wet his hair. 'I am gone already.'

We gazed up through the opening of the silo into the sky above, the sound of lapping water slushing up over our heads.

'What about you?' he said. 'Any word from the University?'

'Still waiting.'

'If anyone can get in, I suppose it's you.'

'Well, it's out of my hands now. I been trying to distract myself from thinking about it too much. Maybe that's why I'm so caught up in this whole thing with KC. I'll tell you something funny. The other day, I went to the Hokkien Association to ask around. Turns out everybody knows who he is, but nobody got the faintest clue where to find him. Don't you find that strange?'

Sonny paddled around to look at me. 'Not this again. I thought you said you were going to forget it.'

'I never said that. You said it. What's it to you, anyhow?'

'I think we need to have a proper talk,' he frowned, peeling the hair from his face. 'Come, let's get out. My father will kill me if he finds out I am swimming in the tank again.'

We sat out on the deck in our underwear and as we dried off, little puddles of water collected at the feet of the rattan chairs in which we lounged. One of the family's servants came out with a tray of snacks and cold sodas, placing it on the table before us. Sonny dismissed her with a wave and sat forward with a serious expression:

'I got to confess something, Ah Tat. But I warn you now, you are not going to like it.'

'Confess what?'

'Remember how I told you I saw KC at the Hokkien Association that day? Well, maybe I didn't tell you everything there was to know.'

'No?'

'If you insist on searching him out, you should tread carefully. See, he wasn't really there to meet with the night session girls. He was there to see some other people.'

'Other people? What other people?'

Sonny picked at the bowl of snacks on the tray and made a face, flinging a couple of peanuts out into the yard. He rubbed his fingers together distastefully.

'Why did she bring these out?' he sighed. 'I tell her every time, not the ones with the peanuts.'

'What people, Sonny?'

'If you must know, he was with Botak Chin and that crowd. Peter and Frankie Yap, Fatty, all of them.' He glanced at me briefly and lowered his eyes. 'I think that Piggy fellow was also there.'

'Piggy? What was he doing with Piggy?'

'Search me. I guess they're friendly-friendly now.'

'Is he mixed up with *pai lang*? Is that what you're telling me, Sonny?'

'I wouldn't go that far. Believe me Ah Tat, it's not as bad as it sounds. Those Hokkien Society Boys are only play-acting. They are not real triads, that lot.'

I got up and walked to the edge of the porch. Through the trellis screen, the gardener was continually crossing in and out of view as he gathered up dead brown fronds shed from palm trees all over the property. A cool breeze drifted through the hills, stirring the mosquito drapes over the back doors. I turned to Sonny. He was picking through the contents of the snack bowl, trying not to look at me.

'You know where he is,' I said.

'No.'

'Yes, you do.'

'No lah, I promise you. I don't know where KC is staying. I wouldn't hide it from you if I did.'

Sonny looked at me for another moment before continuing reluctantly:

'But I do know this girl. She takes FEC accounting classes over at the Hokkien Association on Thursday nights. Maybe she knows where KC stays. That's all I can tell you. But listen, Ah Tat. You got to be careful.'

'Girl? What girl?'

'Are you listening to me, Ah Tat? If you go looking, be careful.'

'What girl, Sonny?'

* * *

I caught her as she was coming out of the lobby of the Hokkien Association building.

'Miss? Excuse me, Miss. Are you June Teh?'

Behind her a gaggle of students streamed out onto Foch Avenue, dispersing at the bottom of the steps while chattering and laughing amongst themselves. She'd been talking with several girls when I called out to her and the group fell silent all at once, turning their eyes on me as I stepped out from the shadows. The lead girl detached herself from the others and came over. She had perfect posture.

'Yes, I am June. Who are you?'

'Lim Kin Tat.'

'Who?'

A few of the girls behind her giggled.

'I'm friends with Sonny Tong. We are classmates over at Methodist Boys School.'

She looked at me without replying.

'He told me you take FEC accounting here,' I pressed on. 'Could we talk for a minute?'

'You mean that fellow with the green sports car?'

'Ah, that's him. The Giulietta.'

She turned to her group of friends, and they all looked back at her with brightness in their eyes, keenly anticipating what she would do next. She dismissed them with a wave of her hand and after a few knowing smiles and whispers, the girls broke off in the direction of the street market. When they were out of earshot, she said to me:

'What does he want now? Tell him I am not interested.'

'No, you don't understand. I'm not here about Sonny.'

She adjusted the buckle on her leather book strap and frowned. There was a little colour on her lips.

'So, your friend with the sports car. He doesn't want to take me out anymore?'

'Sonny? No. I don't think so.'

'Well, tell him I'm not interested anyway.' She turned abruptly and began striding down Foch Avenue at a brisk pace. Over her shoulder, she added, 'But only if he asks.'

I fell in behind her.

'I am looking for Kin Chew,' I said quickly. 'Sonny told me you might know where he is.'

'KC?'

The girl stopped and eyed me suspiciously for a moment. She looked me up and down properly for the first time, as if re-evaluating her initial impression, then after a long pause, said matter-of-factly:

'I got no idea where Kin Chew is. Sorry to disappoint you.'

'But Sonny told me you would know.'

'Well, I don't.'

I followed her up to Petaling Street, where the night bazaar cut a smoky noisy swathe across our path. Each side of the road was teeming with market stalls and a continual procession of people were meandering up and down the *pasar malam*. June slipped into the throng, and I darted in after her, pushing my way through the crowd. Under the awnings and striped umbrella carts, the tables were laden with all sorts of goods: chinaware and pyjamas, shoes, model aeroplanes, six-foot bolts of *batik* cloth and almanac charts, and fried sweets. She turned and glanced back at me:

'Stop following.'

'Please Miss, it's important. I need to talk to Kin Chew.'

'You'll stop following if you know what's good for you.'

'What's that supposed to mean?'

'It means you're asking for trouble.'

'Wait, please. I just want to know where he is.'

She stopped in a huff, looking about cagily for a moment. 'If you're going to pester me all night, the least you can do is be a gentleman about it.'

'Gentleman?'

'I'm thirsty lah. Got to spell it out for you, is it?'

'Oh yes, of course. Where are my manners? Allow me,'

I bought her watermelon juice at the fruit-drink stand and we then continued through the bazaar together in silence. Watching her, I noted the way she held her straw, taking quick little sips as though she were kissing the tips of her fingers. After a while, she no longer appeared intent on losing me, going so far as to throw offhand remarks my way as we perused the various goods on display: 'That's pretty,' or 'remind me to get some sesame oil when we come back this way.' Halfway into our first lap of the markets she began to slow, finally pausing beside a vendor that sold specialist tea. She propped herself against the cart and loosened her flats.

'Wait ah,' she said. 'My feet.'

As she leaned over to rub the arch of her foot, a gap in her shirtfront opened slightly.

'What?' she said.

'Nothing.'

'What is it? Why are you looking at me like that?'

'Like what? I wasn't looking.'

We merged back into the crowd, continuing at a slower pace, and at one point she stopped to adjust her shoe again, placing a hand on my shoulder. I waited by her side as the foot-traffic backed up behind us. Many of the men squeezing past us allowed themselves a backward glance at her. When we started off once more, I took her accounting textbooks, carrying them as we proceeded through the market.

'So, who are you then?' she said. 'Sak Pak Lok? Hakka Fu Chew Society?'

'Ha?'

'Or are you one of those Pudu Road Boys?'

'Pudu Road Boys? I don't know what you're talking about.'

'It doesn't matter who you are. The point is, you cannot get to KC through me. He's too clever for that. Take my advice. If you owe him money, best pay it back quickly. For your own good.'

'No, you don't understand. I am his cousin.'

'Cousin?'

'We're cousins. Lim Kin Tat and Lim Kin Chew.'

She looked at me and laughed. 'Cousins? Ayah, of course! I should have known. You are too innocent-looking to be one of that lot.'

After working our way down one side of the markets, we turned around and started up the other. Often, she would slip her arm through mine and drag me along with her. She stopped frequently at the same kind of stalls: handbags, hair clips, jewellery.

'You know,' she said. 'I am not normally that way.'

'What way?'

'So unpleasant like that. I must always keep my guard up with some of the characters that come around looking for Kin Chew.'

'You were not unpleasant back there.'

'I wasn't?'

'No.'

We went by a stretch of food stalls, and I ordered some *rojak* from an old Indian woman who was squatting by the kerb, her toothy grin stained bloody with wet betel leaf. She sent out streams of saliva into the roadside ditch, wiping her mouth with the back of a sleeve as she expertly prepared the paper plate. June and I sat side-by-side at one of the counters on bright orange plastic stools, skewing chunks of pineapple and cucumber with toothpicks while watching the unending parade of faces proceed past the little *rojak* stand. The smell of fatty spiced meat wafted all around us.

'You finished all the bean curd,' she cried.

'Course I did. The fritters are the best part.' Our knees were touching. 'Can have the mango, if you want.'

'I don't eat green mango. Too sour for me. It makes the insides of my mouth wrinkle up, see?' She hooked a finger into her cheek and stuck her tongue out, moving it around to show me, and then laughed and covered her mouth.

'Did you see?'

I smiled. 'You're mad.'

She pulled the paper plate towards her and continued fishing for more pieces.

'It's good here,' she said.

'I know.'

'I can't remember the last time I had good *rojak*.'

'I was just now going to say the same thing.'

We sat together chatting and eventually the crowd began to thin. Across from the *rojak* stand, one of the vendors began to stow his merchandise into the back of a van. As if it were a signal, half the strip was soon dismantling tables and drawing down their umbrellas.

'I'm still hungry,' she said.

'You want something else? I can get it for you.'

'You'll get something for me?'

'Your foot hurts, doesn't it? I'll go get more snacks before everything closes. What do you want? Nuts? Fried bread?'

'Surprise me.'

I got up and hurried down to the middle of the street, fishing through my pockets for change. Off to the side, a pair of thin harried-looking men were still furiously working away behind a cook station. One of them was deep-frying cuttlefish in a little modified vat, carelessly waving mosquitoes from his face with a wire mesh skimmer that was steaming with hot oil. The other was barbequing sweetmeat, stoking the coals on the brazier with a paper fan. I waited in line and ordered two skewers of chicken livers and he put them in a greasy paper bag for me. But when I got back to the *rojak* counter, June was gone.

* * *

'Did I tell you? I met June the other day.'

Sonny stopped what he was doing and looked across at me. 'You did? June Teh?'

We were in his bedroom and the sun was streaming in through the large bright window. All around us, the artefacts of Sonny's childhood were littered across the bedroom floor and numerous large storage containers, each caked in a thick grey sediment of dust, had been brought up from the garage. The topmost shelves of his wardrobe had been cleared out and, in one corner, a brand-new set of luggage sat with the price tags still attached to its handles. I was helping him pack for his move to London.

'I talked to her Thursday night,' I said. 'After she finished class at the Hokkien Association. I took her to the night market.'

'The two of you? Together?'

'Yeah, what. Just the two of us.'

I was sitting on the floor, rummaging through a box of Sonny's old records. I looked up at him and grinned:

'She told me you were constantly pestering her to take a ride with you in the Giulietta.'

'She said that?'

'That's what she told me.'

Sonny grunted and went over to change the record on the stereo.

'She's great looking, isn't she?' I went on. 'Don't you think?'

'She's okay.'

I scoffed. 'What, she's not pretty enough for you?'

'Pretty got nothing to do with it, my friend. I know better than to fool around with those Hokkien Society types. They will cut you up for looking sideways at one of their girls.' He went and dragged an empty container into the centre of the room and started pressing several pairs of shoes into it. 'Too much trouble for my taste.'

'You mean, she's going with one of them? One of the Hokk-Sock Boys?'

'Of course she is. She's with Kin Chew.'

'Kin Chew? Bullshit.'

'Didn't I tell you? I thought I told you. Anyhow, I bet she didn't say a word about where your cousin is hiding, did she?'

'Come to think of it, no.'

'No, didn't think so. She will never betray her sweetheart. Better to forget the whole thing now, don't you agree? You tried your best. Besides, Kin Chew's not your responsibility.'

He crammed the rest of his shoes into the box and began taping it closed. Grinning to himself, he said:

'So, she remembers me, does she? I knew it. What was she wearing?'

'You think she purposely tricked me?'

'I know that look and I'm telling you, Ah Tat. Let it go lah. You won't find him if he doesn't want to be found.'

* * *

I decided to find out for myself whether there was any truth to the rumour that June and KC were going together. I knew that she volunteered on Sundays, teaching Chinese language classes at the Hokkien Association on Foch Avenue, and when I arrived, the lobby was filled with children, all Chinese, ranging from between five and twelve years of age, running around in identical yellow hats. Before long, a supervisor appeared at the top of the flight and the children hastily arranged themselves into two lines and filed up the stairs. I fell in behind them, up to the second floor where they divided themselves up into separate groups. June was waiting in one of the classrooms. She came out to me.

'What are you doing here, Ah Tat?'

'I came looking for you.'

'How did you know I was here?'

'I asked about you.'

She smiled. 'You asked about me?'

'Sure,' I cleared my throat. 'Sonny told me you teach Sunday school here, so.'

'So?'

'So, I come lor.'

We stood alone in the hallway. Through the glass panel door, the children were observing us from inside the classroom with great smiles on their faces. June looked back at them and pressed a finger to her lips. Then she turned to me, blushing slightly.

'Lessons are about to start, Ah Tat. I better go in before they get too noisy. You can come inside if you like.'

'Can I?'

'Can. Of course, you can. You can help.'

I sat at the back of the room and watched as June took the younger children through their exercises. She held up big index cards on which colourful pictures of various objects had been printed: trees and bicycles, orangutans, clocks, churches. After each set, she reversed the cards to reveal the Chinese denotive on the back. Every now and then, I could hear a chorus of small voices travelling down the length of the corridor from one of the distant rooms; the children were reciting poems in Mandarin. During a break in the lesson, I went up to June.

'What's all this? Communist camp?'

She rolled her eyes, smiling. 'We're only teaching them about their own heritage. What's wrong with that? They can all read and write English—no problems—but ask them to draw their own name in Chinese and most don't have the first clue.'

I looked around the room. On the back wall, a portrait of Dr Sun Yat Sen hung in a fine glass picture frame.

'Did you know,' she went on, 'I got a boy from Johor who speaks Bahasa better than Chinese. Close your eyes and he sounds just like a Malay. Can you imagine, ah? A Chinese that cannot speak Chinese.'

After the children had finished their lessons, June and the other volunteers set up a couple of long folding tables in the reception area. They put out plates of chopped starfruit and papadums and parcels of sticky glutinous rice in the shape of little pyramids, wrapped in black banana leaf. I helped by handing out cups of warm powdered milk. One boy, around nine or ten years of age, stopped me as I was fiddling with the electric kettle.

'Is that your sweetheart?' he said.

'Who?'

'Her. Miss Teh.'

I looked over at June. She was talking to another volunteer while a small child was holding onto her hands and standing on her feet.

'Yeah lah,' I said. 'Sort of.'

The boy looked me up and down, a newfound respect on his face. There were purple ink stains all over his mouth and fingers.

'Do you French kiss with her?' he said.

'Where did you learn that?'

'Don't you even know about French kissing? It's like English kissing but ruder, one.'

I pushed him away. 'Finish your milk and go play with your little friends over there. And wash up, you got ink all over your mouth.'

Over the next hour, parents trickled in to collect their children and we tidied the rooms of the Hwee Ahn Hokkien Chinese Association Centre, stacking chairs and dusting chalkboards, before locking up for the day. Afterwards, I took June out for lunch. We walked up to Mountbatten Road where the banks and big office blocks of the business district loomed incongruously over the deteriorating shophouses.

'Where are we going?' she said. 'Petaling Street is back that way.'

I laughed. 'All those coffeeshops—in Petaling Street and Old Market Square—they're all the same. Wanton mee, Hokkien mee. Bloody curry mee. I thought I would take you someplace different.'

We entered the air-conditioned lobby of the Whiteaway Laidlaw Department Store and I led her downstairs into the basement. We found a table by the carvery.

'I didn't know you can eat here.' She looked around.

'Sonny's not the only one who knows the trendy places. What do you think?'

'I feel like a real English lady. It's air-conditioned even.'

We brought two clean white plates up to the carvery and came back with roast beef and small potatoes and green beans lathered in gravy. I paid extra for Yorkshire puddings and a couple of glasses of ginger beer. It cost almost five dollars. She looked across the table at me as we ate.

'You didn't have to pay for me, Ah Tat.'

'I wanted to.'

Over by the entrance, a well-dressed elderly Chinese man descended the stairs into the dining court followed by a young woman. She was carrying several shopping bags on which the Whiteaway Laidlaw monogram was printed, and the woman set the large square parcels down at one of the tables across from us. The old man took off his hat and sat down opposite her, lighting a cigarette. There was nobody else in the basement. June whispered:

'You think she's his mistress?'

'No lah. Too young. Must be his daughter.'

'Daughter?' June laughed. 'How come the sweet ones are always so naïve?'

After a while, several groups of people made their way down into the basement and the staff busied themselves out back, bringing out fresh trays of roast potato and peas and carrot. One of the cooks emerged from the kitchen to inspect the soup, lifting the lid of the elegant white tureen and looking out over the floor. June kept glancing over at the couple sitting across from us. They were drinking coffee from little white ceramic cups on saucers. The old man was reading his newspaper and the woman stared ahead silently, the bags of shopping stacked neatly in the chair beside her. June inclined her face over at them.

'Do you think she's pretty?'

'She's fine, I suppose.'

'I like her shoes. She must be his mistress. Too young to be his wife, too pretty.'

'You're prettier than her.'

June pressed her leg against mine under the table.

'Let's pretend we are sweethearts,' she said.

She cut one of her potatoes into little quarters and leaned across, placing her fork in my mouth. Then she reached across and touched the corner of my lip as though she were wiping away a crumb. I laughed.

After lunch, I walked her back along Mountbatten Road, to her stop outside Sultan Street Station. We waited for her bus together, watching the tides of scooters and motorcycles come in from Cross Street and Pudu Road. She then surprised me by taking a pack of cigarettes out from her handbag. They were Viceroys.

'You smoke?' I said.

'Sometimes.' She snapped the wheel of her fine, expensive looking lighter several times but couldn't get it to spark.

'This damn thing,' she muttered.

I took the lighter from her and, getting in close, cupped my hand over hers and produced a thin wavering flame. Our faces were inches apart. Then she stood back and looked at me for a moment with one hand cradling her elbow, the other toying with the cigarette. She winked at me.

'So suave. Just like in the picture shows.'

Eventually, June's bus pulled in.

'This is mine,' she said.

She kissed me on the mouth and skipped up the steps, disappearing into the back of the bus.

Afterwards I strolled aimlessly down Foch Avenue, basking in the warm afternoon sun. I couldn't stop my fingers from roaming around my mouth, continually searching out the precise spot where her lips had touched mine. As I passed by, an old Chinese shopkeeper came outside to light some incense at a pocket shrine by her store's entrance. The woman stopped me, waving the joss sticks around.

'Lang jai,' she called out, shaking an empty matchbook. 'Do you have a light?'

I realized then that I had inadvertently pocketed June's lighter and, smiling to myself, reached out and lit the incense for the old lady. She patted my arm in thanks and proceeded to bow several times before the shrine, the thin fragrant reeds held up to her forehead.

It was only when I was halfway down the street, dreamily touching my mouth and turning June's silver lighter over in my palm, that I finally noticed the engraving etched on the base.

It read:

J,
Love, KC.

Eight

The Suleiman Court flats were the very first high-rise tenements to be built in KL, back in 1957. I recall having watched their construction with great anticipation at the time, along with everybody else in town, as barricades sealed off Campbell Road and queues of cement trucks rolled into that massive lot every other day. Seeing those tower blocks gradually climb up, floor by floor—above the little dwellings and quaint shophouses and finally, even over the very palm trees—was like witnessing the birth of an entirely new kind of Kuala Lumpur. The Prime Minister must have thought so too, for the Tunku himself was there to officially open Suleiman Court. I remember thinking the days of attap houses and kampongs would soon fade into our past and from then on, we'd all live up in the skies.

As it turned out, Hasan would end up becoming one of the early tenants of Suleiman Court. His uncle had been assigned a government subsidized flat in the new complex, where the rent was much cheaper, and Hasan was delighted with the move, tentatively allowing himself the hope of scraping together enough savings for a trip home to Mimpi. Soon after moving in however, Zainuddin got himself fired from a decent job and so, to cope, the pair were forced into secretly sub-letting the flat to extra boarders. The way I remember it, a procession of random men was continually rotating through their cramped little unit, filling the apartment with the smell of their unwashed laundry and bickering over the rent money.

As I got older, it became apparent to me that it was Hasan, rather than his uncle, who assumed responsibility for the household. One of his abiding concerns throughout our high school years, for instance, was not grades or girlfriends, but how much he could squeeze out of Zainuddin each payday for the groceries. I can recall one afternoon when I'd suggested he ask Sonny for help in this regard.

'You know his father owns the Tong Hing Soon & Son chain,' I said. 'He gives me groceries whenever I want. All for free. My mother loves him.'

'Sonny?'

'Sure, you should ask him next time.'

Hasan made a face. 'Sonny Tong is the last person I'd ever ask for help. Always talking down to me and flashing his wallet in my face. No lah, I wouldn't give him the satisfaction.'

'Why have so much pride? We are all good friends.'

Hasan snorted. 'Good friends? If you say so.'

We were sitting in his stuffy flat in Suleiman Court, waiting out the rain. Looking around the sitting room, I noted that the living area appeared more cluttered than ever, as it had recently been converted into a space in which to sleep. Two empty bedspreads lay at our feet and in the far corner, someone was snoring in a hammock by the window.

'Hey, Hasan,' I whispered. 'Who's that?'

'Him? The new housemate.'

'You got another one?'

Hasan shrugged. 'He pays rent on time and doesn't take up too much space. He's from the same province as me, near Mimpi. My grandmother knows his grandmother.'

I watched as Hasan went about the room, clearing used cups and plates off the floor and disposing of soda cans that had been stuffed full of cigarette ends. He picked up work boots and dirty laundry and then swept up. When he was finished, the place looked rather tidy. Then he put some music on and settled down with a comic book. Outside, the deluge continued clapping noisily into the concrete surroundings so that I could barely hear the radio. *Smoke Gets in Your Eyes* came on and I turned the volume up and started singing along.

Hasan looked up from his comic. 'What's with you?'

'Nothing,' I grinned.

'Must be that June girl. You *angau* or what?'

'I took her to see *Cleopatra* at the Cathay yesterday.'

He frowned and went back to his comic. The rainstorm continued to rattle the frail awnings outside.

'I thought she was going with your cousin,' he said. 'The gangster.'

'No. She doesn't love him.'

'How do you know that?'

'I just know.'

We sat for a while longer, idling the afternoon away. The light began to fade and we soon fell asleep in the muggy heat, listening to the clatter of the rain. Later in the evening, a pair of Hasan's housemates returned to the flat. They went outside and sat on the balcony where the air was now cool, a giant portion of *nasi lemak* heaped on a sheet of newspaper between them. They mashed up little clumps of rice with *ikan billies* and *sambal* and sucked it off their fingers. After they'd finished eating, the older of the two men lit a cigarette and looked at Hasan.

'Your uncle's not home yet?' he said in Bahasa.

'Not yet.'

The man checked his wristwatch. 'It's late.'

'He's probably downstairs drinking,' Hasan said. 'He doesn't like it if I interrupt. I'll collect him later.'

The housemate frowned. 'Well, make sure he doesn't wake everyone up when he stumbles in tonight. The rest of us got work in the morning. And tell him if he's going to smoke *ganja* until all hours, he'd better leave his window open. The place stinks for days.'

Hasan nodded apologetically and the older man's face softened.

'Have you eaten dinner?' he said.

'Not yet, *pak cik.*'

The man bundled up the remains of his coconut rice and handed it to Hasan.

After he'd eaten, I followed Hasan into the bedroom that he shared with his uncle. The tiny room had been divided in two by a large PVC sheet; several shower curtains duct-taped together and suspended on a rod that hung across the middle of the bedroom. One half of the room contained a rumpled bedspread, blotted with yellow sweat stains, and strewn all over the floor was dirty laundry and loose change and several crushed cans of Guinness Stout. Hanging on the back of the bedroom door was a bus driver's uniform, a cap and belt, and a lewd calendar of Rose Chan. We stepped over the mess to Hasan's side of the room. It was bare and neat by contrast. There was a simple dresser and a desk and chair. He had a small window looking down over Campbell Road and a prayer mat rolled up at the foot of his bed. Hasan sat on his narrow cot. I spotted his old fish trap in the corner of the room and picked it up.

'Ah, the fish trap,' I laughed. 'Remember when you tried to use this thing in the Klang?'

'I remember.'

'How come you keep it? It's useless.'

Hasan took the trap from me and carefully put it back in its place.

'Donno,' he said.

Tacked to the wall behind him was a generic landscape print, the type that could be found in thrift stores for fifty cents, depicting a traditional attap house in a rustic provincial kampong. There were *pinang* trees over the thatched roof and a dirt track out front; cotton curtains and starlings on the eves, a laddered plank running up to the veranda. The hint of a river in the distance.

Hasan went to the window and stared down on the street below.

Opposite the apartment block was the Odeon Cinema. A large crowd had packed themselves under the foyer entrance to escape the rain, the soaked banner for a William Holden double bill sagging above them: THE SEVENTH DAWN and THE WORLD OF SUZIE WONG. From the roof of the building opposite, a giant functioning clock was engineered into a billboard for MIDO LUXURY TIMEPIECES. Cars were pulling in and out of the Odeon, honking and rumbling. People crawled the sidewalks below, as small as beetles, with the colourful little circles of their umbrella tops moving in orderly lines across the wet steaming concrete.

'Sonny was right,' he muttered, still staring out the window. 'My mother doesn't want me to go back to Mimpi.'

'No?'

'She wants me to stay in KL and find a job here. She wrote last week. My father hurt his back and they need money for the doctor.'

'Money? You don't have any money.'

'I know.'

'What will you do?'

He shrugged. 'Get some money lor.'

Nine

I can recall exactly what happened the day I found out I'd been accepted to the University. I remember I had walked across to Ah Hong's shop, all the way on the other side of the kampong, so that I could be alone when the results came. When I got there, Ah Hong's grandson was sitting behind the counter, cleaning his bugle with a dirty rag and a small round tin of brass polish. I remember saluting him as I came into the shop:

'And in Christian warfare
We would hon-our thee,'

The young man fitted the mouthpiece into his bugle and began trumpeting while I sang on:

'Underneath the ban-ner of the cross arrayed,
Lord we ask thy bless-ing on the Boys' Brigade.'

He smiled at me. 'Today's the day, is it?'

I nodded nervously.

He got up from behind the counter and showed me into the stock room, where a small radio was hanging by its handle from a nail in the wall. Before closing the door behind me, he said:

'No one will disturb you here. Best of luck. And don't worry, Ah Tat. I am sure your Ma Ma and Ba Ba will be proud, no matter what happens.'

I remember tuning into the public station, my fingers trembling, and setting myself down at the desk in front of the radio. The announcer's voice had seemed to drone on interminably, each name enunciated with a painfully assiduous exactness, and when finally he'd come to the L's, I remember getting up and pacing around the tiny closet-like storeroom.

'Lalwani, Arun. University of Malaya. Faculty of Law.

Leman bin Ishak. University of Malaya. Faculty of Law.

Li, Ah Ping. University of Singapore. Faculty of Economics and Business.

Liam, Thomas Meng Chee. University of Malaya. Faculty of Education.

Lim, Kin Tat. University of Malaya. Faculty of Engineering Sciences.'

I remember sitting there silently for a long time, just as I remember coming out of the stock room in a daze. I remember the way Ah Hong's grandson had looked at me when I told him I'd made it. How his face had dropped and his eyes went a little dead for an instant, before he came beaming at me to shake my hand, all trace of envy instantly masked. I remember racing home through the kampong, running up the stoop and into the big room where the whole family was crowded round the radio set. The announcer was still reading out the list of names over the air. My mother came to me, taking my hands in hers and holding them to her cheeks. I remember them coming away wet.

* * *

That very night, I took June to the pictures. When the film finished, we remained in our seats as the lights came on and the applause died away. She turned to me, saying:

'Did you like it?'

'I liked the Italian fellow's car. The red Ferrari GT. Better than Elvis' one.'

'That Ann Margret's got great legs. It makes me want to go out dancing.'

Patrons started streaming past us up the aisles.

'Come on,' I said, taking her hand.

'Where are we going?'

'Makan.'

Outside the Odeon, a queue had formed behind a satay stand, snaking counter-parallel to the line for the next showing of the picture. I bought a few chicken satays, and we crossed the road to the Suleiman Court apartment block and sat underneath the tamarind trees in the courtyard. I returned her cigarette lighter.

'Ah,' she said. 'That's where it went.'

She looked at the lighter, quietly running her thumb over the engraving.

'Then it's true.' I said. 'You're going with Kin Chew.'

She didn't look up.

'Are you two sweethearts?'

She gave a little nod. I got up and turned away from her, staring at the crowds milling about the Odeon across the street. I paced around the courtyard for a while before going back to the bench and sitting down again. I took her hands.

'I'm going places, June.'

'I know.'

'I'm going to make something of myself. I am going up.'

'I know.'

'Where's he going?'

* * *

The month following went by in a dream-like blur. I spent most days relaxing at Sonny's house in the hills, the two of us occasionally taking his Giulietta out on long leisurely drives with no particular destination in mind, then picking up Hasan in the evenings from his new job at the FEC book-hire, or June if she was free, for *kuey teow* one night, *roti* and *laksa* on others. My fondest memory from that period was splurging on all-you-can-eat durians at the Shaw Brothers' studio parking lot, sitting in an improvised open-air hawker plaza beneath stage scaffolding adorned with strings of winking-coloured bulbs, snacking and drinking beer and chatting unconcernedly into the early hours. When I received my formal invitation to the University in the mail, my mother had me sit down and translate every line of the letter for her. It was perhaps the happiest I've ever been. Then one night, during this run of blissfully carefree days, Hasan told me there was something serious he needed to discuss and asked me to meet him at his flat early the following day.

He was sitting on a bench in the courtyard when I got there. Towering over him, three blocks of flats rose on all sides to complete the triangle of structures that made up the Suleiman Court apartment complex.

'This better be good,' I said, slumping down next to him on the bench. 'I hardly ever get to sleep in. What are you doing out here anyway?'

'I always sit out here in the mornings. Watch everyone get up and about.'

Above us, figures appeared and reappeared on the balconies of the surrounding flats: hanging up laundry, batting drifts of dust from rugs, smoking cigarettes in the first shards of sunlight. Hasan watched the other residents for a moment and then turned his attention to the opposite end of the common square. There was a long stretch of concrete upon which a row of large rectangles had been marked out in white paint.

'See the courts over there?' he pointed. 'I used to watch people playing badminton out here every morning. Used to. You can see for yourself nobody plays anymore.'

'Get to the point, Hasan,' I yawned, rubbing my eyes. 'It's too early lah. What's so important you need to discuss right this minute?'

'I'm trying to tell you, if you will listen,' he sighed. 'Something happened here a couple of weeks ago. Something bad.'

'Bad?'

'Out on the badminton courts,' he continued. 'A group of *samseng* types started showing up, claiming the courts for themselves. Making trouble for the residents.'

'Samseng? You mean Triads?'

'Not Chinese. Malays.'

'Malays?'

'Ya, Malay gangs. From Kampong Baru, I heard.'

I frowned and looked at Hasan. 'What kind of trouble?'

'They were harassing the Chinese residents. Telling them the badminton courts are only for Malays to use, throwing eggs, calling them *cina babi*, things like that.'

'Bastards.'

'Everyone in the block was complaining about it. You know how these things are. One person talks to another person, they tell some loudmouth, soon everybody is gossiping. Word spreads.' Hasan paused, as if weighing his next words carefully, 'The Hokkien Society Boys started hearing about the trouble here, Ah Tat. The Chinese gangs are involved now. They been coming around ever since, crying out for Malay blood.'

I looked at him. 'The Hokk-Sock Boys?'

'Aw.'

'You mean? Kin Chew?'

Hasan nodded slowly before going on:

'From what I heard, your cousin is one of the ringleaders. Him, together with some lunatic everybody calls Piggy. A whole gang of them. Bringing knives and bottles and baseball bats, going all-out war with the Malays. I heard some Chinese kid showed up with a pistol the other day. Can you imagine, lah? Over bloody badminton courts.'

'Ringleader? Kin Chew?'

'I'm sorry, Ah Tat. I didn't want to be the one to tell you. But now, every few days, real fights break out over this turf. They even posted a police car out on Campbell Road it's got so bad. People are getting scared. None of the residents, Malay or Chinese, not even Indians, dare play badminton out here anymore. Simply sitting here right now, I don't feel safe.'

I closed my eyes.

'Kin Chew,' I said. 'Kin Chew, you bloody fool.'

'There's something else,' Hasan went on.

'What is it?'

He stood up and started walking towards one of the tenement blocks. 'You have to see for yourself or you won't believe it. Come with me.'

I followed him into the stairwell of building C and we climbed the flights, stopping at a landing on one of the upper floors. Hasan walked me over to the fire escape. Sitting on the steps of a flimsy iron gangway, a group of younger boys were talking quietly amongst themselves. They stopped when they saw us.

'I knew I'd find you all here,' Hasan called out.

There were four of them, all Chinese, all around thirteen or fourteen years of age.

'Who are they?' I whispered.

'Your witnesses.'

Hasan turned to the group and beckoned to them.

'Come,' he said. 'Tell abang what you told me. Come, tell him. No need to be afraid.'

The boys fell silent and eyed me suspiciously. One of them was wearing an eye-patch, under which was taped a wad of white gauze. The skin underneath, where the bandage peeled slightly from his cheek, was painted bright pink with mercurochrome. Out of nowhere, the boy with the eye-patch started to cry. He buried his face in the crook of his elbow and would not look up. I turned to Hasan.

'What happened to his eye?'

'No need to cry, young man,' Hasan said. 'Stand up now. Stand up straight and tell us what happened. It's not manly to cry in front of strangers.'

I pulled Hasan aside.

'What happened?' I said. 'Hasan, what happened to his eye?'

Hasan looked at me for a moment and frowned.

'Who did this to him?' I said. 'Tell me.'

'I think you know who.'

The boy had started to bawl in an embarrassingly immoderate way and his companions crowded around him, patting his back helplessly as he gasped for air. Hasan looked at the boy, shaking his head.

'Your cousin's been paying visits to Ah Fook and all his friends. Demanding membership fees to the Hokkien Association. He tells them it's for making the badminton courts safe for Chinese again.'

Hasan sighed to himself, 'Ah Fook here was the only one brave enough to stand up to him.'

'What happened to his eye?'

'He cannot see out of it anymore. Maybe never again.'

'My God, no.'

'He used a brick, Ah Tat.'

'No.'

'It's true. A brick.'

Ten

We went to a little coffee shop in Old Market Square and sat at a quiet table facing the rain-wet side street. June took the seat opposite me and dumped her accounting texts on the table.

'You shouldn't have dragged me out of class in front of everyone like that. The other girls already talk about me enough as it is.'

The waiter wandered across the diner floor, pushing his mop under the tables and chairs. I ordered a couple of *teh tarik* and the man nodded wearily and shuffled out back.

'No more games, June. It's time you took me to see my cousin.'

'They say I got two boyfriends now,' she grinned. 'That I am some two-timer. Isn't that funny? They're just jealous, of course. Most of them can barely even one-time.'

'Where is he hiding? Tell me.'

She sighed and sat back, tying her hair in a ponytail. 'We've been through this, Ah Tat. I promised I would never tell anyone where he stays. For his own safety. If you care about him, you'll stop asking.'

'This is serious now, June. Did you know he beat a boy so badly he lost an eye? A fourteen-year-old boy, June. Did you know that?'

She laughed. 'Kin Chew? People are always saying things like that about him. None of it is true. Strictly for his reputation lah.'

'The police seem to think it's true.'

'Police?'

'An inspector came to our house the other day asking about him. Took me and my aunt into Station Street for questioning.'

'What did you tell them?'

'Nothing. What could I tell them?'

'You could have told them I knew where he was,' she mused aloud, and even as she uttered the words, a look of dread overtook her features. 'You didn't tell them about me, did you?'

I leaned over and took her hands into mine. 'I would never do that.'

'You didn't?'

'Never.'

A group of customers wandered into the coffeeshop at that point, laughing and chatting amongst themselves. They took a table by the tiled arch entrance and called out to the waiter who was still out back preparing our drinks. June let go of my hands.

'What do we do?' she said.

'You have to take me to see him. It's the only thing to do. Let me help him, June. Please.'

The ceiling fan was ticking rhythmically overhead, and P. Ramlee was singing tinnily over the radio. The customers at the other table started making a lot of noise and June turned away, staring out onto the street. The last of the evening light was dwindling in Old Market Square and the plaza had taken on the hue of an old tobacco stain. People were crisscrossing their bicycles through the intersection, leaving wet muddy streaks all over the road.

'Alright, Ah Tat. You win. I'll take you to see him.' She stood up from the table and looked down at me. 'But I hope you know what you're doing.'

* * *

It was late by the time we'd reached Chow Kit. The main road running through the district was still and quiet, darkened by the evening drizzle. June led me up the stairs of a pedestrian bridge and we descended on the other side of the road along a row of squalid shophouses. Farther down we came to an alleyway enclosed by two tall terrace houses. The shadows from the buildings rendered the narrow lane almost pitch black and the smell of stale urine was overpowering. June slipped into the alleyway without a second thought. Out of the dark, a dog's paws padded rapidly out of our path, and we were soon passing through the rear lots of various small businesses, mounds of garbage in shiny wet black plastic accumulating on the pavement and toppling over into the gutters. Haggard busboys smoked cigarettes and gazed vacantly at us as we hurried past. At the end of the lane, we turned into the backyard of a tall shophouse with a vivid blue facade. The yard was filled with trash, much like the others, with a rickety wooden stairway leading into the rear of the blue building. I followed June up the stairs. Before we went in, she whispered:

'Keep your head down and don't look anyone in the eye. They don't like outsiders in here.'

Once inside the blue building the low murmur of conversation was immediately discernible, punctuated regularly by the clack of kissing snooker balls. June led me through what appeared to have once been a large restaurant kitchen, yellow rust stains marking the tiles where cooking fixtures previously stood, now crowded with boxes of liquor and cigarette cartons, luxury handbags flattened into plastic sleeves and rolls of leather upholstery. We went through a narrow hallway that opened out to a spacious room containing a row of billiard tables. The room was murky with shifting smoke and young men in singlets were standing about, leaning on their pool cues, sharply illuminated by trapezoids of white fluorescent light. As I passed by, I noticed one of the young men at the near table. He was wearing a pair of heavy black combat boots. June quickly turned from the billiard room, heading instead for the stairs. Underneath the stairwell on the second landing, a group of middle-aged men were playing mahjong by the light of a hurricane lantern. One of them made a kissing noise at June.

'Eh, *amoi*,' he called out in Hokkien. 'Did you hear? I am finally leaving my wife tomorrow.'

June laughed as we rounded the flight.

'Win some real money first, uncle. Then we can talk.'

Their chuckles followed us up to the topmost floor. There were several rooms on either side of the landing and June proceeded down one of the wings. We came to a door. She felt along the top of the doorframe and retrieved a brass key, letting herself into the room. I followed in after her and she shut the door behind us and locked it.

It was tiny.

There was a thin sunken mattress in the corner and a chest of drawers, on top of which sat a lamp with the shade torn out of the wire frame. June switched on the naked bulb. Geckos darted along the cornices of the room and then froze, stunned by the sudden light. A miniature electric fan had been left to run throughout the day.

'He's not here,' I said.

June shrugged. 'I am not his keeper. You wanted to know where he stays. This is where he stays.'

I went to the window and pulled the curtain aside. It looked onto the back of another building.

'What are you doing here, Kin Chew?'

I closed the curtain and turned and surveyed the room.

'Admit it,' June said. 'It's not as bad as you thought. He's even got electricity. Can't say that for the kampong, can you?'

I went over to Kin Chew's thin mattress and lifted it up off the floor to see if there was anything underneath it. I stripped the sheets and shook them out. Then I went and knelt by his small chest and rummaged through each of the drawers: there were cigarettes and matchbooks inside, rolls of small change, dice, screwdrivers, parking stubs and lottery tickets and a key chain from the Majestic. There was a silk necktie-handkerchief gift set from Robinsons and little sample bottles of Dunhill cologne. I slid the drawers completely off their runners and ran my palm around the inside of the empty frame.

'What are you looking for?'

'Who knows.'

June knelt and replaced the drawers of the chest.

'That's enough, Ah Tat. Stop it.'

She went over to the mattress and refitted the sheet over it. Then she sat on the bed, against the wall, and removed her shoes. She beckoned to me.

'Come,' she said. 'Sit here.'

I sat beside her.

'His mother is climbing the walls,' I said. 'All this time, she's been searching. For years not one word from him. And now the police.'

'They won't catch him. He's too clever.'

I put my head in my hands, 'I was supposed to look out for him.'

'It's not so bad, Ah Tat. You can see with your own eyes. The Association owns a few buildings like this. They put up troubled youngsters, give them a place to sleep. He's even got a room of his own. And the Hokkien Association helped him get a job too. KC is probably over at the Cathay as we speak.'

'The Cathay?'

'He's a parking lot attendant there.'

'A parking lot attendant?'

June shrugged. 'It's money.'

'It's nothing.' I looked at her and could see every one of her short fine lashes in the dim light. 'Are you in love with him?'

'We're going together.'

'How can you love him?' I said, turning away. 'He's got nothing to offer. Anybody with two eyes in their head can see he got nothing to offer. Not even eighteen years old yet and his whole future is down the toilet already.'

'Is that what you think?'

'You want to know what I think? I think, how can someone like you be in love with someone like him?'

'Someone like me?' She slid her legs to one side, tucking them under herself. 'What do you mean someone like me?'

'Someone like you lor.'

She looked at me for a moment.

'You never kissed a girl before,' she said. 'Have you?'

'Course I have.'

'A proper kiss, I mean. It's nothing to be ashamed about.'

'I have.'

She laughed. 'I'm sorry, Ah Tat. It's only that, all this talk of love. You sound so sure of yourself. And yet, you never even kissed a woman before. Isn't that so?'

'It never felt right before.'

'You're not curious?'

'Curious got nothing to do with love.'

'So, you're not curious?'

'I never thought about it.'

She smiled. 'You never seen what a woman looks like, have you?'

'I've seen.'

'A real woman lah. Not like in one of those *haam sup* rags.'

'I don't read those.'

'Do you want to see?'

'Don't be stupid.'

'I can show you. If you want to see.'

She leaned back and shifted her skirt up. I looked across as she pulled her underwear down over her knees.

'June, cover up. It's too indecent.'

'Come, never mind. I'll teach you. It's only a lesson, what.'

I sat motionless beside her.

'Don't be silly, come sit close to me. See? Put your hand here, like that.' She closed her eyes. 'You see?'

'Aw.'

'Is it nice?'

'Aw, it's nice. It's warm.'

'When it's like that, it means the girl likes you.'

I worked my fingers around tentatively. She took in a sharp breath.

'Does it hurt?'

She smiled. 'No.'

'No?'

'No, Ah Tat. It doesn't hurt. Do you want to kiss me now?'

'Yes.'

'Yes?'

'Yes.'

1965

Eleven

On an early August morning, I woke as the sun was rising and took the bicycle into town for breakfast, to the Cheong Kee coffeeshop on Foch Avenue near my old high school. The owner recognized me from my days at MBS and hurriedly came out front to show me a table.

'Ai, it's the university man. What news of the world today?' He pulled both his daughters out from the kitchen and had them wait on me. 'Go bring the young gentleman his breakfast.'

One of the girls set some coffee on the table, smiling demurely, while the other placed a bowl of steaming congee beside it, with a plate of *yau char kuey*, cut into crisp greasy squares. I sipped slowly at the hot thick porridge. A couple of men were stooped over the counter reading papers, their neckties tucked between the buttons of their shirts, sweat spreading in dark patches across their lower backs. I signalled to the street vendor outside and the boy ferried a selection of newspapers to my table.

'What did you sell them?' I said, indicating the men at the counter.

'*Straits Times, encik.*'

I paid for the *Times* and the boy shook a fan of lottery tickets in my face. I waved him away. Leafing through the paper, I glanced occasionally at the serious-faced men at the counter.

After breakfast, I stepped out onto Foch Avenue and noticed a small crowd gathered outside the Phillips Electronics store. I wheeled my bicycle up to the shop window. All the television sets on display were tuned into the news station, where a man was being interviewed.

'What's this? What's happening?'

One of the bystanders muttered something to me without shifting his attention from the screens. He walked up to the window and rapped on the glass irately, cupping a hand to his ear. The sales assistant nodded and turned up the volume on the television sets. The plate glass hummed louder but the words remained muffled and distorted. We stood outside the Phillips store and continued to watch.

'What is it?' I said.

'Lee Kuan Yew.'

The man on the television was blinking constantly and staring glaze-eyed into space. He spoke a few sentences haltingly then sank back and crossed his legs, lapsing into a dazed silence. He dabbed at his eyes with a handkerchief. The camera remained on his face.

'That's it then,' the bystander muttered. 'Unanimous vote already. What more to do? Lee's out, poor bugger.'

'Out? What do you mean out?'

'I mean out. Singapore, *cabut*. They're no longer part of Malaysia, as of today. Too many Chinese there for UMNO's liking.'

'Singapore, out? But how can that be?'

'So much for Malaysia for Malaysians,' he said. 'Malaysia for Malays, more like.'

I took the *Straits Times* from under my arm and looked over the front page.

'How come I didn't read anything about it?' I said.

The man turned and spat on the sidewalk. 'It's happening now. Right now. Before your own eyes.'

At the university, I rode past the Arts and Social Sciences block on the way to my first lecture. As they leaned out the windows of the third floor, some students were singing angrily to the rest of the campus. It was a song I recalled learning in my high school days.

'Land of the free, marching as one
Ready to share in every way, let's get it done, done, done
We're all in the same boat, steady as you go
Let's pull together, everybody row, row, row
Let's get together, sing a happy song
Malaysia forever, ten million strong.'

1969

Twelve

As fate would have it, the first time I was able to vote was in the 1969 general elections. Truth be told, I was not particularly interested in the result. I had gone down to the booths that day for the novelty of fulfilling some woolly notion of manhood more than as any genuine exercise in political enfranchisement. I cast my lot in with the Malaysian Chinese Association, as I assumed most Chinese would be doing and indeed, had been faithfully doing in the years since Independence. The MCA would form their coalition with the Malay party, UMNO, and the Indians of MIC, and that three-party Alliance would continue governing as it had always done. Business as usual. But when the results came out for Selangor, it turned out my vote was in the minority. The Malaysian Chinese Association had lost a staggering fourteen seats. Apparently—or at least this was how it was explained in the newspapers—the Chinese in KL had become disaffected with MCA and their Alliance, instead flocking en masse to the opposition DAP. The DAP made unprecedented gains in the election that year and in the aftermath, much was made of the Alliance losing control of the country. The Malays seemed alarmed by the results; for the first time since Merdeka, they would be forced to contend with an actively hostile Chinese opposition, galvanized by their surprise success. Still, none of this particularly concerned me at the time. My memory of the Monday after the elections was of being preoccupied with other matters entirely.

I was with the Briggs Engineering firm back then and, being my first job out of university, I suppose I was eager to impress my superiors. I had been clocking up some tremendous hours in those first couple of years and was just starting to feel as though I was distinguishing myself from the other new recruits. Nevertheless, I remained acutely aware that I wasn't the only one looking to stand out from the crowd. Quite often, the floor was filled with junior engineers working late into the night, stinking up the offices with the smell of their cigarettes and curried fish brought up from the hawker stalls downstairs. Despite the competition, I was confident Dr. Hayashi and many of the higher-ups at Briggs regarded me as one of their brighter prospects.

That Monday had gone much as usual. I'd come in early to get a head-start on a new project and was making some good progress, but as evening approached, I began to notice that many of the men in the office were packing up their desks early. Unfazed, I remained hunched over my desk, a large sheet of graph paper spread out on the bureau before me. Across the floor my supervisor, Ramesh, stood up and pulled on his jacket. He switched the power off at his desk and stretched and buttoned down his briefcase. On his way out, he stopped by my workstation.

'What's all this?' he said, peering over my shoulder.

I shrugged. 'Just something I'm working on.'

Ramesh placed his briefcase on the floor and leaned over me, adjusting the angle-poise lamp. He squinted down at the schematic.

'That doesn't look like your project,' he said.

'Because lah. It's not.'

He frowned and bundled me aside. Putting on his glasses, he spread his arms out over the drawing. Slowly, his frown deepened. After another moment, he stepped back and looked at me.

'That's not your project, Ah Tat. Dieter and his team are supposed to be working on the headstock. What do you think you're doing?'

I made a few refinements with my mechanical pencil.

'This is better than Dieter's design,' I said. 'What do you think?'

Ramesh took the sheet from the table and rolled it up hastily. He pulled a rubber band over the graph paper and slid it into a cardboard tube and tossed the tube into a corner of the workstation.

'I think you should be careful of stepping on too many toes. You're still new here, Ah Tat. There's no need to make enemies so soon. What happened to your own project?'

'I put the drawings on your station already. Finished last week, boss.'

'Last week?' Ramesh looked at me for moment and then reached up to switch the lamp off over my desk. He allowed himself a little smile. 'Alright, no need to get cocky, young man. Come on. Walk me out.'

'Did you talk to Dr Hayashi for me?' I said, packing up my things.

'I will. Be patient, Ah Tat.'

'You put in a good word for me, right?'

'He's seen your work. He knows about you. Just be patient, Ah Tat.'

On the other side of the office floor, somebody popped open a bottle of champagne. The election results had been announced over the weekend and many of the Chinese engineers who hadn't had the opportunity to celebrate with their colleagues now gathered together in Chin Woon Lai's office, toasting the DAP noisily. A group of our foreign engineers watched on with amused expressions. The vast majority of employees at Briggs were either local Chinese or UK nationals. As for the Malays, I can only recall two of them being under contract at the time—Abdul Harun and one of the interns whose name I've since forgotten. I had noticed they'd each slunk away very meekly that afternoon, just before the election celebrations had begun in earnest, finishing early on some pretence or other.

Ramesh looked across at his colleagues gathered in Chin Woon Lai's office, neckties loosed, drinking and guffawing.

'Maybe I should join them,' he said.

I looked at him, slightly surprised. 'You voted DAP?'

'Sure,' he shrugged. 'Malaysia for Malaysians.'

* * *

After work the following day, I went down to the Indian tailor behind Loke Yew Road to collect a *sari* I'd taken in for some alterations. Several months ago, Ramesh had invited me to his niece's wedding, going so far as to pick out a pair of costumes for the occasion on my behalf: a *kurta* for myself, and a beautiful emerald-green sari for June.

'Cannot have you turning up to my niece's wedding looking like some bloody *Mat Salleh*, can I? Do you like it?'

I ran my fingers along the delicate material and lifted the pleat of the sari to reveal the backless blouse underneath. Light passed through the semi-transparent chiffon.

'It's beautiful. June will love it.'

Ramesh patted me on the back. 'Good. Now listen, don't forget to mark the date. Last weekend in October, just before Deepavali. You're in for a treat. Indian weddings are best of all. June should have a good time.'

'I know she will. She adores weddings.'

'And who knows?' he grinned. 'Maybe the two of you will be next.'

I carefully folded the sari and laid it back in its box, flattening the tissue over the garment.

'Funny you should say.'

* * *

After collecting June's newly altered sari from the Indian tailor, I walked out to Loke Yew Road under the stretch of flats near the big *angsana* trees. A bank of ramshackle fruit stalls had been set up along the road and I passed through the small milling crowd, under the hanging hands of banana and green plantain, and watched as one of the merchants chopped up the shell of a jackfruit, scooping out the giant yellow bulbs for a discerning customer. I continued through the backstreets and came out at the local shops. A ratty marquee served by several *Mamak* hawkers had been erected in the middle of the road and two narrow lanes of traffic squeezed round either side of the tent. It had been hot during the day and the smell from the open gutters mingled with that of fried chicken and turmeric. I took a seat under the pavilion and ordered some tea from the waitress. Then I put my briefcase on the table and took out the sari to look over the alterations, carefully unwinding the *pallu* and holding it out in front of me between outstretched arms. The waitress came back with my tea.

'That for your girlfriend?' she said.

'Aw. We are invited to a wedding come October.'

'Mamak wedding?'

'Hindus.'

She nodded and put my change on the table. 'It's very pretty. You got good taste for a Chinese.'

I smiled and carefully returned the dress to the garment bag before draping it on the chair beside me. Getting up, I went over to one of the stalls and ordered some roti and brought the metal plate back to the table with its little wells full of watery curry. I tucked my necktie into my shirt and ate slowly while waiting for Kin Chew to arrive. Lately, we had been meeting every other week so that he could give me money to pass on to his mother. KC was earning a little more these days, though I never probed with too much scrutiny the source of his income, and for the past couple of years he'd been able to send a little home to Sam Ji on a regular basis. He was convinced that my own mother neglected to take proper care of her.

When KC finally arrived, he ordered a coffee *kosong* from the waitress and lit a cigarette.

'You're late,' I said.

'I am on time. You're early.'

He went into his shirt pocket and fished out a couple of banknotes and leaned across the table, pressing them into my fist.

'Remember,' he said. 'That's only for Ma.'

I took the rumpled notes and flattened them, fitting them into my wallet.

'You should come back to the kampong with me and pass it to her yourself,' I said. 'Your mother hasn't seen your face in don't know how long. She has bad spells when you don't visit, you know.'

'I saw her at New Year.'

'It's already bloody May, Kin Chew.'

He sighed and looked across the table at me. 'Just pass her the money, Ah Tat. Tell her I'll visit soon.'

I watched the street outside as we talked. A young boy was washing his feet in a bucket by the roadside scullery, his mother beside him on a milkcrate, trimming the tops off some okra. On the other side of the road, a pair of monks went into the druggist with a cake box from the Royal India sweet shop. I tore off a strip of roti and wiped the last bit of curry off the metal plate with it.

'When was the last time you cut your hair?' I said, looking at Kin Chew with a frown.

'Donno. You keep track of your haircuts, do you?'

'Or the last time you shaved even.'

He smiled to himself, shaking his head.

'I could get you a job at Briggs,' I went on. 'If you bothered to keep up your appearance once in a while. We need a file clerk. The money's not too bad, considering.'

'File clerk?' Kin Chew looked at me.

I sighed. 'Ayah, suit yourself.'

A small group of Malays stepped under the marquee and seated themselves at a table across from us. The waitress went over to ask them what they wanted but the men barely registered her presence, drowning her out in a spirited discussion over the recent elections. She stood by patiently until they'd settled down enough to place their orders, at which point their conversation became hushed and rather circumspect. They appeared to have noticed that Kin Chew was eavesdropping. KC turned to face me, indicating the Malays with his thumb.

'You hear what they're saying over there?'

'Keep your voice down,' I murmured. 'Don't provoke them.'

He shrugged and sat back, sipping languidly at his cigarette. After a moment he noticed the garment bag draped over the chair for the first time.

'What's that you got there?'

'This?' I looked at the bag. 'Oh, it's nothing. My boss invited me to his niece's wedding. I got a few alterations done, that's all. It's nothing.'

'A new suit? Let me see.'

'There's nothing to see, Kin Chew. It's not a suit.'

'What is it, then? Why are you being so mysterious?'

I looked at him and sighed. 'If you must know, it's a sari.'

'A sari?' he laughed. 'What are you doing with a sari?'

When I didn't reply, KC's eyes narrowed and he sat forward, watching me curiously for a moment. Finally, I said:

'It's for June.'

Kin Chew turned away reflexively. He ground the rest of his cigarette down in the ashtray and then, not knowing what else to do, immediately lit another.

The Malays' conversation at the table across from us started to flare up once again but Kin Chew barely noticed them this time. He was facing me, staring out onto the street beyond, smoking his cigarette pensively. I too lapsed into silence, watching the goings-on over KC's shoulder; we might have been mirrored images of one another. Neither of us said anything for a long time.

Later, we were interrupted by Piggy. He strode up to our table under the marquee, combat boots striking the ground with a heavy menacing clop, and slapped two packs of Viceroys onto the table. Kin Chew looked up at him.

'You got my change?'

Piggy grinned and fished out a fistful of coins and notes from his pocket and handed them to KC. He took a seat beside my cousin and the waitress came over and smiled at him.

'Drink?'

Piggy looked at her.

'Boss? No drink for you? Come lah. On a day like this?'

Piggy continued to glare at the waitress. After a moment, she frowned and lowered her eyes, backing away quietly. I watched as she retreated behind one of the cooks at the rear of the marquee.

'Can't you be civil?' I said. 'The girl simply asked if you wanted a drink, she didn't insult your mother. I suppose they don't bother to teach you good manners at the pool hall.'

Piggy spat on the ground. 'Good manners is like begging.'

We hadn't been sitting there for very long before Piggy started to overhear snippets of the conversation at the table of Malays across from us. He looked over at my cousin and slowly, a smile started to spread across his face.

'Are you listening to this?' he laughed.

'Leave them alone,' KC sighed. 'I'm not in the mood for a fight.'

Piggy grinned and began going through the ashtray. He picked out a single crumpled cigarette butt and straightened it out, standing it upright on the table. Then he flicked the butt over at the group of Malays. The cigarette end sailed in a long arc across the eatery, dropping like a tiny grenade onto their table. The second one landed in their food. Piggy continued flicking cigarette butts over at them.

'What's the matter?' he called. 'You all are sour, is it?'

For a while, the group of men tried to ignore what was happening, but Piggy continued to flick butt after butt at them, laughing gleefully. The waitstaff watched on, backing away behind their counters. I looked across at my cousin. Kin Chew's face had taken on a grim set, and I noticed that he was now sitting very upright, gripping the edge of the table. He looked pointedly at me and gave a discreet shake of his head, as if to warn me against interfering. Piggy continued to taunt the Malays:

'Why don't you cabut back to the jungle where you belong?' he laughed. 'KL belongs to the Chinese now. Haven't you heard?'

To my relief, after we left the Mamak place, Piggy went off on his own. He'd heard a rumour that thousands of Malays were gathering for an UMNO supporters rally in Kampong Baru in response to Chinese gains made in the election. Ever spoiling for a fight, Piggy had assembled his own little impromptu march, full of Hokk-Sock members and gangsters from the triads in Chinatown, to show that, in fact, there were some Chinese in

KL who would not be intimidated. He tried to convince Kin Chew to join them, but my cousin had refused to be drawn:

'Do I look stupid to you? I got more sense than to poke a tiger in the eye.'

Later, KC and I waited at the bus stop on Loke Yew Road. It was getting dark and the surrounding neighbourhood seemed quieter than usual. I sat with my briefcase on my lap, the garment bag with June's sari folded neatly on top of the briefcase, while Kin Chew smoked a cigarette and counted out the banknotes in his pocket.

'Why must you always bring that Piggy along?' I said.

'Don't ever call him that to his face, Ah Tat. That name is only for us.'

'He makes my skin crawl.'

Kin Chew shrugged and folded up the notes, returning them to his shirt pocket.

'He got his uses.'

'Useful? What use has Piggy got? He's nothing but a sadist.'

'Even a sadist got use sometimes.'

I shot an irritable glance at Kin Chew. 'Why must you say things like that to me? If I told you once, then I told you a hundred times. Keep all that pai lang nonsense to yourself. Nobody's impressed by your tough man act.'

We sat underneath the shelter, waiting quietly for my bus. Above us, a tall bank of tenements loomed over the street, the lights in the identical windows winking on one at a time in the darkening evening. High-rise blocks were springing up all over KL lately: the Pekeliling flats, the Razak and Pudu Road flats. And most recently, these on Loke Yew Road.

'Why don't you come back to the kampong with me tonight?' I said. 'For old times' sake.'

KC shook his head. 'Not tonight. It's late already.'

'Come on. I'll borrow the truck from Ah Teng and send you back afterwards. Siew Mooi is always badgering me to bring you home to visit. Your mother is not the only one who misses you.'

He smiled. 'I've always had a soft spot for Siew Mooi.'

'Even the twins ask for you. Nobody to kacau them anymore.'

Kin Chew glanced at his watch and wandered over to the bus stand, peering down the timetable. 'Where the hell has this bus got to?'

We waited almost half an hour for the bus that evening.

I can recall the particulars even today.

When it became clear the bus was no longer coming, Kin Chew and I decided to walk towards town to see if we could find a cab instead. Very quickly, we noticed something odd about the traffic. Our side of Loke Yew Road was virtually empty and yet in the opposing lane, a succession of vehicles was continually streaming by, busier than ever, heading for the outer suburbs. We'd gotten as far as the intersection with Birch Road before Kin Chew finally spotted a taxicab. Stepping out onto the road he went to hail the driver, but instead of slowing down, the cab unexpectedly roared up the gears. It charged right at Kin Chew, like some enraged mechanical beast.

'Watch out!' I shouted.

KC leapt back onto the sidewalk as the vehicle swerved away at the last instant. It fishtailed alarmingly for an instant, then righted itself and peeled off.

I looked at Kin Chew.

He looked at me.

'The hell was that about?'

We stood around taking turns looking at one another.

'Did you see the look on his face? It's like the bastard wanted to run me down.'

We continued up Birch Road, with the high walls of the Chinese Assembly Hall coming into view, when all at once it dawned on me that there was nobody out on the street. It was eerily still; the only movement, a traffic light hanging over a deserted intersection that ticked from green to amber, and then amber to red. We'd walked almost halfway into town before finally getting our first glimpse of other people: two figures in the distance, running across the road—sprinting really, as if being chased—before disappearing into a parking lot structure. Kin Chew stopped me.

'Something's not right. You hear that?'

I strained my ears, staring down at my feet.

'It's a loud-hailer,' he said. 'Come on.'

KC started to walk quickly up the street. I hurried after him. Soon, we were both of us running.

'Kin Chew?'

'I don't know,' he said, scanning the surroundings warily.

'Kin Chew? Why are we running?'

'I don't know lah. I don't know.'

We emerged on High Street, slightly out of breath. About a block away a sizeable crowd had gathered at the police station and the sounds of activity gradually returned to fill the KL streetscape. A group of officers had corralled the agitated crowd by the station corner and one of the policemen was standing on the bonnet of his car, repeating something I couldn't quite make out over a megaphone. Behind the officers, the main road north into town had been barricaded and a queue of vehicles was being redirected into Station Street. Though there were many people, the gathering seemed oddly subdued. KC pushed through the back of the murmuring crowd. Finally, the message over the megaphone became intelligible:

'Return home quickly and calmly. News will be reported on RM and Malaysia Television. Do not form up around the police station. Return to your homes quickly and calmly.'

The officer repeated the announcement in Bahasa and then Cantonese. Another policeman was translating into Tamil and Hindi. Near the front of the police station, a young woman was wailing, attempting to breach the barricade; I could hear her pleading with the officers. In all the commotion, I lost sight of Kin Chew as he disappeared into a clot of bystanders. I stopped a man who was trying to leave the gathering.

'Uncle, what's happening?'

He looked at me blankly for a moment.

'What is it, uncle? What?'

He was slowly rubbing his temple, as though something had struck him in the head.

'Killings,' he said dazedly.

'Killings? Who is killed?'

'Donno. But there are many. Up near Kampong Baru and Chow Kit area. All uptown.'

'Chow Kit?' I grabbed him by the shirtsleeve to prevent him leaving. 'What about Batu Road? Did you hear anything about Batu Road?'

'Batu Road. Campbell Road. Killings.'

The man extricated himself from me. Before taking off, he hesitated a moment and then patted me sympathetically on the back. I stood alone at the edge of the crowd and watched everyone gazing dumbly towards the north end of town. Many were clinging onto one another, unable to stand on their own. One woman sat on the kerb with her face in her hands, a little boy beside her, tugging at her sleeve. On the horizon, two thin tendrils of smoke were rising straight into the sky.

At that point Kin Chew reappeared, seizing me by the arm and pulling me into a quiet part of the street.

'Kin Chew,' I said. 'Kin Chew, what's happening? What did you hear?'

He turned to look at me, his expression hardening.

'I heard there are riots. People killing and setting fire to shops up north. Police won't let anybody go uptown. What about you? You hear anything?'

'I heard Batu Road.'

'Yes. I heard that too.'

'What do we do?'

He turned away, lost in thought.

'I don't know, Ah Tat.'

* * *

It was clear there was no way into town through the blockade on High Street and so Kin Chew led me down the embankment towards the river. He reasoned we could avoid the authorities by skirting the main road, following the Klang upriver past Chinatown and Petaling Street, before crossing one of the bridges up north. From there we would make our way to Batu Road. My mother was likely to be at home, together with Di Di and the twins. Kin Chew's mother rarely left the house and so she too could be expected to be in the kampong with the others. My father, on the other hand, worked evenings, as did Siew Mooi. At that moment, he might have been across town at BB Park while my sister was probably still finishing her shift at the medical hall on Cecil Street. I couldn't decide if they were better off in the Batu Road house with the rest of the family, or as far from the trouble as possible. Kin Chew grimly pointed out that without either of us, or my father, the women would be at home by themselves.

'I didn't even think of that.'

I also worried about June. Her family lived in Imbi but there was no telling how far the rioting had spread. Kin Chew must have known she was on my mind. Still, neither one of us mentioned her name.

As we scrabbled along the riverbank in the steely evening light, I saw clearly for the first time what had initially appeared to be bags of garbage floating downstream. The chillingly familiar shapes made their slow passage on the water's surface, three of them in a small cluster, silently adrift. Some ways south of the crossing, on the opposite bank of the river, a man was with his dog, struggling to guide the dead bodies to shore with a long bamboo barge pole. The floating lumps merely bobbed and turned in the brown waters before continuing on placidly. The dog paddled out toward them, tongue lolling happily.

'It's getting dark,' Kin Chew said. 'We shouldn't be out in the open like this.'

He stood up tentatively and surveyed the area to gain his bearings. Another body appeared at the top of the river.

'Better get across while we can.'

* * *

'Maybe it's the Communists come back.'

'Communists? Ayah, all that study at the U and for what? Still got nothing but rocks in your head.'

'If you know so much, then what?'

'Why not the Japs even? Maybe they've also come back. Why not?'

'You tell me, since you're so bloody clever.'

'The bodies. In the river.'

'What about them?'

'They were wearing yellow shirts.'

'So?'

'So, Ah Tat. Those are DAP colours. It means they're killing Chinese.'

* * *

At the Mountbatten Road crossing, the bridge was blocked off by squads of police vehicles attempting to contain the spread of the riots. We watched with dread fascination as a massive mob of Malays descended on the barricade, parading UMNO banners and brandishing all manner of improvised weapons: clubs and *changkol*, hoes, tire irons, *parang*. At first it appeared as though the police would stem the onrushing tide, the mob bucking restlessly against the line of defence, seeming to vacillate at the moment of truth. But then, on the fringes of the crowd, a handful of rioters began climbing onto the bonnet of a police van. I heard two gunshots snapping off in quick succession and in the next instant, the mob was surging through the checkpoint, as if a starter had been fired for some violent footrace. They swarmed the police officers and their units, mounting the rocking hoods of their cars, upending steel barricades and driving them through the windshields. One policeman had the clothes torn from his body and was forced to leap into the Klang, naked, arms waving panicked shapes in the air. In a matter of minutes, the Mountbatten Road bridge was overrun. We looked on horrified as the vanguard began pouring south. They were sprinting over the bridge, hurling themselves at the first shophouses they came across, glass bottles splashing on the streets and against the facades of the buildings all around them. They tore down Chinese signs and urinated on them.

Kin Chew pulled me away.

'Time to go.'

'What are they doing? Are they all gone mad?'

'Time to go, Ah Tat. Run for God's sake.'

No longer able to reach Batu Road, we were pushed out further east, scurrying from shophouse to shophouse along Ampang Street, the abandoned buildings watching our retreat in perfect stillness, as if stoically awaiting their own fate. We slipped into an alleyway and wove through the backstreets. Before long, I'd completely lost my sense of direction. Somewhere along the way I must have dropped the sari.

Finally, we emerged in the open, somewhere off Bukit Nanas Road. It was deep into the evening by that time and Bukit Nanas hill rose in the dark before us like the black hump of a surfacing whale. Encircling the base of the hill was a narrow road leading out to the forest reserve; an ill-lit, heavily wooded area that we hoped might provide some cover, but as we followed the deserted road, Kin Chew spotted a felled palm tree in the distance, lying across our path. The tree trunk had prevented a silver Volkswagen from getting any further up the road and the car was idling there in the dark, emitting a bright ruby haze from its taillights. Something was wrong. Out of the silence, rapid footfalls could be heard echoing through the reserve, and several shrouded figures darted behind the Volkswagen, their silhouettes fleetingly backlit by the car's brake-lamps. Kin Chew and I backed away. We watched as men surrounded the vehicle, hauling the driver out of the cabin along with two other passengers, one of whose shrill screams pierced the otherwise ominously noiseless night. The sound made the hairs spring up on the back of my neck. Abruptly, the screams were cut short and the smell of petrol filled the air. Soon the Volkswagen was smoking in a thick black fug. Man-shaped shadows stood in the light of the flames while a couple of smaller shapes, boys perhaps, began chasing each other around the road, hooting and shouting and pitching glass bottles at one another. A colony of bats scattered from the trees.

Kin Chew crouched beneath the level of the road. He turned and looked up at Bukit Nanas. The church sitting atop the hill was looking back.

*　*　*

A middle-aged Indian nun let us in. At first, she'd only opened the heavy teak door a crack and, seeing Kin Chew standing there long-haired and unshaven, remained hidden within the building:

'What do you want? This is a house of peace.'

I bundled Kin Chew aside with my briefcase and stood before the nun. The sister's severe expression softened immediately when she saw that I was wearing a shirt and tie.

'We're Methodists,' I blurted out. 'Please, Sister.'

'Come in then,' she frowned, ushering us in hastily. 'Even Methodists are welcome here.'

It was dark inside the church, the electric lights having been switched off in favour of a handful of candles lighted at the altar. Multiple stone reliefs were fixed high on the walls at evenly spaced stations around the building, and in the wings of the church, two glassy-eyed statues stood in their dioramas: one of Mary, the other of Jesus. The life-sized statues had an unnerving appearance in the gloomy, flickering light. There were half a dozen children sitting in the front row of the church, seven-year-old girls in school uniforms who seemed spooked by their surroundings. They'd been waiting for their parents to collect them from the school at the bottom of the hill when the rioting had broken out. The nun had subsequently spirited the girls up to the church for refuge, claiming their mothers and fathers wanted them to stay behind for scripture lessons. There they waited, a couple of them clearly sceptical of the story they'd been told, and of the vaguely anxious adults milling about and speaking in hushed tones.

'They're coming soon, girls,' Sister Claire reassured them. 'Your parents will all be here to pick you up soon. Everything's fine. Everything's normal.'

The priest, one Father Bernard Loong, spent his time at the top of a ladder, peering worriedly out the tall arched windows onto the church properties at the bottom of the hill: the rectory, the convent and the school. Every now and then, he would drift off into the tiny room behind the altar where he checked to see if the telephone line was still down. He carried a portable radio wherever he went, refusing to surrender it even to the nun, and as the bulletins started coming over the air, began officiously repeating the announcements to the rest of us, almost word-for-word:

'Mountbatten Road is closed. Batu Road is closed. Nobody is to go into Kampong Baru or Chow Kit. We are to stay indoors and await further instructions.'

Kin Chew and I passed the time sitting by the statue of Mary, watching Sister Claire read stories from a children's bible to the little girls in the candlelight. It was warm and quiet, and the steady rhythm of the nun's low voice had started to put the girls to sleep, her storytelling interrupted only by the odd siren that would wail and then recede into the night. I myself was beginning to drift off when, out of the corner of my eye, I noticed the cat that had been curled up on the ledge of one of the tall stained-glass windows. It sat up suddenly with its large yellow eyes round and alert, and then darted into the shadows, ears flat against its head. A moment later, a group of faint voices could be heard approaching the church. Kin Chew sat bolt upright. He got up and went to the entrance, crouching warily behind the teak doors. The glossy sheen of sweat on his face caught the sallow candlelight as he listened. When there was no longer any doubt the voices were travelling up the hill, he made me drag the heavy pews over from the back of the church and we began stacking them against the door. The priest hovered around us, complaining irritably:

'Careful with those. You will scratch the floor, dragging them around like that. Stop it now. You panic for nothing.'

'Father's right,' I said. 'They're probably just like us, Kin Chew. Just people looking for shelter.'

'Can't you hear them?' KC hissed at me. 'They're laughing out there.'

The little girls started waking, roused by the commotion and urgent whispers. They sat up and watched us bracing the benches against the door, their expressions slowly changing one by one, from curious to nervous, culminating finally in something highly disturbing; their innocent features twisted into a picture of unconcealed dread. Then, surprising us all out of the dark, a man's voice rang out clearly through the church, as if the speaker was just on the other side of the door.

'Census!' he shouted in Bahasa. 'Come out, come out for the UMNO census!'

Kin Chew looked at the rest of us and put a finger to his lips. Sister Claire gathered the children together and they scurried into the corner of the church by the statue of Mary. Moments later, several sharp blows rattled the frame of the door and one of the girls inadvertently let out a frightened yelp.

'Come out, all you Chinese and Indians. All Christians stand up to be counted for the census.'

There was laughter on the other side of the door and then one of the high windows at the back of the church shattered. We all turned to stare at the stained glass now littering the linoleum floor. Several more rocks flew through the window, followed by more laughter and a second window splintering. The schoolgirls scuttled behind Mary's statue, whimpering and trying to hide. The statue's outstretched arms made it appear in the gloom as though it had momentarily come to life. From outside, one of the Malay voices switched languages, taunting us in perfect Cantonese:

'We know you're in there. Come out, there's nothing to fear.'

Kin Chew stood away from the door. He reached around the back of his trousers and withdrew a scuffed metal object that had been strapped to his body, concealed in the waistband.

It was a pistol.

He pointed the gun at the door and fired two rounds into the wood—one, two—in a measured, almost detached way, as if it was like any other kind of ordinary tool. I had been standing right beside him when he'd discharged the weapon and I leapt back instinctively, flinching after each shot with my hands over my face. I stared at Kin Chew. We were all of us, Sister Claire and the priest, staring at him. Even the little girls had ceased their mewling and writhing to look on breathlessly, hands clapped to their ears. After a moment, KC climbed over the stacked benches and put his ear to the door. He turned and looked back at me before pressing his head against the wood once again.

'I can't hear,' he half-shouted. 'Can you hear anything? I think they're gone.'

I couldn't reply, overcome as I too was, by an eye-watering tinnitus.

* * *

The priest spent the next half hour on his hands and knees, painstakingly collecting every shard of stained glass from the broken windows onto a large white altar cloth. When he was done, he carefully folded the cloth over the coloured jags of glass and placed the bundle in the tabernacle, before hurrying to inspect the pair of bullet holes in the main door. While the priest was busy, Sister Claire came over to Kin Chew and took him aside.

'Shame on you,' she said. 'Guns have no place here. Who are you? Tell me the truth now.'

'I am nobody.'

'I wasn't born yesterday. We won't have triads bringing violence into the Lord's house.'

I could see the nun's hands were trembling and she clasped them together in an effort to bring them under control, as if seized by a sharp attack of rheumatism. She stood there a moment, shifting her gaze from Kin Chew to myself. When she next spoke, her voice emerged with a surprising degree of authority:

'I've had a discussion with Father Bernard. We both feel it is best if the two of you leave as soon as possible.'

'Leave?'

'I am sorry but that is our decision. Take your gun and go elsewhere. Join that madness if you must. But there are children here to think of.'

'You don't expect us to go back out there?' I said.

'You go now, please. It's for the best.'

I looked at Kin Chew. Before my very eyes his whole demeanour changed, and he suddenly transformed into the vicious hoodlum I'd only ever heard rumours about. Still gripping the pistol in his hand, he took a step towards Sister Claire and raised his arm over her. He was on the verge of bringing the butt of it down on her head when she fell away, cowering at his feet.

'Mercy!'

'Who do you think you're talking to? I am no schoolgirl, woman.'

In that instant I knew, unequivocally, the stories surrounding Kin Chew to be true. He was what they said he was. Sister Claire backed away on her knees, eyes downcast.

'I was only trying to—'

'Shut up,' he barked. 'Find us a place to sleep. I am tired of dealing with you lot.'

She took us up a narrow staircase to an attic above the church where it was agreed we would stay out-of-sight. The arrangement suited everybody, as Kin Chew's presence had begun to unnerve the others, and he himself preferred to be around as few people as possible. The attic was long, spanning the length of the church, with the rafters slanting steeply to the ceiling-boards on either side of the building. We brought a pack of candles up with us and set up in the middle of the room, where a series of dormer windows looked out on the surrounding hillside. They provided an unexpected view of much of the town below: the roofs of the houses on Ampang Road and Malacca Street, illuminated by a row of streetlamps; and the Mountbatten Road bridge, from which we had been repelled earlier, now deserted but for a cluster of burning vehicles. Just across the river, the minaret and domed towers of the central mosque watched on. I could see, every now and then, the façade of the great sand-coloured building being lit up from below in bright pulses of cellophane red, cast by the revolving beacons of ambulance cars. I turned quietly to Kin Chew.

'You weren't really going to hit her, were you? She's a nun for God's sake.'

'I'll hit whoever I want,' he said.

Looking north, it was very dark. Despite our high vantage, all that could be seen of the area was the faint glow of numerous fires, and the thin spires of smoke that had billowed black during the day, now billowing cotton white.

'I didn't know you had a gun.'

'I don't wave it around for everyone to see.'

'What do you need a gun for, Kin Chew?'

'What for? Ask those animals kicking at the door just now, what for. Unbelievable. What for.'

He turned away muttering to himself and lay down to rest.

'I'm not even asking for a simple thank you lah. Just not so many dirty looks.'

* * *

I woke with a start around ten that night. From somewhere out in the kampongs surrounding us, the metallic thrum of distant *kendang* drums clanged menacingly in the air. Kin Chew was sitting over by the window, smoking a cigarette in the dark.

'I couldn't sleep properly,' I croaked.

'Me too.'

More than a dozen butts littered the space around Kin Chew's feet and the attic reeked of tobacco smoke. He sat with his head pressed against the glass of the window, gazing down on the street below.

'Kin Chew?'

'What is it, Ah Tat?'

'I need to use the bathroom.'

He turned to look at me in the dark. The candles in the attic had long since melted into a flat pool of cold wax so I couldn't quite make out his expression, merely the shape of his motionless figure in the window, backlit by the moon.

'You want me to take you?' he said.

'Yes, please.'

A couple of hours later I was woken again, this time by a pattern of clipped popping sounds, rapidly snapped off in the distance. The sound put me in mind of Chinese New Year festivals, when the paper lion would prance before all the shophouse doors in Chinatown, each garlanded with reams of the little red firecrackers.

A second burst followed.

Kin Chew peered out the window, hand cupped to the glass.

'Automatics,' he murmured.

We hurried down the stairs into the church proper. Sister Claire and the priest were in the small room behind the altar, sitting on either side of the radio. The priest looked up at us as we came in.

'A state of emergency is declared,' he said. 'Twenty-four-hour curfew.'

We listened to the warnings issued on every station. The Royal Malay Regiment had been deployed with orders to shoot-on-sight any civilians found out on the streets. Father Bernard was sitting on a high-backed chair at his desk, smoking a cigarette.

'About time,' he said, under his breath. 'Shoot the bastards.'

Kin Chew went over to the priest and reached for the man's cigarettes, but Father Bernard snatched his pack of Camels away, saying:

'There's only a few left. Who knows how long we'll be here now with curfew? You should have rationed yours, like I did.'

The radio announcements began to repeat themselves after a while. Sister Claire returned to the main hall of the church. The schoolgirls were sleeping in the front pews and the nun went around rousing each child where she drowsed fitfully, leading the little girls—confused and half-asleep—before the altar. She lit several candles and had the children kneel in a row, removing the glass rosary from around her neck.

'We must pray for your parents,' she said solemnly. 'And the country also.'

* * *

The following day Kin Chew and I sat in the stuffy attic awaiting news. Out the window, we glimpsed convoys of olive-green trucks roving slowly through the streets around Mountbatten Road, but across the river to the north, many of the fires continued to burn despite the military presence.

That afternoon, Kin Chew and I saw from the window of the attic an old Malay woman brazenly trudging up the hill. She was alone, carrying a rattan handbasket whilst casually making her way towards the church. An army truck was posted at the foot of the hill and one of the soldiers had climbed onto the bed of the truck, shouting out at the woman through a loudspeaker.

'Back to your house, auntie! Don't you know it's curfew? Go back now or we will fire.'

Kin Chew and I watched as the old woman plodded on determinedly, through the little cemetery in the yard, right up to the front doors of the church where she deposited her handbasket. She then turned around and started right back down the hill, giving the onlooking soldiers a cheerful wave.

The woman had brought us a big pot of yellow rice with raisins, along with some biscuits and chocolate bars. As Sister Claire sat the little girls down in a circle to eat, Father Bernard paced around the back of the church, patting the pockets of his trousers.

'Where did my cigarettes go? For the life of me, I can't find where I left my Camels.'

* * *

That night, the second running we spent in the church attic, I woke to find that Kin Chew had gone. Blinking in the dark, a cold sweat washed over me, and I got up and stumbled downstairs in the dark to look for him. The children were all asleep along the pews, Sister Claire lying on the floor of the aisle beside them. From the room behind the altar, the priest's snores emerged brokenly. Searching frantically, I eventually noticed the side door, framed by pale blue light coming from outside. An empty pack of cigarettes was flattened against the latch. I opened the door and stepped outside and then replaced the bit of cardboard, wedging it back into the jamb. Scurrying along the walls, I kept to the shadows. In the middle of the small churchyard cemetery, Kin Chew was sitting on a headstone in plain view, staring down the hill.

'What the hell are you doing out here? You trying to get yourself shot?'

He turned and put a finger to his lips. Several cigarette butts littered the gravesite, the last of which was still smouldering on the ground.

'Let me guess,' I said. 'Camels?'

He grinned and looked off into the distance once more.

'We are supposed to stay inside, Kin Chew. It's not safe.'

'Don't worry so much. I been watching the patrols. The next shift won't be here for another hour.'

Bukit Nanas fell away beneath us. At the bottom of the hill, the white buildings of the convent and school appeared oddly luminous in the moonlight and from a distance, an indistinct garble echoed eerily in the stillness; somebody's radio set, its lone voice afloat in an ocean of silence. The air smelled of ash.

'When I woke and you were gone, I thought you cabut.'

'Where would I go?'

'Wouldn't be the first time you disappeared without a trace.'

Kin Chew got up and paced around the cemetery, stopping to scrape the bottom of his shoe on one of the plaques.

'I never did tell you why I ran off,' he said. 'Back then, I mean.'

'You went to Carey Island.'

'How did you know?'

'Siew Mooi told me.'

'Ah Mooi told you, did she? How did Ah Mooi know?'

'She knows everything.'

Kin Chew smiled. He nodded and stared vacantly over the dark hillside and lost his smile after a moment.

'When I found him in Carey Island, I realized he was leaving us. After that, everything changed for me. I decided, I am on my own now.'

'I heard he got a whole new family over there.'

'Aw. He married some local girl. A Malay. Changed his name to Ahmad Adi. They even got children now, last I heard.'

'Walao, he converted? Siew Mooi never told me that. Ahmad Adi. And I always thought he hated Malays.'

'Ahmad Adi.' Kin Chew shook his head.

'What did he say? When you found him?'

'Nothing. He asked me how was school. Introduced me to his woman. He told her I was his nephew, can you believe that? Didn't want her to know about me, I suppose.'

'What did you say?'

'Nothing. What's to say?'

KC walked to the edge of the hill and looked out over the grey landscape. A line of headlamps was crawling along Mountbatten Road towards town. Military trucks. Across the river, the rest of Kuala Lumpur continued to burn.

'I've got to tell you something, Kin Chew.'

'What is it?'

'I'm getting married come November.'

'Yeah lah. I know.'

'You know?'

Kin Chew looked at me in the dark, 'Siew Mooi told me.'

We each smiled to ourselves for a moment.

'I should have told you about the wedding myself. I don't know why I didn't.'

He nodded and fell silent. After a while, I said:

'Aren't you going to say anything?'

'What's to say? Congratulations?' he shrugged. 'Congratulations.'

'Will you come to the wedding? We both want you there.'

'No, Ah Tat. I am not coming to the wedding.'

'Come inside and we can talk about it. I bet you'll change your mind.'

He sighed.

'Alright, never mind. We'll talk about it some other time.'

'There's nothing to say.'

'You want me to leave you alone?'

'Yeah lah. Leave me alone.'

'You'll come back inside soon, won't you? It makes me nervous you being out here, all these trigger-happy soldiers about. Kin Chew?'

'I heard you, Ah Tat. Go back inside. I'll be in soon.'

* * *

Curfew was lifted for a few hours the following day. The batteries in the priest's portable radio had died overnight and so it was only when several people showed up at the church doors, anxiously asking after their children, that we became aware of the news. Kin Chew and I immediately prepared to set out for Batu Road. As we were leaving, I noticed that all but one of the schoolchildren had been collected by their parents. The image of that last remaining girl standing beside Sister Claire in the church courtyard has stayed with me to this day. The child was staring fiercely at the road, practically willing her parents' car to appear around the bend. I'd overheard they owned a silver Volkswagen.

Rather than head back through the centre of town, Kin Chew and I decided to cross the river at Campbell Road. We had almost reached the bridge when we passed by a row of shops on the perimeter of a nearby kampong. A handful of bystanders were poking around the ransacked stores: its windows smashed out and the shelves brought down, the floor strewn with stock. Behind the shops, a car had been turned upside down. A thatched roof bus shelter stood at the end of the shop row. Something had caught Kin Chew's attention and he went over to the bus stop. Lodged sideways into the leg of the wooden structure was the blade of a parang. It had bitten into the grain a good couple of inches and Kin Chew took the handle with both hands and pried the long knife out, pushing off the plank with his foot. It came away suddenly and he held the flat of the parang up to the sunlight. A tuft of fine hair was plastered to the sharp edge by a black crusted-over stain. Kin Chew looked at me. He knelt and peered into the gash sectioned out of the wood beam of the bus shelter. Embedded deep within the groove of the cut were three white teeth—molars—still attached to the shattered remnant of a jaw. Kin Chew dropped the parang. Its clattering seemed to ring out through the street. He wiped his hands on the front of his shirt as curious onlookers started making their way over. I backed away, my heart suddenly racing. There were drag marks all over the dusty earth and a few feet away, concealed in the shadow of one of the provision shops, a peculiar-looking pile was covered over with palm fronds and flattened cardboard boxes. Several pairs of feet stuck out from under the coverings, and when one of the bystanders pulled the top layer of sodden cardboard away, a seething cloud of flies filled the air with their murmuring. Underneath was a horror-film monster with many heads and limbs. Kin Chew had to wait for me while I was sick by the side of the road.

Afterwards, we finally crossed the river and made our way up to Batu Road. We joined a large crowd that was shuffling along the main road, waves of people ahead of us and more coming behind, all steadily heading north, watched by army wagons stationed every hundred yards or so, soldiers hanging off running boards with their submachine guns braced, ready to open fire. Rows of shophouses had been scorched, a fine white soot covering the charred remains, and a delicate layer had settled on all the flat surfaces: the roofs of cars, the pavement, the window-ledges and tree branches. As the surrounding areas became more residential, we passed by people standing transfixed in doorways or squatting under the eaves of their houses, watching without expression the silent crowds march along Batu Road. I noticed the facades of some of the houses had been peppered with bullet-holes, the glass shot out of windowpanes on the upper storeys and from the windshields of the cars sitting in the driveways. Further on, a man was arguing with a pair of soldiers outside his home. One of the soldiers suddenly struck him in the chest with the butt of his rifle. The passing crowd moved on quickly.

When we came to the turnoff leading to the family kampong, I reached out for Kin Chew's hand. We walked down together, grown men hand in hand, through the little village street among the lime trees. The attap houses stared back at us, empty and silent but for the timid clucking of fowls. We passed by Ah Teng's house on our way through the kampong. His truck, usually parked out the front, was missing. I went up to his door and called out for him, peering through the window, but there was no reply.

I knew we wouldn't find anyone at our house either. But as we stepped through the front door, I half-expected my little brother to come running, or hear Ma Ma cursing from the backyard, demanding to know where I'd been. The rooms were dark and motionless. All the dresser drawers had been pulled out and bundles of clothes were heaped on the bed and floor. The large trunk that my parents kept on top of the wardrobe was gone, along with all the money in the house. Everything else seemed untouched. I went out the back into the yard. The stone mortar was sitting at the bottom of the stoop with a mouldering yellow paste still in it. The pestle lay in the dusty earth. Kin Chew came outside and looked at me:

'Let's go to the shop. Maybe Ah Hong has news.'

The village shop was unusually busy, with several people I'd never seen before rummaging through the shelves and filling their small wheelbarrows with supplies. Ah Hong's grandson was behind the counter.

'Most of the families got relocated early on,' he said. 'I think your mother and the rest of them got shifted to Stadium Merdeka.'

'Was Siew Mooi with her? And Ah Di and the twins?'

'That's all I know.'

'What about my father?'

'That's all I know lah.'

'Let me use your telephone. I want to check on my sweetheart.'

'The lines been down since Tuesday, Ah Tat. Still nothing today.'

I stared blankly at the customers in the shop. A couple of them were bickering over some milk powder. On the shelves surrounding them, rows and rows were empty of stock.

'How is your grandfather?' I said.

'He's fine. Especially now the shop is making a killing.'

I looked at him and frowned.

'Okay lah, not a killing. Poor choice of words. But we can charge anything we like and look, people will still pay. The shop hasn't been this busy in years. Must be the only place open around here. Eh, did you hear or not? They set fire to Ah Teng's truck.'

'Is it?'

'I saw the plates myself. The only thing left to see. Let me tell you, he won't be driving that thing around anymore.'

'You got any rice?'

'Got. Sure, I got. It's more expensive now, of course. Emergency surcharge and all. Okay or not?'

'Fine, fine.'

I went into the aisles amongst the other customers and returned to the counter with several packets of dried mushroom and cans of fried fish. Ah Hong's grandson put a small sack of rice onto the counter. Kin Chew came over and stood beside me:

'Give me a carton of Viceroy.'

'Cigarettes?' he laughed. 'Cigarettes are long gone, my friend.'

* * *

Curfew was reinstated that evening, the klaxons sounding off intermittently from Batu Road for an hour. There was not enough time to make it all the way to Stadium Merdeka in order to begin our search for the family, so we decided to spend the night in the kampong and start out early the following day. I made lumpy congee and tidied up around the house while Kin Chew scanned the radio for news, lying in the spot where he used to sleep as a child. I remembered the pack of Viceroys that Sam Ji always kept on the altar in the big room and went to get it. Tossing the pack at KC, I said:

'Look what I found.'

'Oh my God,' he sat up. 'Ah Tat, I could kiss you.'

'Thank your mother. I told you, you should come home more often.'

That night was a strange one. I remember waking up sometime in the early hours, as the sky was beginning to gain some colour outside and found Kin Chew wandering aimlessly about the dim blue rooms with his pistol drawn. He was glistening with sweat. I called out to him:

'Kin Chew! What are you doing? Kin Chew, wake up for God's sake!'

He looked at me as if from a great distance.

'Piggy?'

'It's me! It's Ah Tat! Your cousin, it's your cousin.' I sidled up to him, taking care to stay as far away from the pistol as possible, and gently eased the gun out of his hand. 'Come, let's go back to sleep. I'll take you back to bed.'

I led him through the corridor into the other room. As he got down on the bamboo mat, still half asleep, he continued to mutter at me:

'We could have let him go, Piggy. He was begging, the poor bastard.'

'Quiet now, Kin Chew. Go back to sleep.'

'He had kids. Did you know he had kids?'

The next day, we heard over the radio that curfew had been relaxed once again and before setting out for the stadium, I reheated the pot of congee I'd made the previous night. Kin Chew sat on the floor before the low table and I placed a bowl in front of him.

'You still walk around in your sleep,' I said.

He was blowing gently on a spoonful of the thick porridge and paused to look up at me.

'Do I?'

'You don't remember?'

I went to the shelves where the crockery was kept and took down one of the big clay pots. I removed the lid of the pot and took out his handgun, holding it out to him with two fingers. Kin Chew got up from the low table. He came over and snatched the pistol from me, carefully opening the slide and peering inside the chamber. Then he locked it and shoved it in the back of his trousers, covering it over with his shirttail. He sat down and continued eating.

'That's where it went.'

'You were saying some strange things in your sleep, Kin Chew.'

He shrugged. 'You know what dreams are like.'

'My dreams are not like that.'

'Finish eating and let's get to the stadium. I'm almost out of cigarettes again. Maybe we can find some on the way.'

* * *

We arrived early at Stadium Merdeka, joining crowds of people already milling outside the entrances, waiting to enter the grounds. Soldiers had been stationed out front under the great concrete arches, searching people as they shuffled slowly through the gates. Their uniforms were slightly different to the ones I'd seen on the street patrols: capped with red berets and brassards, the letters MP boldly printed high on their sleeves. We were almost at the front of the queue when, with a cold start, I remembered Kin Chew's pistol. I turned to warn him off, but he'd already disappeared.

Surprisingly, the stadium inside had something of a carnival air. The playing field was filled with hawkers, rows of traders spaced evenly apart, kneeling on newspaper mats with vegetables and sweets and sacks of rice laid out before them. Old women with carrying poles walked among the allotments, long bamboo rods see-sawing precariously across their shoulders, weighted down with buckets of tofu and red bean paste. Crowds of people were wandering through the field, inspecting the food on display as young barefoot boys ran back and forth, ferrying change and purchased goods up to the stands. It could have been a weekend market.

Up in the north and east stands, displaced refugees had erected cardboard box houses in the aisles and standing areas. Tarpaulin sheets were fashioned into improvised tents that encircled the grounds, thin wisps of cooking smoke emerging from within them. Children were hopping from seat to seat along the bleachers and teenagers sat grouped on the terraces, playing cards and catcalling the young women that happened past. An ambulance car was parked at one end of the stadium, military trucks at the other. I climbed the steps to the uppermost tier of the structure for a better view. Below me, the tops of a few thousand heads jostled through the grounds, the red berets of the military police dotted amongst them. Streams of people continued to pour into the stadium, some desperately clinging to a few precious belongings, others seeking out friends and family members. Every once in a while, great exclamations of relief, in Cantonese, Hakka, Tamil and Hindi, Bahasa and English, could be heard coming from the various sections of the stands.

I had already been walking the aisles for some time when seemingly out of nowhere, Kin Chew appeared by my side.

'How did you get in?' I said.

'I know people.' He was smoking a cigarette.

'Did you find them?'

'No. Nothing yet.'

'I see you found yourself some smokes though.'

He grunted. 'Listen, Ah Tat. Keep your wallet close. I recognize some of the fellows in here. It's open season.'

For the next half hour, we picked our way through the grandstands, gazing across row upon row of the brightly painted seats—banks of red, white, yellow and blue—the colours of the flag. As I walked around the blue section of the stands, it occurred to me that I was passing through the very same bay in which I had been seated with my family many years ago, during the ceremony for Malayan Independence. Then, as now, thousands of people had packed into Stadium Merdeka. I stopped to gaze over the stadium. We'd all cheered at the time.

Before me now, an old man was dozing across a line of faded blue seats, perhaps the very same seats my family had occupied back in 1957, with a flattened cardboard box lying on top of him as if it were a blanket. Flashing unbidden across my mind's eye, I saw the old man rotting in a pool of tar-like blood, covered in a writhing pall of flies. The ground beneath me tilted, veering up sharply for a moment. I sat where I stood, looking up at Kin Chew.

'What if they're not here?' My hands were shaking.

Kin Chew tried to get me to stand up, but my legs wouldn't take the weight. Farther down in the stands, beside one of the makeshift cardboard shelters, a pair of white men, reporters possibly, were talking to a woman who was beating her chest and wailing inconsolably. A naked infant was squirming around on a cardboard mat beside her, face contorted in the act of crying, a hoarse rattle emerging from his throat. Suddenly, it seemed as though there were people crying all around me.

'What if something terrible happened to them?'

Kin Chew hauled me up by the armpit and pointed over to the south entrance of the stadium.

'Stand up, you fool. Look. Isn't that your mother over there? They're all over there lah. Look!'

I hurried down through the bays and leaned over the field wall, looking along the banks of the stadium. Leaping over the railing, I fought my way past the crowds, hand waving frantically in the air. Siew Mooi was the first to spot me across the field. She hurried over, pushing past hawkers and meandering refugees. We embraced.

'We thought the worst,' she laughed.

I stood back, taking in the sight of my sister, then glanced over her shoulder at the tunnel by the south gate. My mother was haggling over some vegetables with one of the hawker boys. Di Di and the twins were with her.

'Ba Ba?'

'He's alright. He left to check on the house.'

I told her the house was intact, that I'd spent the night there just past and that the rest of the kampong seemed to have escaped damage. Siew Mooi in turn told me that she'd run into one of June's old high school friends in the stadium; she was safe, in Petaling Jaya with some relatives. One by one, the rest of the family spotted me across the crowded grounds. Sam Ji was next to arrive at my side. She looked at me, eyes full of apprehension:

'Have you heard from my boy?'

I laughed. 'He's fine, Sam Ji. He's right here.'

I turned around to call him over but of course, Kin Chew was nowhere to be seen.

* * *

In the wake of the May Thirteen riots, the Malaysian Parliament was suspended. An emergency caretaker government was installed, and Prime Minister Abdul Rahman was forced to step down from office. When Parliament reconvened, a year later in 1970, the new ruling coalition began devising a raft of measures intended to close the economic gulf between the various ethnic groups in Malaysia, namely the Chinese in urban areas and the largely rural Malay population. Collectively these initiatives were known as the New Economic Policy, or the NEP.

1971

Thirteen

When Hasan told me he was moving out of the Suleiman Court flats, to some new housing further out from the city, I don't know what I expected the place to be like. I'd never heard of Kampong Pasir and assumed it was simply another one of the new low-cost housing projects springing up all over KL at that time. I must admit, I wasn't prepared for what I was to see.

I recall getting my first inkling as I came off the Federal Highway, driving along an exit road that seemed to get narrower and dustier the further along I went. Eventually, the paved road disappeared altogether and I parked my Mercedes on a bare patch of dirt and got out. I took out my pocketbook and looked over Hasan's directions. Cupping a hand to my brow, I squinted across the bleak landscape. Far away, down by the river's edge, a dense clutter of faded rust-stained rooftops sprawled out from the western bank like a ragged patchwork blanket of browns, reds and sheenless metal greys. I glanced back at the Mercedes, its wheels and undercarriage now caked in the dusty earth, and winced. I'd washed the car only a day ago. Pressing my handkerchief to my temple, I tracked down the craggy hillside toward the river.

At the edge of the squatter area, a group of shirtless men were crowded round a shopping trolley loaded with second-hand transistor radios. An old man was sitting on a footstool nearby, mending the stitching on a pair of worn brogues. I went over to him and showed him the page of my pocketbook.

'Aneh, do you know where Kampong Pasir is? Am I in the right place?'

The old man muttered something in Tamil, peering at the thin gold pen clipped to the spine of the book. He started beckoning to me, looking now at my suit pants and Italian leather shoes. I hurried on.

Several dwellings, little more than shacks, had been erected on the outskirts of the settlement. A woman was squatting over a big round metal tub, dyeing strips of cloth in dark red water, while another was sweeping out her doorway with a tuft of attap. They both stopped what they were doing to watch me pass.

Further in, the shanty houses became more crowded, the air stuffier and rancid, and I made my way through the narrow spaces separating them. Magazines and cigarette butts and empty potato crisp packets littered the ground at my feet. A pale dirty stray roamed the ruelles, lifting its nose inquisitively here and there. It looked at me for a moment before trotting away. And then from behind, a familiar voice:

'Ah Tat? Is that you?'

* * *

It was stuffy and cramped inside the shack, the cloistered space irradiated with heat trapped by the tin walls. There was not much inside: a simple wooden shelf, crammed with pots and bowls; a second-hand coffee table and cases of beer stacked in a corner. The floor was lined with old newspaper, peppered with tiny cockroach droppings, and against the side wall was a row of large tubs, each filled with fresh water. Throw pillows and a bedsheet were bundled on the mat where he slept in the back.

Hasan watched me, sitting on the floor opposite him at the little coffee table.

'What is it?' he said. 'What's the matter?'

'Nothing.'

He frowned. 'You look like something's bothering you.'

I peered about the room as Hasan followed my gaze. After a moment, he chuckled to himself:

'Sometimes I forget what this room looks like.'

'How can you live like this, Hasan?'

'It scares you, does it?'

'Scared?' I shifted on the floor and brushed the dusty earth from the seat of my suit pants, looking around uneasily. 'Scared is not the word.'

'It's not as bad as it looks.'

'Isn't it? Even the houses we grew up in were better than this. I mean for God's sake, Hasan. You got tin sheets for walls.'

'I know.'

'We are supposed to go up. Not down.'

He scratched his belly and frowned.

'Things could be worse,' he said. 'The Reserve Unit used to come by every day to tear down shelters. That's what the old-timers tell me. But since we moved in, the government hasn't come to hassle anybody, inshallah. Apparently, the settlement's grown too big.'

I sat hugging my knees. 'What happened to your flat in Suleiman Court?'

He shrugged. 'We were evicted when Zainuddin lost his job. You know him. Cannot manage life back in town, my uncle.'

I pulled aside the blotched muslin curtain that looked out onto the river through a square hole sawn out of the corrugated siding. A grey layer of scum and litter collected along the Klang waterline. Perched on the edge of a crumbling culvert, a group of young sun-blackened children were edging their way down to the water's edge, screeching and pointing at something in the river.

'What's all the fuss out there?' I said.

'Ignore them. It's a game. Ever since the riots they cannot get enough of it.'

The children continued screaming and stamping, running along the bank. I turned from the window and looked at Hasan. He laughed:

'They're trying to convince the adults they spot dead bodies in the river.'

'What, you mean like another May Thirteen?'

He shrugged, reaching for his tobacco pouch. 'Nothing much else to do around here.'

Filling a cigarette paper with grainy green tobacco, Hasan licked the ends of his fingers and twisted the paper into a smoke. He lit it and pulled steadily on the cigarette, its sear end crackling. I started coughing and unbuttoned the collar of my shirt.

'What brand is that you're smoking? It stinks to all hell.'

Slowly, the shack began to fill with smoke; a dreamy haze shifting sluggishly in the hot air. A big blowfly charged into the room and we watched it ricochet noisily from corner to corner, repeatedly butting itself into the low ceiling before finally finding its way out through a gap in the joint. Just outside, somebody was singing to the tune of the American national anthem, improvising some of the lyrics in Bahasa. Hasan smiled at me.

'Zainuddin,' he said.

'That's your uncle singing?'

'Not bad, right? He's practising for his audition.'

'Audition?'

'He's decided he wants to be a big film star now. I'm going to go into town with him later today. Maybe try and audition myself. Who knows, Ah Tat? You could be looking at the next P. Ramlee. My voice is not too bad, if I do say so myself.'

'You're not serious.'

He frowned. 'You never know. Lightning can strike.'

A moment later, Hasan's uncle appeared at the entrance of the shack, ducking his head under the door. He peered in at the two of us.

'What's this?' His face was lathered in soap, and he was pointing a plastic razor at us. 'You two *cibai* smoked the last of my *dadah*, is it?'

'Dadah?' I said.

'Don't play ignorant with me,' Zainuddin snapped. 'I can smell it from outside.'

Hasan giggled and lay back against the corrugated siding of the room, the cigarette still burning between his fingers. His uncle was shouting at him now:

'You better not have smoked the last of it, Hasan. My audition is coming up soon. You know how it helps me loosen up my vocal cords.'

Hasan lay contentedly on the floor with his eyes half-closed. He looked up at me, grinning through heavy lids:

'Don't look so worried, Ah Tat. A little ganja never hurt anyone.'

'What are you doing to yourself?'

'This? This stuff is weak as old tea leaves. Remind me to tell you about my first time with Lucy. Zainuddin's friends over at the studio backlot got us some a few weeks ago. I tell you, truly. There are other worlds beyond this one.'

'Other worlds? What are you talking about?'

'Don't be so close-minded, Ah Tat. The Beatles dropped acid.'

I looked at him, shaking my head. 'You're some kind of bloody hippie now, is it?'

Later, Hasan walked me back to my car, and we hiked up the hillside to the sound of the Federal Highway roaring in the distance. Stopping on the crest of a high ridge, we gazed back on the shanty houses in silence. The settlement merged contiguous with the river and looked from afar like an infected boil, swelling out of the Klang itself.

'Where did you park?' Hasan said.

I looked along the dirt track. 'Back there, where the road ends.'

In the distance, the regular geometry of the KL skyline was visible through the heat haze.

'You should come back to town,' I said. 'There are low-cost flats in Pekeliling now. Nicer than Suleiman Court even.'

'No, I don't think so. My destiny is here now.'

I looked at him. 'Cannot cukup makan forever, Hasan. I know people. I can get you a job in the filing room at Briggs. Don't waste your life here.'

'All is well, Ah Tat. I am getting by.'

'I'm worried about you, old friend. You need money?'

'Worried?' he smiled, sadly. 'What are you worried about? I'm going to be a big film star one day.'

I started along the path towards my car and then stopped to look back. Hasan was watching me leave with his hands on his hips.

'You're turning into your uncle,' I called out to him. 'Drinking all the time, smoking that poison. You better watch out, Hasan.'

He grinned and saluted me before turning and starting off home. He was singing at the top of his voice as he sauntered away:

'Oh say can you see,
By the dawn's chau ci-bai,'

* * *

Driving home, I watched the river birds streaking through the honey-coloured light, against the tiered furrowed clouds that were banked row upon row in the sky, like giant golden papadums. As I sped along the highway, my thoughts drifted to the three-storey house I was building in Kenny Hills. The family would be moving in soon, packing up the old attap place off Batu Road. There were flushing toilets in the new place; electricity and a kitchen with running water for Ma Ma, a television set waiting for the old man. Even Sam Ji would get a room to herself. It would be a beautiful home, nestled in the cool majesty of the hills district, just down the road from the Prime Minister's former residence. More importantly, there would be space now, for children.

I'd finally made it out of the kampong. Not everyone had what it took. I thought about Hasan living hand-to-mouth in the slums by the river, and of Kin Chew, who continued to eke out a life of petty crime in the parking lots and flophouses of KL. It was a sad thing, really, but I consoled myself with the knowledge that at least one of us had been blessed with the will—and enough brains and good sense—to truly make something of himself.

1977

Fourteen

By 1977, the small engineering firm I had started was teetering on the brink of bankruptcy. Around that time, the government was pushing domestic rice cultivation very hard and so I'd decided to take my one big chance, investing heavily in the production of a small-sized harvester, specially engineered for use in the Malaysian paddy fields. It was a wonderful machine; to this very day, I still maintain that. I had been so confident of its success that we had a small fleet manufactured on spec. I suppose that had been my undoing. Impatient to grow the business, I had taken a step too far too soon. It turned out the rice farmers preferred modifying the massive combine harvesters imported from Holland and Australia, never mind the fact that they had been designed to cultivate wheat, not rice. Those clumsy foreign tractors were plainly too heavy to work the Asian soil, constantly trapping themselves in the soft Selangor paddy fields and destroying everything underneath them in the process, but they were big and impressive-looking and in the end, nobody was much willing to take a chance on my curious rinky-dink design. For a time, we tried off-loading our harvester on some of the smaller tenant farmers on the outskirts of KL but they were sceptical of anything other than their ploughs and water buffalo, and I woke up one day to find that I'd turned over my basket and all the eggs that were in it. It was a humiliating defeat. Suddenly, after years of steady incremental progress, I was going out of business.

To make matters worse, the government's New Economic Policy was in full swing by that time. All the contracts we might have been vying for were being preferentially awarded to Malay companies, as the government

looked to improve the lot of the *Bumiputra*. Bumiputra—sons of the soil—
that's what the Malays were calling themselves now. Everybody in my
engineering firm was ethnically Chinese, bar one, a German. Bumiputra
we most certainly were not. Still, I'd heard there were ways around the
NEP. My colleagues informed me of an underhanded practice whereby
companies would pay-off Malay businessmen to act as fronts: the Malays
could go and win government contracts using their Bumiputra privileges
and then afterwards pass the work off to companies like ours, ostensibly
'Chinese' companies. Everyone got paid. Around the time when things
were getting really bad for us, Dieter Hoffman and Terrence Tan had
started warming to the idea:

'At least consider it, Ah Tat. We've all got to eat, one way or another.'

'Absolutely not, out of the question. I refuse to work my fingers off
while some Bumiputra bastard got one hand in my pocket.'

In hindsight, perhaps I should have heard them out. It wasn't long
before I was forced to sell my three-storey house in Kenny Hills and move
to a more modest dwelling in the outer suburbs.

It was next to a landfill site.

* * *

I came home in a hurry, barging through the back door and running
straight up the stairs without pause. At the top of the flight, I kicked a toy
xylophone into my daughter's bedroom and then let myself into the study.
I'd left some paperwork on my desk and was anxious to get back to the
office with it as soon as possible. As I was rifling through my files, the door
creaked open and Rosie wandered in. She looked up with a frown and put
her arms out to me.

'Not now, Rosalind. Ba Ba's got work to do now.'

Pulling the lining of my pockets out, I dumped my keys and loose
change on the table, along with a handful of cellophane-wrapped candies.
I gave one of the boiled sweets to my daughter.

'Here, here. Go back downstairs, Rosie. Ba Ba is very busy right now.
Where is your mother?' I went to the door and called out downstairs. 'June?
Ah June? You let Rosalind come up the stairs again. June?'

Rosie twisted the cellophane apart and sniffed at the piece of candy
before discarding it and mouthing her soft fat knuckles. She started to
whine.

'June,' I called out. 'June?'

I hoisted the girl up onto my hip and went downstairs. The sitting room was unusually dark. All the curtains had been drawn and my father and Sam Ji were both dozing in front of the television with the volume turned down. The flickering images were playing like ghosts off the walls. My mother shuffled in from the kitchen, wiping her hands on a damp tea towel, and went over to the television set and snapped it off.

'Who let Rosie come upstairs?' I said. 'Where's June?'

'She's sleeping. Hasn't gotten up yet, believe it or not.'

'Sleeping?' I looked at my watch. 'It's two o'clock in the afternoon. Who's taking care of Rosalind?'

My mother sighed, reaching across to take my daughter from me.

'Who do you think?'

*　*　*

On the eve of the Hari Merdeka holiday, I left the house and went for my daily walk through the neighbourhood. The first fireworks had just begun to appear at the horizon, and I stopped to watch the small bursts of coloured light raining silently on the distant city centre. When we had been living in Kenny Hills, I'd been able to smell the gunpowder from my balcony during the Independence Day celebrations, hear the booms exploding from the Municipal Town Hall and the Supreme Court building just across the river. Here in Happy Garden, nothing was in the air but the creaks and low nattering of hidden katydids.

Across from the house, an enormous tract of uncleared land the size of a football field stretched out to the end of the block. It was overrun with all manner of wild fecund growth: jungle trees and black ferns, banana palms and lalang, and stunted thatches of bamboo shoot. On the far side of the dense strip, the land had been levelled for new developments; a row of identical terraces gradually coming up, each at varying stages of construction.

When I came to the bottom of my street, a bread scooter came puttering by, weighed down by a teeming colourful skirt of packaged snacks and biscuits. The roti man bleated his horn repeatedly and a group of young children suddenly materialized from the surrounding houses, swarming the little motorcycle and waving their parents' money in the air. Several more people started trickling out of their homes so that eventually, a small crowd had soon gathered on the street corner. A man I vaguely recognized from the neighbourhood came over and stood beside me.

'Selamat Hari Merdeka,' he said.

'Selamat.'

'How's your holiday been?'

'Holiday? What holiday? Spent the entire day cooped in the office.'

The man chuckled, watching the children jostle for potato crisps and doughnuts and roti bengali.

'My wife sent me to get some bread,' he smiled. 'But it looks like I got a fight on my hands. I've seen you around from time to time. Which one are you?'

I pointed back up the street. 'With the red gate.'

'The house with the Mercedes?'

'That's the one. Just moved in with my family at the beginning of the year.'

'Well then,' he said, lighting a cigarette. 'Welcome to the neighbourhood. We've been here three years now. One of the first, before all these new lots coming up. Happy Garden is a good area. A nice up-and-coming area. You'll like it here.'

I looked at him. 'You think so?'

'Sure, what. No?'

'It's fine, I suppose. Someone should really do something about those wild monkeys that keep going through the trash. And the smell. I can't get used to the smell coming from the landfill site. How do you all put up with it?'

'I don't even notice the smell anymore.'

'I used to live in Kenny Hills myself. You will never get a smell like that up in the hills, let me tell you.'

The man raised his eyebrows slightly, looking me up and down.

'Kenny Hills?' he said.

'That's right. Not near the main road either, but right in the hills. Where the Prime Minister's house used to be. I built a big three-storey house over there a few years back. I loved that place.'

The man grinned to himself. 'What are you doing all the way out here then?'

'I been asking myself the same thing.'

We watched as the roti man hurried to the tall, mounted cabinet on the back of his motorcycle, bringing out all his holiday merchandise: sparklers and cap-guns and reams of pop-pops. The children were soon chasing each other up and down the street, fizzing and snapping through puffs of smoke. My neighbour watched them with a big smile spreading across his face.

'Still,' he said. 'It's not so bad around here. A lot of young families. Happy Garden is a nice up-and-coming area.'

I spat on the road. 'Imagine building houses down the road from a rubbish tip.'

'You'll get used to the smell.'

'You know the problem, don't you? It's this country. And the bloody NEP.'

He looked at me, frowning thoughtfully.

'But I don't have to tell you,' I went on. 'You're Chinese. You know what I'm saying. Still, you'd be shocked lah, by how far things have gone. You know how many government contracts are simply handed out to Bumiputra companies these days? Simply handed out. Like Malays are the only ones must put food on the table. What chance the rest of us got, I ask you.'

I took my neighbour's arm and walked him a little way down the street.

'Let me explain the situation to you since you seem interested. I am an engineer, you see. In the agricultural sector. And ever since they rolled out this New Economic Policy, it's like my firm has been throwing money down the gutter.'

The man glanced away for a moment, waving at someone in the distance.

'This government will never award a contract to my company. And why? Because they say I am Chinese. Chinese? I was born in Pahang Road. Bloody Kuala Lumpur Hospital. I am just as Malaysian as the next man. If I'm not a *son of the soil*, then what am I?'

My neighbour nodded distractedly.

'You see how it is now?' I went on. 'If you are not Malay, then you are nothing in this country. You see what I'm saying?'

The man continued nodding at me and dropped his cigarette, half-smoked, at his feet. He stamped it out and then turned and waved again to someone up the street.

'My wife is calling,' he said.

I looked at my watch. 'Off already? We only just met.'

'What can I do? The youngest has to be fed the same time every night or he wakes up screaming at three in the morning,' he sighed, smiling at me. 'I should have stopped after the second. You got any children?'

'A daughter. Stay a minute, your wife can manage the house herself. We can talk more about serious matters. You seem to know what's what.'

He turned away, jogging back up the street. 'Another time, maybe. See you around the neighbourhood. Take care.'

'Sure, sure. Next time then.'

I watched him go up the road and disappear into one of the houses at the top of the street. Suddenly, the stench of rotting garbage from the landfill site overcame me yet again. Sighing to myself I continued my walk around the block. Passing my neighbours' houses, I spied the silver-blue light of their TV sets glimmering behind drawn curtains one after another, like faint sparks of lightning, bottled up and domesticated. I heard canned laughter, smelled dinners cooking. A barefooted woman, trousers rolled up to her knees, waddled out the front of her tiled yard and tipped out a basin full of washing water. The grey soapy puddle crept to the street. She waved,

'*Lei ho.*'

From inside her house, I could hear the television, the program announcer declaring: 'Twenty years independence! United and Progressive. Hari Merdeka! Hari Merdeka, Malaysians all!' Another lot of fireworks was being set off and I looked to the horizon, the sky over the distant city glittering with pink and green constellations.

As I came back around the block, I saw my mother waiting for me at the front of our house. She was holding onto a dinner plate, waving it hysterically at me as I approached. The gate had been unlatched and the Mercedes was gone. Rosie's high-pitched squeal was piercing the serenity of the street and my neighbours were peering out their windows in the direction of my home. I hurried over to my mother.

'What's the matter? Can't you hear Rosalind crying? And where's the car gone?'

She continued to brandish the plate in my face, unable to speak.

'Ma Ma? Are you alright?'

'Your wife!' she shrieked. 'Your wife, your wife!'

'What happened for God's sake?'

'Look. Take a proper look. This is the last good piece of china in the house. Come inside, see for yourself. She shattered every bowl and plate in the kitchen and then took the car and left. Come, see what I've been telling you all along.'

My mother collapsed in a heap on the road.

'Look what she did. See how she treats me.'

I took the plate from her and stood in the middle of the road, staring back at the house. The neighbour's dogs were barking, setting off a chain of baying that was repeated all the way down the street.

'I warned you when you married her,' she wailed. 'I warned you, didn't I?'

Fifteen

At the end of the year my business partner, Terrence Tan, was much excited by an invitation he'd managed to procure to an exclusive MCA party function being thrown for some of Kuala Lumpur's major players in the manufacturing and trade industries. He claimed the dinner would be attended by the city's most influential businesspeople and politicians, many of whom operated in the agricultural sector, and said it would be a good opportunity for our little company to make much-needed contacts. By that stage, my firm was well and truly on its last legs and I'd not seen the point in making an appearance, but June had long been complaining about being cooped up with my mother every day, and claimed that I never took her out anymore. Though I was convinced little would come of the function business-wise, I finally agreed to go along and make the best of it, if only to get June out of the house for a night.

When we arrived, the main function hall of Hotel Merlin was half-empty. Round twelve-person banquet tables had been spaced evenly across the wide elegant floor, but the majority of tables remained conspicuously unoccupied. Several immaculate tablecloths, each yet host to little more than a circle of rice bowls and teacups upturned on pink serviettes, ran right through the middle of the enormous room. Our own table on the periphery was only occupied by the three of us.

'I told you,' I sighed. 'A waste of time. Barely anyone bothered to show up.'

Terrence glanced at his watch. 'It's early yet, Ah Tat. Keep an open mind.'

The few guests in attendance had formed a small crowd at the base of the speaker's platform, near the front of the function room, and most of them were swiftly getting drunk. An ostentatious red and gold banner was strung up over their heads:

THE MALAYSIAN CHINESE ASSOC. (MCA) WELCOMES ITS PARTNERS IN THE KUALA LUMPUR BUSINESS COMMUNITY

Waiters dressed in black and white attire stood idly by the kitchen doors chatting amongst themselves, hands behind their backs with nothing to do. June leaned across the table and picked out a piece of fried yam from among the selection of entrees and placed it on my plate.

'Eat darling,' she said. 'You don't eat anymore.'

'I'm not hungry.'

'Fretting no use lah. What will be, will be. Meanwhile, all this good food is gone to waste.'

She reached for some cold seaweed, carefully drawing the slippery translucent filaments into a bowl, and put the bowl in front of me. I pushed it aside.

'I'm not hungry. Didn't I just say?'

June sat back and stared at her tea. Terrence frowned and looked at her, then he looked at me.

Meanwhile, the group of drunken guests gathered by the foot of the stage continued to toast one another noisily, every sentence prompting a belligerent cheer from those nearby. The racket became louder and louder, drawing wary glances from the waitstaff on the edges of the room and drowning out the faint tinkling of piano keys that drifted in from the hotel foyer. Terrence nudged me and nodded over at the disorderly crowd.

'Ah Tat, you see what I see?'

'Just a bunch of bloody drunks.'

'No lah, not them. Look carefully.'

A spectacled man in a *songkok* was seated at one of the prominent tables, slightly removed from the rowdy guests.

'It's the Dato,' Terrence said.

I shifted in my seat and peered across the room. 'Who?'

'Hafiz Ali Husin. The Agriculture Minister.'

'The Agriculture Minister is here?'

The Dato was flanked by his wife and several subdued men. They were watching the drunk guests make a fracas at the front of the room, clearly unimpressed with what they were seeing.

'What's he doing here?'

Terrence crossed his thick fingers. 'MCA and UMNO are like this nowadays. We should go over there and introduce ourselves. With the Third Malaysia plan, contracts are being handed out left, right and centre. What can it hurt?'

I turned away, shaking my head. 'That's your big idea? That's how we're going to save the company? Stroll up to the Dato and ask for a contract.'

'Not quite like that. But we should at least hand the man a business card.'

'We'll look like fools.'

'It's networking, Ah Tat. It's how things are done. We've got to try something at this point.'

'All this work talk is so tiresome,' June interjected. 'You two can't take one night off? I am simply pleased to be out and about for once. Did you know, apparently this hotel has a fantastic discotheque?'

I looked at June. 'What?'

'The discotheque, Tomorrow Disco. It's upstairs. All the young people are talking about it. Let's go see for ourselves after dinner. We are not so old, after all.'

'Discotheque?' I slammed my glass of brandy down on the table. 'Why are you talking about discotheques? We're trying to discuss something important just now, for God's sake. What nonsense are you talking about, June? Discotheques?'

June sat back. Terrence looked at me. He looked at June. After a moment, he leaned over and whispered something in her ear. She nodded quietly, brow knotted, and then attempted a weak smile.

At the head of the function hall, the drunken crowd of businessmen had started to become unruly. Noisy cheers arose from that section of the floor and soon one of their members had climbed onto a banquet table, clutching a bottle of champagne in his fist. The man tipped the bottle upside down, emptying the contents all over the people surrounding him who leapt back and clapped, laughed, and shouted. A couple of the man's colleagues tried to pull him down from the table, but he fended them off and reached up, tearing down the MCA banner hanging over their heads. It fluttered to the floor in two pieces, swinging and twisting from its grommets to the sound of delighted cries and applause. A young MCA party official scurried up to the podium and began mumbling into the microphone:

'If we could all please take our seats. Please, madams and gentlemen, *mo yisi*. Could we take our seats and begin the evening?'

The man who'd torn the banner down started screaming abuse at the speaker. His voice broke and he was trembling and red-faced and he continued to shout until it seemed as though he was almost crying. He flung the empty champagne bottle at the podium and then got down from the tabletop and picked up a pail full of ice, hurling it at the stage. The clattering sound filled the function hall and a hush descended, punctuated by a few gleeful jeers. A group of MCA organizers and hotel staff immediately bundled the man away as he continued to screech and curse in Cantonese:

'What have you done for us? What have you done for us? What have you done for us?'

The young MCA host stammered into the microphone, a sheen of sweat giving his face a mannequin-gleam:

'Rest assured, friends. Rest assured. The Malaysian Chinese Association is looking out for your interests. Rest assured.'

I looked across at Terrence. He was shaking his head. A low murmur spread throughout the gathering and eventually, the guests started returning to their assigned tables. A few moments later, the Dato stood up and quietly departed with his entourage.

Following the incident, proceedings settled down. The waiters had hastily reset the front few banquet tables and the MCA welcome banner was patched together and restrung over the stage. An electronic keyboard was brought into the function hall and the pianist from the hotel foyer performed a series of sedate minuets. The Dato's table remained empty.

'Well, I hope you're happy,' Terrence chided. 'We missed our opportunity.'

Guests continued to trickle in for the next couple of hours so that the turn-out for the function in fact proved fairly respectable. The pork dish was brought in, followed by rice-wine chicken and glass noodles in claypots with tofu and mushroom. Speeches were made. Finally, the steamed sea bass was ferried to each of the tables. A few people I'd never met before, representatives from the Tan Chong Motor Group, had joined our table by that time and together we picked away at the fish's soft pearled belly until there was nothing left but its fine quill-like bones. As Terrence discussed the economy with the automobile men, I overheard snatches of conversation from guests wandering the floor, the earlier drunken outburst recounted and exaggerated the room over.

'Who can blame him?'

'If MCA keeps kowtowing to the Malays, he won't be the only one to speak out. Chinese in this country are tired of being side-lined.'

The waiters started bringing out dessert: custard *daan tat* and shrimp paste biscuit, black coffee, and platters of sliced orange and watermelon. Terrence Tan sat back from the table and undid his belt. He belched and scratched his belly. June yawned ostentatiously and, as the others helped themselves to coffee and fruit, excused herself to visit the ladies' room. Terrence watched her leave.

'I used to have a nice-looking woman like that,' he said.

'Good for you.'

'I wish now I was a little kinder to her,' he looked at me for a moment. 'You want some friendly advice?'

'Keep it to yourself, Terrence.'

I signalled for another brandy. When it arrived, I took half of it in one swallow. Terrence was watching me.

'Slow down, Ah Tat. Take it easy.'

'I just want to leave this past year behind.'

He sighed and sat back, taking up his own drink. 'Sure. Could have been better.'

Across the function room people were migrating across the floor, mingling at one another's tables. A young woman in a figure-hugging *cheongsam* was circling the far tables.

'My God, Terrence. That girl over there. You see her?'

'Ha?'

'That girl.'

Terrence turned on his side with some difficulty and glanced over.

'I see her,' he shrugged. 'Some beauty queen probably. So what?'

'Doesn't she remind you of anybody?'

'Of who?'

'Come on. You know. Look properly, *fei lo*. Sit up.'

He adjusted his trousers and sat up and looked over again, squinting. 'You mean June?'

'She looks exactly like June.'

'June?' he laughed. 'No lah. Barely more than a child, that girl.'

I drained the rest of my brandy and signalled to the waiter for another, continuing to stare across the room.

'I am telling you, Terrence. Maybe not so much these days but ten years ago. Ten years ago, I'm telling you Terrence, June got a figure just like that. I wouldn't be able to tell them apart.'

'Just drink your drink and don't be stupid.'

'It's remarkable, I tell you. The resemblance.'

'Sit down, Ah Tat. You're in no condition. Sit down, I am begging you. June will be back any minute.'

I got up and stumbled across the room. A group of guests were blocking my path and by the time I'd fought my way past them, the girl had moved on, disappearing behind a partition that separated the function hall from the greater part of the hotel. I caught a glimpse of her moving briskly along the outer corridor. I followed her out to the foyer before losing sight of her again. The hotel concierge had watched me stagger out from the function room and was eyeing me concernedly.

'Sir? Can I help you, sir? Please be careful.'

He came out from behind the front desk and approached me but I swerved away from him, almost completely losing my balance in the process, and half-tumbled out the main entrance. A pair of foreign guests, dressed as though returned from some distinguished outing, gave me a wide berth. The concierge came up behind me:

'Please be careful, sir. If you are going to be sick, I must direct you away from the port cochere.'

Seizing me by the elbow, he dragged me out of the hotel.

'This is a respectable establishment,' he said.

'Let go of me, I am quite alright now. Just let me back inside. Please lah, I am quite alright.'

The man's grip remained vice-like while escorting me to the visitors' car park. At the rear of the hotel, he pushed me off into the dark, and I looked about feebly as the concierge strode back to his post. A pair of Indonesian hotel workers were smoking cigarettes while manning an empty linen trolley nearby. Their dark faces broke into brilliant toothy grins. Standing there too, was the young woman in the cheongsam I'd seen earlier. She was watching from afar, giggling to herself. I straightened up, adjusting my dinner jacket, and shouted back at the hotel desk man.

'You can't treat me this way! I am a respectable businessman!'

I inched my way unsteadily over to the young lady, who was covering her mouth and trying not to laugh.

'Can you believe that fellow?' I said, thumbing back in his direction. 'Must have mistaken me for one of those drunk guests inside. I never been so insulted in all my life.'

'Is that so?' she grinned.

'I am a respectable businessman.'

'Looks to me like you've gone a little overboard tonight, Mr Respectable Businessman. You going to be alright?'

'Me? I am fine. I'm quite fine.' I looked around again and took a deep breath. 'Although, I suppose I didn't absolutely need to have that last brandy. I don't usually drink so much.'

She smiled. 'Celebrating, is it?'

'Celebrating? What's to celebrate? Ayah, don't get me started.'

I reached back, looking for a wall to support myself with and, finding none, sat hard on the kerb. She crouched down a couple of yards away, the high split in her dress creeping up to her hip and looked at me with her head atilt.

'I can find you some water, if you want.'

'I am fine lah, I'm fine. Do you have a tissue?'

She went through her handbag and handed me a wad of lavender scented tissues. I held the tissues to my mouth and slumped forward with my head between my knees. Closing my eyes, I breathed slowly and deliberately for a moment. When I opened them again, she was turning to leave.

'Wait, Siew Jieh. Wait. Stay a moment, please. I'm starting to feel better now that you're here.'

The young woman frowned and checked her watch. She glanced out over the car park.

'I seen you inside,' I said quickly, sitting up. 'The MCA banquet.'

'Is that what it is? They're all the same to me, these things. Just a bunch of self-important men talking shop. So tedious.'

'Wah, tedious. No kidding. Self-important?'

She winked. 'Not you though, of course.'

As we chatted, I noticed that every now and then, whenever a car drove into the hotel with its headlamps sweeping across the crowded lot, the young woman would crane her neck to peer at the circling vehicle.

'Waiting for someone?' I said.

She nodded. 'He'll be here any minute.'

'If you ask me, he shouldn't be making a lovely young girl wait around for him.'

'Is that so?' she smiled to herself. 'Maybe you can tell him yourself when he gets here. I'd like to see what he says to that.'

'Maybe I will.'

She laughed. 'I am only fooling around. Don't say that.'

'He won't like that?'

'No, he won't like that.' She looked at me with her eyebrows raised. 'He won't like the way you're looking at me either.'

I shook my head, waving the comment away.

'No, you got me all wrong, Siew Jieh. You remind me of someone, is all.'

'I've heard that before.'

'No, it's true.'

'Is it Lily Ho? Men are always telling me I look like Lily Ho.'

'No, no. Not Lily Ho.'

Another car drove into the hotel and the young woman glanced over, watching it take a slow lap of the lot. Eventually, the vehicle pulled into an empty space and a group of older Malay gentlemen emerged, smoking cigarettes, and murmuring amongst themselves as they made their way over to the hotel entrance. The young woman frowned and turned back to me.

'What does he do?' I said.

'Who?'

'Whoever you're waiting for.'

'Why are you so interested?'

'To catch someone like you, he must be very successful.'

'Successful?' she shrugged. 'No, I don't care about that.'

'You don't care about that? Why not? It matters.'

'Not to me.'

'It matters. Believe me, Siew Jieh, you don't want a husband who is a failure. If that happens, everybody ends up miserable. And then what love can there be? Believe me, I know what I'm talking about.'

I turned to look at her but she no longer appeared to be paying any attention to me.

'I just hope he doesn't end up disappointing you,' I murmured.

'Oh, he'll show up soon,' she said, checking the time. 'He better if he knows what's good for him.'

'That's not what I meant.'

She looked at me quizzically. 'What did you mean?'

'Never mind,' I sighed. 'You're too young to understand.'

After a while, a beautiful gleaming Black Town Car appeared at the top of the ramp. Instead of circling the car park and looking for a space, the black Continental drove right up to the hotel and idled by the kerb. The back door swung open and somebody inside half-stepped out, still talking to the driver. The young woman adjusted her hair.

'About time,' she murmured. 'Will you be okay?'

'Much better now. Turns out all I needed was some air. And the company of a lovely young miss.'

'How do I look?' She ran her hands over the cheongsam, flattening the front of her dress down over her legs. 'He hasn't seen this dress before. I want to surprise him.'

'Fine, fine. You look fine. Go ahead.'

'Why don't you come with me? I'll introduce the two of you.'

'No lah, please. I don't want to meet him. I am half drunk.'

'Don't be silly. Isn't that why all you men come to these ridiculous things? To make contacts. I'll introduce you. He's important, a big man.'

In the darkness, a figure emerged from the Town Car and the girl hurried over to him. Their shadows merged briefly, his faint voice running underneath her animated chattering, and soon she had taken him by the arm and was steering him over in my direction. I straightened up, hastily dusting myself off as the couple emerged in the light of a streetlamp nearby. The man was well dressed, wearing a tailored navy-blue suit, fine dress shoes and a gold wristwatch. He stopped in his tracks upon seeing me.

'Ai?' he blinked. 'What are you doing here?'

For a confused moment we stood staring at one another.

'Kin Chew?'

* * *

He looked good.

I'd noticed, in fact, that Kin Chew had started paying much closer attention to the way he was dressed in recent years. He kept himself clean-shaven these days, hair trimmed short and conservatively styled, with blazers and Italian leather loafers taking the place of his singlets and rubber flip-flops. He was even developing a penchant for luxury wristwatches. I remember once going past a jeweller on Cross Street and spotting a Rolex I'd seen him sporting on a previous occasion. Even second-hand, the price was exorbitant. I told myself his own watch must have been a clever knock-off, the type you might find two-for-one at the night bazaar, but there were other signs of his increasing prosperity that I could not explain away as easily.

His mother still lived with us—moving from Batu Road to Kenny Hills, and finally to my house out in Happy Garden—and Kin Chew had kept up his fortnightly ritual of handing me envelopes of cash to pass onto her. Only this last Chinese New Year, the envelope he'd slipped me underneath the dinner table was bulging with clean grey leaves, thick as a small novel.

'What the hell is this, Kin Chew? There must be a thousand ringgit in here.'

'Spend it on the family,' he'd winked, ever so casually.

I brooded on all this as he joined our table at the Hotel Merlin. Every now and then, someone would cross the function room floor specifically to shake KC's hand, as if they were proud to know him, and the rest of us were forced to wait patiently while he drew out the pleasantries. He sat next to the young woman in the cheongsam, arm resting with easy familiarity on the back of her chair, his fine gold wristwatch catching the chandelier light as he talked. Kin Chew was telling us how he'd met her, coming home on a flight from Hong Kong a few months back. Her name was Shirley and she was a stewardess with MAS.

'She kept serving me cold coffee,' he smiled.

Shirley swatted him playfully on the chest and the two looked at one another. Terrence sat forward, puffing affably on his cigarette:

'You're a stewardess with Malaysian Airlines, are you Shirley? I heard they got the new fleet over there. DC tens. You must have had to fight tooth and nail for that job.'

Shirley smiled and nodded.

'I saw a picture in the newspaper a while back,' Terrence went on. 'Queues all around the block at the Koperasi Polis Building. So many women waiting to hand in job applications. Good for you, young lady. Well done.'

I recalled June herself had considered applying for one of those air-hostess positions, back when all the jobs were being advertised. Our daughter was barely more than a year old at the time and June had tried to convince me that my mother was more than capable of taking care of Rosie while she went to work. It was, of course, out of the question.

'A child needs its mother, June. What are you thinking?'

Still, I must admit I was somewhat taken aback by how disappointed she'd seemed after all the applications had closed.

As I sat there listening to the others drone on, still a little light-headed from the brandy, I noticed June behaving strangely. She sat at the table, distractedly tearing up a paper serviette until there was a little pile of pink confetti on her place-setting, while watching Kin Chew's new lady friend very closely, with one of her dark expressions. I assumed it was because she'd been reminded of the Malaysian Airlines job, but after a while, it occurred to me—for no more than a fleeting moment—that her odd behaviour might be due to something else entirely. Suddenly, she interrupted a conversation KC was having, saying to him:

'I barely recognized you, Kin Chew, all dressed up. You look like a completely changed man.'

KC paused and looked at her for the first time that evening.

'Do I?' he said.

'Yes, completely changed. And with such a beautiful young lady by your side too. Kin Chew, she's far too pretty for you.'

KC shifted on his seat. He seemed about to reply when June went on:

'You've come such a long way. Remember, when we were just kids? Running around the Hokkien Association and Foch Avenue together? You always told me you would make it big one day. I never doubted you.'

'Well,' he shrugged. 'Business is good at the moment.'

I burst out laughing.

'Business,' I said, shaking my head.

Everyone at the table paused to look over at me. Perhaps I was still a little drunk, but I went on nonetheless:

'Exactly what kind of business is that, Kin Chew? Have you told Shirley what it is that you do? Go on, tell her. Tell her all about your charming friend, Piggy.'

Shirley turned curiously to Kin Chew.

'Piggy?' she said. 'That's a funny name. Who's Piggy?'

'Go on,' I said, smiling across the table at KC. 'Why don't you tell us? Tell us all how you really make a living.'

The rest of the people at our table cast uncertain glances at one another, lapsing into an awkward silence. KC was glaring at me. Finally, he sat back and crossed one leg over the other.

'If you must know, Ah Tat. My business these days is with a local *towkay*, Mr Yeung Yau Yu. He's taken me on as a kind of advisor.'

Terrence was about to take a drag from his Dunhill but stopped abruptly, the cigarette hovering before his half-open mouth. He sat up and leaned across the table.

'Yeung Yau Yu?' he said. 'You work for Yeung Yau Yu?'

Kin Chew nodded. 'Yes, you know of him?'

'Know of him? Who doesn't know Yeung Yau Yu?'

The men from the Tan Chong Motor group, who had until that point been quietly chatting amongst themselves on the other side of our table, paused to regard Kin Chew with newfound interest. Terrence said:

'Ah Tat, you never told me your cousin is so well connected.'

I stared across the table at KC. He was looking back at me, a wry expression in his eyes. Shirley leaned over and whispered something into his ear and he broke into a grin and looked at me again, nodding and laughing. Terrence called one of the waiters over and had him bring a few drinks. He offered Kin Chew a cigarette and proceeded to fire questions at him, one after another.

'Yes, yes,' KC smiled. 'As a matter of fact, I came here tonight with Mr Yeung so we could hold talks with the Agriculture Minister.'

'The Dato?' Terrence looked at me.

'Impossible,' I said. 'We saw the Dato leave earlier this evening. He's long gone.'

'The Dato is in the hotel lounge speaking with Mr Yeung at this very moment.'

'No, that's not possible. He left already. I saw him leave.'

Kin Chew shrugged. 'If you say so, Ah Tat.'

All around us, the function hall was gradually emptying of guests and the waitstaff had begun dismantling foldaway partitions. The men from the Tan Chong Motor Group rose from the table and bowed to us before making their departure. Waiters began flying about the room, shouting instructions to one another in Cantonese, sweeping away scraps of food from the tables and clearing glasses and beer bottles and plates streaked with cigarette ash. They folded up oil-spotted tablecloths and stacked chairs to the side of the hall. As they were packing up, a young woman from the front desk of the hotel appeared at our table with a message for Kin Chew. He nodded at her, shaking the gold wristwatch free from his sleeve, and glanced down at the time.

'Apologies everyone,' he said, standing up and holding his arm out to Shirley. 'I'm afraid I am being called away. Mr Yeung doesn't like to be kept waiting.'

'Yeung Yau Yu is waiting?' I scoffed. 'On you?'

Terrence raised his glass to Kin Chew.

'You see that, Ah Tat? We could learn a thing or two from your cousin over here.' He belched and took a sip from his drink and held it up again. 'Yeung Yau Yu, can you believe it? Yeung Yau Yu. The man himself.'

* * *

In the car, on the way home from the hotel that night, June said:

'Did you see that dress she was wearing? Shameless. Utterly shameless. She looked no better than a high-class prostitute.'

'Yeah lah, I agree. Not in good taste.'

'How old can she be? Twenty. Nineteen, even?'

'Not even.'

'What is Kin Chew thinking, going with her?'

I stared at the road unfolding darkly before the car. The occasional tea-stall still appeared by the roadside, continuing to draw customers out into the lamplit streets despite the late hour. As we passed out of town, the shophouses were replaced by long stretches of silent neighbourhoods. Closer to home, the rancid odour of the district landfill site drifted into the Mercedes and June screwed up her face, winding the window up. I sped across an intersection without slowing.

'How about that Rolex he was wearing?' I said. 'I tell you, no way can it be authentic. I seen that model in the shops. It costs thousands of RM. Tens of thousands. He probably got one of those fakes over at the pasar malam. Don't you think?'

'Probably.'

'Of course I cannot put it past Kin Chew to steal a real one. Could've held up a jewellery store for all I know. I am not kidding.'

June switched on the light in the cabin and pulled down the sunvisor. She looked carefully at her reflection.

'Do you think I should grow my hair out again?' she said.

'I've read articles in *The Star* about that towkay he works for. Yeung Yau Yu. He's under investigation, you know. For corruption. Everybody in KL knows he's some kind of crime-lord. But you think anybody cares?'

'Short hair makes me look older,' she sighed.

'They'll never pin anything on him, of course. These crooks get away with murder. This bloody country, I tell you.'

'What do you think, Ah Tat? Long again?'

'Ayah, your hair looks fine the way it is.'

I glanced across the dashboard at June. She was still scrutinizing herself in the mirror. After a moment, I said:

'Did Shirley remind you of anyone?'

'Who? No.'

'No one? No one at all?'

June stared up into the mirror, turning her face from side to side and flattening her palms over her head. She started rifling through her handbag.

'Where's my lipstick?'

'What do you need lipstick for? The night's over with already.'

She turned off the cabin light, flipping the sun visor back in place, and slumped down in her seat. She stared out the car window.

'I bet your mother will still be awake when we get home.'

Sixteen

The following week I had a meeting with the bank people. I was shown into the client relations suite of the Maybank branch in Pudu and told to wait for the manager who would be in to see me shortly. I sat there with my hands in my lap, looking around the room. The walls were clad in faux wood panelling and overhead the ceiling fan was spinning at a high speed, wobbling precariously on its axis. The office smelled of fried bread and onions, as if someone had just finished eating their lunch at the table. Before me was a bare desk on which almost nothing lay except my company's file and a mound of peanut shells in a wet ashtray. The branch manager, a balding middle-aged Chinese man, came in and nodded to me and took his seat behind the table. He opened the file and made a quick note in the corner with his pen. He looked at me for a moment.

'You have a good business plan,' he said. 'It's good.'

I frowned. 'But?'

'But you don't exactly have much collateral. The house is not worth all that much, I'm sorry to say. Especially in this climate.' He flipped through the file. 'And from what I can see, your company is not doing so well right now.'

'It's just a temporary set-back, encik. The business is still viable. Did you look at the projections? I'll be able to pay back the loan in a few years.'

The manager sighed and looked at me. He was silent for a long time and the wall clock behind his head seemed to be making an unusually loud ticking. I shifted in my seat. At that moment, a knock came at the door and a heavyset Malay man let himself in without waiting for an answer.

I recognized him from our previous meetings. He was the credit officer. The two bank men exchanged a look and the manager spread his fingers over the application. He pushed the file back at me.

'I am sorry, Mr Lim. The bottom line is the bank must decline to take part.'

'But with a little more investment we can get back on track. Did you look at the numbers properly? It's all there.'

The manager turned slightly to the credit officer who stood unmoving by his shoulder. Both men frowned and looked back at me in silence.

'Did you see the numbers?'

'We saw,' the manager said. 'I am very sorry, Mr Lim.'

He lowered his eyes while the big credit officer stood stiffly behind him, like some bodyguard.

'There must be something you can do,' I said. 'What about this CGC I hear so much about?'

The credit officer spoke up suddenly.

'Only Bumiputra are eligible for the Credit Guarantee loan.'

'Bumiputra?' I looked up at him. 'I see. What you're saying is, if I am a Malay then you can lend.'

'Yes.'

'No.' The manager shot the credit officer an irritable glance before turning back to me and continuing on in a low soothing tone:

'I mean, I wouldn't put like that. It's not helpful to look at it that way. The bank only has a certain amount to loan, Mr Lim. We cannot overextend ourselves at this moment.'

'But still you can give to Malays.'

He held his hands out. 'That money is guaranteed by the government. After all, Maybank didn't write the NEP.'

I gripped my knees.

'I will go under,' I said.

The manager sighed. He turned and mumbled something to his colleague and the big credit officer left the suite, closing the door quietly behind him. The manager watched me for another moment. He got up and walked around his desk and took the seat beside me. The vinyl upholstery creaked under his weight.

'May I speak informally, Mr Lim?'

I nodded.

'You are an engineer, am I right? That's a good profession. Can make good money with a profession like that, isn't it? And you lah, still so young also. Believe me, if it was up to me, I would lend to you. Certainly, you're a better bet than some of the riff-raff that come in here expecting a handout. But take some advice from this old man. Someone who seen what it takes to succeed. Start again. Build capital. These things take patience.'

'All due respect, encik, I don't need career advice. I need the loan.'

'Come back in a few years' time. We will see then.'

'Years?'

The manager stood up and collected my file and opened the door to the office. He waited for me to get up.

* * *

A week later I drove the Mercedes up the steel grate ramp of the Peninsula Auto Group warehouse on Batu Road and parked the car in one of the waiting bays by reception. A man in dark blue overalls greeted me as I stepped out of the vehicle.

'All your belongings out of the car already?' he said.

'Aw.'

He checked my plates and reviewed his clipboard. 'And the papers? Log book?'

'In the glove box.' I handed him the keys.

He pocketed the keys and scratched a few notes on his clipboard. He was tall and wiry and his name-tag YUSUF was smeared with greasy fingerprints. He looked up from his clipboard at me.

'Repossession?'

'How did you know?'

He gave a sympathetic smile. 'The look on your face, what. Never mind lah. Happens to the best of us.'

Afterwards, I walked to a coffeeshop on the corner. I hadn't smoked a cigarette since my university days but I bought a pack of Pall Malls from the man at the counter and took a table facing the street. I ordered black tea and sat watching the cars go by, smoking one cigarette after another, the butts accumulating on the grimy tiled floor around me. An old Indian woman was going from table to table, proffering her wares: embroidered hand towels, car fresheners, paper fans. Outside the coffeeshop, traffic hiccupped along the main road. The afternoon downpour arrived right on time, crashing deafeningly through the streetscape and steaming off the tarmac.

Hasan came running down the street and skipped into the coffeeshop. He shook himself off.

'Sorry I'm late,' he panted. 'So, how?'

I stood up. 'It's done. Let's go, where did you park?'

'But it's raining still.'

'I cannot sit here any longer, Hasan. Take me away already. Please.'

Sitting quietly in the passenger seat of Hasan's rusty old car, I watched the traffic build up around us at the intersection. The Datsun's worn wiper blades were steadily batting the blurred curtain of water off the windshield and every now and then, Hasan leaned over the steering column and mopped the fog building up on the inside of the glass. Outside, the tarmac crackled. It appeared as though the surface of the road was boiling, being simmered by streaks of hot rain. I stared out the window.

'Look at all this traffic. Cannot get anywhere in KL these days without a bloody jam.'

Hasan nodded. 'It's getting worse and worse. But that's the price of progress, isn't it?'

I turned away, shaking my head.

'Progress,' I laughed.

We worked our way slowly out of the city, stop-starting through the rain and congestion. I looked out on Mountbatten Road, frowning. Nobody called it Mountbatten Road anymore. Now it was Jalan Tun Perak. Treacher Road had become Jalan Sultan Ismail, and Batu Road was Jalan Tuanku Abdul Rahman—a ludicrous mouthful if I ever heard one. Everywhere the Malays were taking over. I shook my head, staring out the passenger side window at people darting through the downpour. At the intersection we backed up behind a lorry, waiting for the lights to change. Hasan looked at me and sighed,

'It's not the end of the world, Ah Tat. Just a car, after all. To tell you the truth I always thought it was a little ugly. What possessed you to get it in brown anyway?'

'It's not brown lah, it's gold.'

'Ah gold.'

'I bought it right after I landed my first big contract in Shah Alam. We replaced all their processing machinery out there. It was a good job we did.'

'I am sure it was, Ah Tat. You can be proud.'

'Yes, and now what do I have to show for it?'

Soon, the storm started to peter out and the sun came through the clouds at the horizon, tinged with marmalade coloured light. It might have been pretty but for the jibs of several tower-cranes obscuring the city skyline. Driving on, the congestion eventually eased. We pulled off the main road and Hasan took the exit heading south towards Happy Garden.

'Where are you going?' I said.

'I'm taking you home, isn't it?'

'I can't face everyone at home just yet, Hasan. Take me somewhere else. Anywhere.'

He slowed the car and put on his indicator. 'We could always go back to my place. Sit together a while and catch up slowly-slowly, like old times. I warn you though, the house is a mess.'

I turned back to the window and let my head rest against the glass. All around us cars were slashing noisily past the Datsun.

'Ah Tat? Did you hear what I said? Why don't you come back to my house for a bit?'

'Har?'

Hasan sighed, looking at me:

'Things will turn around, Ah Tat. Everybody goes through ups and downs. Remember a few years ago, when you found me living in that slum area? No job, no money. No running water in that place even. Smoking dadah and drinking beer all day with my uncle. I thought I would never get out.'

He smiled gently:

'But look at me now. All I'm saying is I know how you feel. People have come back from worse.'

Over the last few years Hasan had indeed managed to clean up his act. Fed up with life in the slums, and of waking up hungover next to his uncle in their rickety tin shack on the banks of the Klang, Hasan had one day decided to visit the Social Welfare Department in order to look for work. They'd assigned a nice-looking girl to be his career counsellor and every fortnight he'd gone into the branch office in Imbi, dressed in a tie and the only business shirt he'd owned, to have the nice-looking girl enrol him in the latest employment workshop. Wadida was polite and earnest, and he liked the mild way that she scolded him into taking his life more seriously. She liked his eyes and affable nature. Before long, Hasan had started showing up to their regular appointments with a box of *halwa* from the Royal India Sweet shop.

'Luckily lah,' he'd told me at the time. 'She got one hell of a sweet-tooth, that girl.'

Still, Hasan could never quite manage to get Wadida to agree to see him outside the welfare offices. He began looking for ways to impress her. During their sessions, he'd made note of the fact that she kept a prayer mat rolled up under her desk and seemed to take special pride in wearing a *tudong* to work, and this, at a time before it had become typical for Malay women to do so. He quit drinking alcohol to show her he was the religious-type and started attending Jumu'ah at the Masjid Wakaf Baru Mosque, where he knew a group of Wadida's cousins went for Friday prayers. Her cousins did little to help him with Wadida, although one of them did put him up for a job at Jabatan Telekom Malaysia. Hasan started out on the switchboards at first, keeping his head down, quietly savouring the first steady paycheck of his life, and then one day saw a notice pinned to the corkboard outside the JTM engineers' lunch room:

ARE YOU UNDER 25 YEARS OLD?
AMBITIOUS?
SEEKING OPPORTUNITIES FOR ADVANCEMENT?
JABATAN TELEKOM MALAYSIA'S CAREER FAST-
TRACK PROGRAM MAY BE FOR YOU! QUALIFICATIONS
UNNECCESARY. CONTACT YOUR DEPARTMENT
SUPERVISOR FOR MORE INFORMATION.
ONLY BUMIPUTRA NEED APPLY.

Within six months of his application, Hasan had been promoted into JTM's billing department and by the end of his second year, the company had singled him out yet again, this time moving him into a junior executive training program for Bumiputras. Without realizing it, Hasan found he'd relinquished his nightly habit of smoking marijuana in favour of making it to work on time every morning. He saved enough to buy himself a little Datsun and started driving by the welfare offices to chauffeur Wadida home at the end of her shifts, getting her to laugh at his shrill falsetto while singing along to Uji Rashid and *You Should Be Dancing* on the car radio. She, in turn, got him to pray five times a day and give up pork. They got married right after Hari Raya Puasa in her family's house in Damansara and I was there at the wedding ceremony when Hasan had declared in front of everyone like a love-drunk fool that she'd saved his life. Wadida smiled meekly in her way and said simply:

'It is Allah's will only.'

Her family came from a little money, being distantly related to Malay royalty, and so Hasan's in-laws put up a deposit for the newlyweds on a house in one of the up-and-coming development sites in KL. With help from the government's discount for Bumiputras, the couple were able to afford a modest house in Kampong Pasir. It turned out to be barely a stone's throw away from where I'd found Hasan living only a few years earlier. The slums were still there of course, and in fact, Hasan's uncle continued to live in one of those makeshift shanty houses as before, refusing to conform, binge drinking his nights away and chasing his drug-fogged fantasy of becoming a film-star, but all around the squatter area now, new housing developments were starting to come up, squeezing the tin and wood shacks further and further out to the river. They were replaced by home estates and condominiums and new roads and schools. Certainly, the area had undergone a rapid transformation in the intervening years. It seemed to mirror Hasan's own exponential trajectory.

In fact, the day he picked me up after having the Mercedes repossessed, I remember looking out the window of the Datsun as we pulled up outside his driveway. It occurred to me then that his house was even nicer than my own.

'You want to come inside?' Hasan said. 'Wadida's home. And the girls.'

The sound of the rain continued to batter the steel top of the Datsun and I sat in the passenger seat, listening to the engine tick down.

'Let's just sit here for now,' I said, looking at his yard.

A shopping trolley loaded with large drums of paint sat out front, together with a kitchen sink and a pile of dismantled cabinets. Everything was covered in a chalky layer of cement powder that was dissolving into a silty residue with the rain. I looked across at Hasan:

'You doing some work on the house?'

'It's Wadida's idea. She wants a bigger kitchen. What can you do?'

'But you only just bought the house. How can you afford to renovate so soon?'

Before he could answer, I shook my head, saying:

'Never mind, I can guess. A cheap loan, right? Courtesy of the NEP.'

Hasan looked at me and shrugged. As the downpour thinned to a fine drizzle, I kicked open the door of the Datsun and stepped out.

'Must be nice,' I muttered.

We sat in the living room and his wife brought out a little folding table which she opened out and set down between us. Wadida went back to the kitchen and returned with a samovar of hot black Turkish coffee and two Arab drinking cups the size of shot glasses. She set the tray down on the folding table and smiled and poured out the coffee. She looked at me.

'Are you hungry, Ah Tat? I got some cakes, if you like. Or fruit.'

'No, thank you, Wadida. This is fine.'

She bowed politely and excused herself, returning to the kitchen. A moment later, she came back with a plate of red grapes and set them on the coffee table saying, 'If you change your mind,' and then quietly left the room for the two of us to catch up. Just then, a little black-eyed girl wandered into the living area. She came over and sat in front Hasan, reaching out for one of the coffee cups.

'Akak, that's not for you. Greet pak cik properly now.'

The girl took my hand and touched it quickly to her nose.

'Salaam.'

Hasan smiled at her.

'My youngest is sleeping,' he said. 'You haven't met her yet, have you?'

'Not yet. Another girl, is it?'

'Yeah lah, two girls,' he chuckled. 'Maybe I'll be luckier next time.'

'You and me both.' I looked down at the steaming coffee. 'Got nothing stronger back there? It's been one hell of a day.'

'Sorry, boss. I don't drink anymore, remember? Wadida would snatch off my *rambutans*.'

'You've really turned right around, isn't it? One-hundred-and-eighty degrees.'

He chuckled. 'I am a reformed man.'

I leaned forward and sipped at the coffee. Hasan's daughter was sitting by my feet, observing me closely.

'Can I smoke in here?' I said, taking out my Pall Malls.

'I didn't know you smoked cigarettes. Looks like you turned a few degrees yourself, Ah Tat.'

The little girl watched as I lit up. She wrinkled her nose as the thin wisps emerged from the cigarette and turned to look at her father with a question in her eyes. Hasan winked at her and sat back.

'So, what will you do now?' he said. 'Back to the drawing board?'

'I don't think so.'

'You're giving up, just like that?'

'It's hardly an overnight decision.'

'You cannot give up, Ah Tat. What is it they say? The successful man is only the one who fails over and over. He gets so good at it, he even fails at failing. You must try again, surely.'

'I am finished lah.'

'Be optimistic, old friend. There is great hope for the future. Look around you, Ah Tat. The country is really going places. The government is doing a fantastic job; the economy is stronger than ever. There will be a second chance for your company, you will see.'

I stopped him before he could go on. 'What did you say?'

'I said you will get a second chance.'

'No, before that. About the government. You said the government is doing a fantastic job.'

'Sure,' he frowned. 'Aren't they?'

I burst out laughing, shaking my head mirthlessly. Hasan's daughter, who had been staring at me while I talked, seemed startled.

'Why am I surprised?' I said. 'Of course, you would think that. I forget who you are sometimes.'

'What's that supposed to mean? Who am I?'

'You Bumiputra are all the same.'

Hasan looked at me for a moment and then looked at his daughter. She was sitting in front of us, watching our exchange intently. Hasan set his cup of coffee down on the table and picked his little girl up off the floor. He took her into the kitchen and left her with Wadida and then came back and closed the door. He sat down again.

'What's gotten into you lately?'

I stood up and went over to his front window, looking out onto the street.

'You know what I just realized?' I said, pressing my finger against the glass. 'The district landfill site is over in that direction. Across the river, past Old Klang Road.'

I turned to Hasan, shaking my head as I went on:

'Unbelievable as it is, I think my place is closer to the rubbish tip than yours. Do you not find that unbelievable?'

Hasan remained silent as I turned back to the window, muttering to myself.

'This time last year I was still in Kenny Hills. Kenny Hills! Now, look at me, standing here, looking for the rubbish tip so I can figure out where my house is.'

'Calm down, Ah Tat.'

'All that hard work, all those years. And yet here I am. What was the point of it all? I may as well have been born a Malay. Let the government hand me everything and save myself the trouble. At least I'd end up on the right side of the rubbish tip.'

'Alright, Ah Tat. You're upset. Just calm down.'

Later on, Hasan drove me home in his Datsun. Once again we were caught in traffic as men in orange hard hats crowded round a motorized crane on the main road, attempting to dislodge a tree branch that had fallen onto some power lines during the storm. Finally crossing the river into Happy Garden, I watched people sweeping the water from their tiled yards and clearing giant fronds that had been torn away from battered palm trees. The run-off from the rain was still streaming away along the ground ditches. Hasan turned into my street and pulled up beside the now empty driveway.

'Will you be alright?' he said.

I stared at my house through the passenger window. The Datsun was idling.

'Go around,' I said.

'What?'

'Go around, keep driving. I am not ready to go in just yet.'

Hasan put the car into gear and slowly pulled away from the house.

'Where am I going?' he said.

'Anywhere lah. Just go.'

He drove to the end of the street and turned towards the new housing development. The rain-darkened tarmac trailed off and eventually gave way to a sandy unpaved road pitted with deep tire ruts that were filled with muddy water. I told Hasan to keep driving and we went about in a big circle, making slow laps of the housing project. Half-completed homes stood without their roofs, surrounded by construction materials covered in black tarpaulin sheets. Finally, I said:

'How can I face her?'

'You haven't told them yet?'

'This morning I drove out in a special class Mercedes-Benz. Now I am home in an old beat-up Datsun. It's funny, almost.'

I laughed and as I laughed, my voice caught unexpectedly in my throat. Hasan slowed the car and looked across the dash.

'Ah Tat? Are you alright?'

'Keep driving. Don't look this way, don't look at me.'

Hasan pulled over and yanked up on the handbrake, turning to face me. Before he could say anything, I got out and walked around to the back of the car and stood in the street, blinking up at the sky. I pulled the front of my shirt up over my face. Behind me, I could hear the exhaust of the Datsun murmuring away warmly. After a moment, I turned around and walked back to the car and got in. We sat there in silence for a while. Finally, I said:

'It's just the weather.'

'You want a handkerchief?'

'I'm fine.'

'Listen, Ah Tat,'

'It's been a long day. That's all it is.'

He nodded quietly.

'You can take me home now,' I said, patting him on the knee. 'Thank you, Hasan. Thank you, my friend.'

'It's nothing. I simply drove you home is all.'

'No. You're a good friend. Thank you.'

He smiled as I ran my sleeve over my nose, looking over in the direction of my house.

'I am alright now. You can take me home.'

'Are you sure?'

'Yeah lah, I am sure. Take me home.'

1985

Seventeen

I strolled down the mountainside enjoying the brisk highland air on my face. A path of worn stone steps stretched out below me, skirting the edge of the escarpment in a jagged trail, all the way to the distant tree line. Midway down, the path plateaued to a small rocky shelf that jutted from the face of the cliff and looked out on the valley and surrounding hills. Sitting back from the ledge, a simple wooden bench had been bolted into the rock. I made my way down and waited on the bench. June was taking her time, dallying near the top of the rise. A cool breeze riffled the fabric of her blouse. She came down the stone steps and sat beside me, taking in a long deep breath.

'It's so beautiful here,' she said.

'It is.'

'I am so glad we came.' She lifted the sunglasses from her face and perched them on her forehead, looking at me. 'And you? Are you glad?'

'I am. I'm glad.'

I unshouldered my knapsack and took out the camera. June was gazing out on the view in silence, absently tracing her fingers over an etching in the wooden bench between us: BUNNY AND OTTER FOREVER. She sighed and kicked her feet out. I took a few snaps of her, framed by the steep verdant cliffs. Below, a gauzy mist dispersed imperceptibly over the rolling hills; it looked as if everything was laced with cobwebs.

'How high are we do you think?' she said.

'High.'

She stood up and sidled to the precipice, glancing back at me. 'Would you catch me?'

'You're too old for fooling, June. Come away from the edge.'

I got up and went to her and caught her by the wrist.

'Would you or not,' she smiled. 'Topple off after me?'

A group of elderly sightseers coming up the mountain appeared out of the tree line and June and I broke away from one another sheepishly. One of the men in a *dastaar* smiled as he passed us on the way up. When they were out of sight, I said:

'So playful today. Like a young girl all over again.'

'I am just in a good mood.'

'I can see that. It's a nice change.'

'I suppose I really needed the break.' She looked at me for a moment and sighed, 'I guess we both did.'

I opened the knapsack and unpacked the lunch pail I'd brought along for the hike. I laid the pork buns and mandarins out on the bench between us and went into the bag again and brought out the hot flask. We sat looking out over the hills, eating quietly.

'Do you think the kids would have liked this?' I said.

'Never mind the kids.'

'But they would have liked it, all this space. I realized on the drive up here they never been outside of KL before. I'll start making more time for them, when things settle down. You want some coffee?'

I unscrewed the lid of the flask and poured the coffee out into the large metal lid. The liquid came out steaming in the cool mountain air.

'Kieran is too young to appreciate the hills,' she said.

'And Rosalind?'

'Maybe Rosie would have liked it. But I've had about as much as I can take from that girl.' June took a sip of the coffee and sat back, turning her face up to the sky. She closed her eyes for a moment. 'She's a real handful lately. I'm glad it's just the two of us.'

After we'd finished eating, I packed the leftovers into the plastic lunch-pail and tossed the dregs of coffee out over the bluff. I shrugged on the knapsack, and we continued our languid trek down into the valley. Sections of the maroon guardrail guided our descent in amongst the trees. Farther down, the foliage began to thin, and the narrow trail ended abruptly, opening out into a large rest-stop area. A paved road ran through the clearing and a tour bus was rumbling beside a block of toilets.

A quaint little canteen-cum-souvenir shop stood on the other side of the road and passengers were filing out of the bus, stretching and chatting and taking in the view. As we entered the rest area, June looked up the mountain-face.

'Look,' she said, pointing. 'Can see our room from here.'

Perched at the peak of the mountain, the enormous white façade of the hotel looked down on us. The prominent red monogram and signage GENTING HIGHLANDS HOTEL was erected on the deck of the roof, held up by a cross-hatched array of supporting wires. I took a photograph. Nearby, a woman in a sun-yellow hijab was also staring up at the hotel. I asked if she'd take a photo of us and we stood smilingly underneath a multi-arrowed signpost, one arrow pointing to HIGHLANDS HOTEL & CASINO, the others to WATERFALL and CHIN SWEE TEMPLE. Afterwards, I went and ordered an *ais kacang* at the canteen and the vendor prepared it using an old-style cast iron shaver with a hand crank. He drenched the ice and red beans in root beer syrup with condensed milk and June and I ate the dessert at a row of tables nearby. We quietly watched people wander about the rest-stop.

'It's so cool up here in the Highlands.'

'I know.'

'Let's never go back, Ah Tat.'

'I can be persuaded.'

June smiled. 'If only lah.'

The condensation from the kacang started to run down my wrists and I placed the paper cup on the table, rubbing my fingers together.

'These things are always so sticky.'

'Ayah, Ah Tat, look at you. Even Rosie would do a better job. Go wash your hands before you touch me.'

I got up and walked across the lot. There was a long queue snaking out of the toilet block, with visitors from the tour bus lining up behind the only two bathroom stalls available. I went to the basin to wash my hands. As I was rinsing them off, an older Indian gentleman came up behind me and tapped me on the shoulder. I turned around.

'I thought that was you,' he said.

'Ai? What are you doing here?'

The man smiled warmly at me. He was wearing a thin linen shirt that appeared to have been buttoned out of alignment and there was a folded brochure map of Genting sticking out of his front pocket.

'On vacation, of course,' he laughed. 'Why else does anyone come up to the Highlands? My daughter and her family are somewhere around. We're with the bus.'

'My God, I haven't seen your face in years.'

'I know. It's been a long time.'

I dried my hands on the back of my trousers and together we walked back across the lot to where June was sitting by the canteen.

'June,' I said. 'June, look who I bumped into in the bathroom. You remember Ramesh, don't you? My old boss at Briggs.'

'Oh yes, of course,' she smiled. 'Ramesh. How are you, uncle? It's been such a long time.'

'A very long time. In May it will be sixteen years already.'

'Sixteen?' I said, shaking my head. 'Where did the time go?'

Visitors from the tour bus were dispersing over the rest-stop to explore the surroundings. Some of them wandered over to a bank of metallic coin-operated binoculars to get a better view of the hillside while others lined up at the canteen or browsed the wares at the souvenir stand. Ramesh and I sat underneath the shelter of the eating area, reminiscing about the time we worked at Briggs together. June listened obligingly as we went on and on.

'Ah Tat here was one of my best young engineers,' Ramesh was telling her. 'Always hunched over that tiny workstation of his. Working until all hours of the night, staying later than anyone else. Always working, he was.'

June shook her head, looking at me. 'I'm afraid nothing's changed, uncle.'

'I'm not surprised,' Ramesh chuckled. 'You always worked too hard for your own good, Ah Tat. Too hard.'

'I wasn't that bad.'

'Not that bad? You were obsessed with getting ahead. So ambitious, you were. You could be ruthless too, Ah Tat. Remember how you tried to steal poor Dieter's project away from him? I had to step in between the two of you.'

'That's all water under the bridge. He works for me now, did you know? Dieter Hoffman.'

'I remember you always hovering over my shoulder back then, forever kacau-kacau me to put in a good word for you, looking to climb. Remember those days?'

'I remember.'

'But I suppose if you were not that way inclined, you wouldn't be where you are today.'

I shrugged. 'It's all finally starting to pay off.'

'I'll say,' Ramesh smiled. 'I read that profile about you in the *New Straits Times* last year. What was it they said? A young rising star. At the forefront of Malaysia's next commodities boom.'

'You saw that, is it?'

'Sure, I saw it. Everybody at Briggs saw it. Our former colleagues posted me a copy when it came out. They keep me updated on your career. I am so proud to hear about your success, Ah Tat. A fantastic story.'

I looked at Ramesh. 'They still talk about me? Over at Briggs?'

'Not all of them are still at Briggs, of course. But I hear from some of the old team now and then. We are always boasting about knowing you in the early days. Everywhere I go now, whenever I see industry people, I tell them, you know Lim Kin Tat? Of LKT Holdings? He was my protégé. I taught him everything he knows.'

June smiled at me.

'Is that right?' I said.

'That company of yours, LKT Holdings. Doing great things for this country, Ah Tat, great things. I always knew you would be a big success one day.'

Ramesh was holding onto my arm as he talked and kept squeezing me with his bony fingers after everything he said. He was beaming at me. I smiled back at him.

'Well, it wasn't all plain sailing. The early years were difficult.' I glanced at June. 'It's been a long journey.'

Above us, a thin cloud passed in front of the sun and the leeside of the mountain was cast into shadow for a moment, as if a curtain had been drawn over the hillside. All around the rest-stop, tourists paused momentarily in the darkness. Then the mist evaporated, and the sun shone through again, brighter than before. The tour bus started up and groups of people made their way over and formed a queue outside its doors. Ramesh's family was among them, waiting to board. His daughter waved to him.

'I think your bus is leaving now.'

He looked over and sighed.

'I suppose I better get going. These tour conductor types are like little dictators, everything must run on time. Anyway, it was good to see you again, Ah Tat. Keep up the good work. You make us all proud to know you.'

I stopped him as he was turning to leave.

'Ramesh, wait. Before you go. I wanted to tell you. I was sorry to hear about what happened. It was a terrible thing.'

He turned back to look at me and I paused for a moment, hesitating, before going on:

'I just wanted you to know, I keep your family in my prayers.'

Ramesh nodded and smiled weakly at me.

'Thank you for saying that, Ah Tat.'

The bus gave several short sharp blasts from its horn.

'You better go,' I said.

June put her arm through mine, and we watched as Ramesh boarded the bus with the rest of his family.

'What was that about?' she said.

'What was what about?'

'Keeping him in your prayers. You never prayed in your life.'

'I pray sometimes.'

We waved at the bus as it heaved up the steep incline in low gear, roaring round the curve of the hill. For a long time after it had disappeared, the engine could still be heard circling the mountain. I looked around the rest-stop. It had suddenly become deserted. June tugged gently at my arm.

'That's all you're going to say? What did you mean, "keeping him in your prayers?"'

'Nothing.'

'We agreed to start talking to each other more, Ah Tat.'

I frowned and nodded. 'He had a nervous breakdown. Back when we knew each other.'

'Breakdown?' June gave a small shudder and drew close to me. 'Oh dear.'

'I remember when he left Briggs. It was right after the riots. No warning, no nothing. Didn't even hand in his resignation. Just vanished, like that. I haven't seen him since. Not until this very day. I heard he had a breakdown and cabut off to Australia with his whole family and never looked back.'

'How strange. He seemed quite happy to me. Quite normal.'

'He's aged so much since then. I hardly recognized him.' I turned to June and sighed. 'How quickly time flies.'

'So true.'

The rest-stop had become eerily quiet and the only sound we could hear was the muted rustle of canopies billowing in the surrounding hills. I sat there staring at the empty space vacated by the tour bus. A moment later, a minivan with SMK TELUK INTAN BADMINTON printed in bright blue letters on its doors appeared from around the corner, coming up the mountain. It parked by the toilet block and opened its doors. A squad of lithe young girls jumped out, wearing formfitting white tee-shirts and little blue shorts. They all started jogging on the spot and bending over and stretching out their long, muscled legs. June needled me in the ribs.

'Like what you see, do you?'

I turned to June.

'His only son was killed in the riots. Did I ever tell you?'

'Ayah, how awful.'

'It was. Awful, so awful. I remember he told Dieter and some of the others at Briggs about it, right after it happened. They found the boy in a ditch out at Selak South. Ramesh didn't get his body until a week after May Thirteen. A week, can you imagine? Never even found out what really happened to him. The examiner said that he was probably trampled to death. I remember Dieter saying at the time, just between us, the trampling thing was just the examiner being kind. The poor bugger must have been beaten to death. Why else would they try to hide his body in a ditch?'

'Enough, Ah Tat. Stop it.'

'What?'

'It's too depressing lah.'

I took June's hand, and we got up to leave.

'You wanted me to talk more, so I am talking. That's how come we got so many problems between us, isn't that what you're always telling me? So, I'm talking.'

'Not about that. God, anything but that.'

We walked across the clearing, heading for the trail that led back up the mountain towards the hotel. The girls from the badminton team raced past us in a blue and white blur, loping up the stone steps two at a time. June watched them jog up the hill.

'We should exercise more,' she said. 'Take up badminton. That would be something we could do together.'

I shrugged.

'If you think it would help.'

Eighteen

I ordered coffee and sat down at a table in the food court, on one of the upper floors of the Genting casino. I'd brought a catalogue from the Mont Blanc showroom to pass the time while I waited, and I leafed through its glossy pages, turning down the corners on the belt buckles and calfskin attaches, watching people mill about the dining area. It was still bright outside and so it was relatively quiet in and around the casino complex. A group of off-duty croupiers were eating noodles together outside one of the makan stalls, dressed in their red and black silk vests, and the janitor was doing slow laps around them with his mop, stopping every now and then to chat. I drank my coffee and smoked a cigarette and waited. An overweight Chinese man in a rumpled VISIT MALAYSIA! T-shirt was sitting in front of me, slobbering down a bowl of cheap mee. As soon as he was done, he rose and sloped back down the escalators into the gaming dens. Kin Chew arrived with Piggy just as I was getting up for more coffee.

'You waiting long?' he said.

'Half an hour already. What took you?'

'How's June?'

'She's fine. She says to tell you to thank you for the cable car coupons.'

KC sat down opposite me and looked around at the stalls. 'You want something to drink? Makan?'

'I was just now getting more coffee.'

He nodded and turned to Piggy who was standing off to one side, wearing his sunglasses indoors. Kin Chew held up two fingers and said 'kosong, dua,' and Piggy stood unmoving as though he hadn't heard, eyes masked by the dark shades. KC raised his voice:

'Did you hear me? Kopi kosong lah, two of them.'

Piggy grunted and went over to the drinks stand to order our coffees.

'You really got that Piggy trained now I see.'

'Not so loud, one. He is sensitive about that stuff still. And I told you already, he doesn't like to be called that.'

I looked over. Piggy was waiting in front of the coffee stall but there was no one there to serve him. He began slapping his palm repeatedly on the countertop and a few people in the food court glanced over at him.

'You should teach him some manners.'

'Forget about him. Listen, Ah Tat.' KC reached across and took a cigarette from my pewter case. 'The boss wants to see you.'

'What, tonight?'

'Tonight. His helicopter just landed and he's still checking in and resting and all the rest, but yes. Tonight. He likes to play at the tables after dinner, but he asked you to join him in his suite later. Say, eleven.'

I looked at Kin Chew. 'Do I have to?'

'What's the problem?'

'It's not a good time right now. June is only just starting to warm up to me again. I told her this vacation is a chance for us to make amends. I don't want her to know I planned this trip around a business meeting.'

'Don't worry about that. She knows.'

I looked at him. 'She knows?'

'She knows about the meeting. I told her. She's fine with it.'

'You told her?'

Kin Chew shrugged. 'It's an important meeting. She understands. Work is not the problem between the two of you, anyhow.'

Piggy came over and set two cups of black coffee down in front of us and then went to sit at a nearby table. As the janitor was mopping up around him, Piggy spat on the floor at the man's feet. The cleaner stopped and stared at him. Piggy stared back.

'Since when do you and June talk?' I said.

'Are you listening to me, Ah Tat? The meeting is at eleven tonight. It's nothing official lor, but don't come dressed like you're going to the buffet either.'

'You cannot talk to the old man yourself?'

'Not this time. He insists on seeing you personally.'

I sipped at the coffee and looked down the empty aisles of the food court. 'Are you asking or telling?'

'You cannot refuse. He came up to Genting just to see you.'

I frowned, looking away. Kin Chew stubbed out his cigarette and leaned across the table, taking hold of my wrist:

'You cannot refuse, Ah Tat. Do I have to remind you what would've happened to your company without his help? A man like Yeung Yau Yu never forgets.'

I pulled away. 'Yes, I know. I heard you.'

'Don't make me look bad, Ah Tat,' he said, standing up. He gestured to Piggy and Piggy got up and buttoned his jacket.

'You're off already?' I said.

'I got some things to attend to.'

'But your coffee.'

'They make it too bitter here.' He reached over and took a couple of Pall Malls from my cigarette case. He put one in his mouth and slid the other behind his ear and he and Piggy started off towards the escalators together.

'Eleven tonight,' he called over his shoulder. 'Penthouse level. You'll be there, isn't it?'

I watched them sink down the moving stairs.

'Don't make me look bad, Ah Tat.'

* * *

A young woman answered the door to the penthouse suite. She was wearing a pressed white shirt, dark maroon waistcoat and bowtie, and on her hotel badge, the name ROSE was printed.

'My daughter's name is Rose,' I said. 'Rosalind.'

The attendant smiled wordlessly and indicated the low rack by the entrance. I removed my shoes, placed them on the wooden slats, and followed her in. The corridor walls were adorned with framed pictures of the Genting Highlands Hotel: black-and-white stills during its construction, architectural schematics and an aerial photograph. The young woman led me into a spacious suite that was dimly lit by a pair of massive lamps fashioned after arguileh pipes, each seven feet tall and highly polished, their metallic honey gold sheen rippling like amber water on the walls of the room. An elderly man was sitting on a rattan sofa in the centre of the suite. He was eating a mandarin, its peel and pips accumulated on a folded-over newspaper. Yeung Yau Yu waved me over to a seat opposite him.

'Ah Tat,' he said. 'Come, sit. Yum jao, ma?'

'No. Thank you.'

'Have, have. There's good whiskey here.' He gummed a piece of wet fruit in his mouth. 'Myself I don't drink, but my associates all commented on how good the whiskey was before they left just now.'

At a small table off to the side, Kin Chew and Piggy were counting out casino chips and packing away mahjong tiles. There was a circle of half-empty glasses on the table and the room smelled of cigar smoke. Kin Chew and I nodded to one another as I took the seat facing Mr Yeung.

'I don't drink either,' I said. 'Not at meetings.'

The old man finished off his mandarin and immediately began peeling another.

'Smart,' he said.

I glanced around the suite. Behind the old man, the room let onto a balcony which, in the sunlight, might have overlooked a glorious view of the surrounding hillside. At night however it returned only the sight of a dark unknown terrain. Yeung Yau Yu looked at me.

'It's a nice change of scenery up here, isn't it, Ah Tat? Away from the bustle of KL.'

The old man was almost completely bald, though a few hoary iron-grey wisps clung on around his ears and temples. The thinning hair contrasted sharply with the jet-black shock of his moustache: trim and prominent and effete.

'You're a difficult man to get a hold of,' he said. 'It's been months I've been trying to arrange a meeting.'

'I've been busy.'

'I understand how it is. How's the family?'

'Fine.'

'That's good to hear. Kin Chew tells me your wife is here at the hotel with you. You should have told me she was coming. I might have arranged for the two of you to stay at one of the executive suites. The wives always like that sort of detail. How is she doing anyhow?'

I shrugged, crossing my arms. 'She's fine.'

The old man frowned. For a while, there was an awkward silence that lingered in the room. When Kin Chew and Piggy had finished packing away the mahjong tiles, they came over and each took a chair beside

Mr Yeung so that all three men were facing me. Kin Chew shot me a look and said:

'June recently gave birth to a boy. Kieran is soon to have his first Chinese New Year.'

Yeung Yau Yu smiled. 'Healthy, I hope.'

'Yes. Healthy.'

'Health is important. Maybe most important of all.'

I nodded.

'If I had known, I would have sent a gift.'

'That's not necessary. After all, we hardly know each other.'

Yeung Yau Yu frowned again and looked at me carefully. He drained the rest of his herbal tea and then signalled for the attendant. She came over and refilled his cup from a large kettle.

'Thank you, young lady. That will be all for now.'

Reaching for his elegant cane, Mr Yeung struggled to lift himself up off the rattan sofa before personally escorting the young woman to the door. He made a considerable racket as he hobbled clumsily down the corridor, the sound of his cane rapping disjointedly against the floorboards. By the time he returned, he'd worked out the stiffness in his gait, but I realized for the first time how debilitating the old man's handicap truly was. I was no longer certain whether he even possessed a real limb under that loose-fitting trouser leg. He settled into the rattan sofa once more and looked at me.

'It's worth the effort to show courtesy to young ladies,' he said. 'Now, I assume Kin Chew told you why I asked you here tonight.'

'I got some idea.'

He nodded slowly. 'And what is that?'

'Oil palm.'

He leaned across the coffee table and took up his tea and sipped from it thoughtfully. He set it back down.

'Partly,' he said. 'Yes.'

'Partly? What's that supposed to mean, partly?'

The old man studied me for a moment. The gold ring on his small finger, set with a large rectangular stone of milky jade, drew the eye as he caressed the wings of his moustache with thumb and forefinger. He leaned back and looked over at KC with an amused expression.

'I can see there's no point in wasting time on niceties with your cousin. Okay lah, so be it. Show him.'

He made a small gesture with his hand and Piggy immediately got up and went to a bookshelf in the corner of the room. He brought over a large black binder and dropped it unceremoniously on the coffee table in front of me. Yeung Yau Yu pointed to the binder.

'It's your copy.'

'What's this?'

I opened the cover and thumbed through the pages rapidly. It looked to be a legal document. Terrence Tan and Dieter Hoffman's names, together with my own, appeared on multiple pages. There were also several names that appeared in the paperwork—many of them Malay—that I did not recognize at all. I stopped flipping through the binder and closed the cover and set it on the table.

'I don't understand.'

'Your company is expanding,' he said.

'Expanding?'

'It's all in the document, Ah Tat. A lot of money is to be invested into LKT Holdings soon. The company will be needing a proper corporate structure. You will remain as managing director, of course, but there will be a board of directors now, with some new people sitting. Associates of mine, don't worry, all capable men.'

Yeung Yau Yu was watching me closely as he went on speaking:

'Your cousin,' he said, nodding at Kin Chew. 'He will be your chairman. The rest of you can report to him. Kin Chew will be my representative at LKT since, after this, I will become the majority shareholder.'

'The what?'

'Congratulations are in order,' he said.

I looked up at the others. Piggy was grinning stupidly at me while Kin Chew sat very still in his chair, almost as though he dared not breathe.

'You knew about this?' I said to KC.

'It's inevitable, Ah Tat. Don't overreact.'

'And if I refuse? You cannot make me sign the company over.'

The comment seemed to have a strange effect on everyone in the room. Kin Chew and Piggy both turned to look at Mr Yeung. The old man had not stopped peeling and eating mandarins since my arrival, but he stopped now, frowning, and leaned forward to run his hands along his weak leg, groping and pressing it as though it were a foreign object, or some slab of meat unconnected with the rest of his body. Finally, he managed to lift the lame leg, repositioning it on top of his good one. He sat back, legs now crossed, and stared at me as if I hadn't said a thing. It was Kin Chew who was the first to break the silence:

'Don't worry, Mr Yeung. He will sign the agreement. Believe me, he'll sign. Won't you, Ah Tat? He just doesn't understand, is all.'

'I understand perfectly. I am not signing anything.'

I stood up to leave.

Piggy immediately stood up as well, taking a step towards me and squaring his shoulders. In the spotless glass of the balcony doors behind the old man, I could see our reflections superimposed on the dark falling hillside. I hadn't realized until then just how much bigger Piggy was than me. I stiffened and backed away. Kin Chew leapt out of his seat and stood between us, holding off the bigger man.

'Stop, you damn fools. Stop.' Mr Yeung reached for his cane and swatted Piggy in the back of the legs. 'Enough! I won't tell you again.'

KC and Piggy broke off from one another, panting slightly, and looked to the old man.

'Get out,' he barked. 'Go on. I'll see you two buffoons in the morning. I want to talk to Ah Tat alone. Like bloody children, the pair of you. I am trying to have a civilized conversation.'

He was leaning heavily on his cane to lurch to his feet and Kin Chew immediately went over, sliding his hand in an almost tender way under the old man's armpit to help him up. KC and Piggy then gathered their money-clips and cigarettes, hastily swallowing down the rest of their drinks, before marching to the corridor. Kin Chew shot me a pointed look as he left the suite. The latch to the room door snapped shut after them.

'The energy in this room is too stagnant,' Mr Yeung sighed.

He hobbled over to the balcony doors and pulled them apart, letting some air in. A chilly mountain breeze surged inside, transforming the serene lamplight into a paroxysm of flickering shadow. The old man stepped out onto the balcony and motioned for me to follow.

'Join me outside. I'll explain everything.'

I looked at him.

'For heaven's sake, Ah Tat. Come outside, we will talk together.'

Out on the balcony, the rest of Genting fell away in the dark. I stepped to the guardrail and peered down the mountainside but there was nothing to see; merely the sound of moving trees. The wind whipped about us and I looked at the old man, who seemed unperturbed by the cold.

'Did Kin Chew ever tell you what happened to my leg?' he said.

I looked down at his trousers.

'He mentioned it. Polio, I think he said.'

'Polio, that's right. I caught a fever when I was very young and soon afterwards, it started to wither away. At two years old I was walking around, running even, but by three no more. There was nothing you could do in those days. Of course, my mother didn't understand such things. Too much damp heat, she said. Too much *yeet foong* for a child. She was only a simple kampong girl after all. Not educated, you know. I got to rely on one leg ever since.'

'I see.'

'My first memory is from that time. Most people cannot remember much past when they are ten years old, but I am seventy-six now and still, I got a clear picture of that doctor's room back when I was three. Can argue I see it clearer than I see you now, if you look at things a certain way. That is what it is like for people who have illness so young. We never forget.'

'I am sorry to hear.'

He waved the comment away. 'By rights, I should be a worthless beggar today. A gutter rat. But then, that is how we differ from the Malays.'

Yeung Yau Yu leaned on the banister railing and stared down the sharp declivity. A dark chasm stretched out before us in all directions, completely black but for a tiny speck of yellow light—some lost tourist, perhaps— crawling round a bend in the mountain road.

'You know about Genting, don't you?' he said.

'A little.'

'Lim Goh Tong, same family name as you. He conjured this resort out of thin air. It took him almost four years to cut the road up through Ulu Kali. Some places they even have to dig manually.'

'It is impressive.'

'Impressive the least of it. The bastard damn near got himself killed trying to get up this mountain. Literally lah.'

I nodded quietly.

'But you understand that, don't you, boy?'

The distant trees had been swaying rhythmically somewhere beyond the balcony, buffeted continually by invisible undulating waves. Then, suddenly, the wind died away completely and there was no sound to take its place. A deep silence followed. It was as though I had lost my hearing.

'Don't you, boy? You understand it, that drive. That unstoppable need. To forge a road through a wild mountain where there was none before.'

'Yes. In fact, I do.'

'Good, yes. I understand it also. So, it stands to reason, we should understand each other.'

I stood up straight and turned to face him. 'Go on, Mr Yeung.'

He nodded approvingly for the first time.

'This latest investment,' he said. 'It is simply the next natural step for you. If you do not seize this opportunity, LKT Holdings will be a second-class operation until the day you die. Believe me. You are not the first rising star.'

'Do I have a choice?'

'I am not your enemy, Ah Tat. I'm lending a helping hand only. Not for the first time either, if I can remind you.'

I looked away.

'We all need friends,' he murmured.

'And what do you need?'

'Nothing is for free, young man. Big investment means big return, after all. Yes, I will control the company after this, but again, you miss the bigger picture. Oil palm is the new rubber. Do you know how many hectares been earmarked for oil palm plantations in Selangor? More than a hundred thousand. If that doesn't impress you then you only need to look east. Borneo got ten times as much land. Sabah, Sarawak. That is your future. If whales like Guthrie or Harrisons take up the machinery we manufacture, well, I can let you imagine for yourself.'

Yeung Yau Yu was staring at me in the dark, a flinty glassiness coming over his black eyes. He went on:

'I am an old man already. I got no sons. You understand what I'm saying to you?'

The hills of the highland ranges sprawled out darkly around us and we stood on the balcony as though it were the bow of some great ship, gazing out on an immense midnight sea of hills, like waves frozen mid-swell in the moonlight. Yeung Yau Yu took a deep breath and turned to face me, suddenly larger and more robust.

'Think it over, Ah Tat. No need to sign anything right away. The transition process is slow anyhow. But I will tell you this once only and we never need mention it again. The gwai los got a saying, about the carrot and the stick. You know it, this saying?'

I nodded quietly.

He started shuffling back towards the hotel room.

'Good,' he said. 'So, now you know about the carrot.'

Nineteen

June stepped from the shower wrapped in a hotel bathrobe and went dripping past me, tidying the room. She collected the liner from the dustbin, together with the dirty dishes from our room-service dinner and left all the trash piled neatly outside our room door.

'You don't have to do that,' I said.

'I know.'

'We're on holiday. That's what the housekeeper is for.'

'Yeah lah, but if I leave it then your mother's voice will be in my head all night.' June made a face, twisting her voice so that it came out ugly and contorted, 'What kind of wife are you, cannot even keep the house tidy for your husband and children?'

She wandered back into the bathroom and wiped down the fogged mirror, staring at herself in the glass. Her bathrobe had fallen open and thin cords of water were still running from her hair down her collarbone and breasts. I watched her through the open door. When she noticed me looking, she tied up her robe and closed the door.

'You want me to sign it, don't you?' I called out to her.

'I don't want anything.'

'You want me to sign and take the deal and hand everything over to the old man. If that's what you want, just say so June.'

'I don't want anything, Ah Tat. Don't put words in my mouth.'

I sat on my side of the bed, flipping through Mr Yeung's proposal.

'It's a hijacking,' I said. 'Simple as that. All my sweat and tears, for what? For Yeung Yau Yu's personal glory, that's what. He thinks he can come along and buy up everything I built. The gall of the man.'

June came out of the bathroom, hair still sopping wet, and sat on the edge of the bed. She crawled underneath the sheets and snapped off her bedside lamp. I looked at her across the headboard.

'It's exhausting thinking about this,' I said.

'Then sleep, Ah Tat. Think tomorrow.'

I sat for a moment, leafing listlessly through the pages of the proposal, then closed the binder and set it on the bedside table and turned out my own lamp. I stared at June in the dark. After a moment I turned over, shifting on all fours, and crawled on top of her, pushing her knees apart with my knees.

'I thought you said you were tired,' she said.

I reached out and pressed my palm against her throat. 'I am so tense. I need to get it all out.'

Squeezing her eyes shut, she rasped, 'Be quick about it.'

Afterwards, I fell on my side and rolled over. Lying in the darkened room I listened to the wind out in the hills and let the sound lull me to sleep. Later, I woke with a start. June's terrycloth robe had come off sometime during the night and was now twisted in a rope around my arm, between my legs. Her pale naked form lay motionless beside me. I turned on my side and dozed off once again. When I woke for the second time that night, it was still dark out.

'Are you awake?' I said.

'I never fell asleep.'

'Maybe a take-over wouldn't be the worst thing. We'd have more money.'

'If that's what you want, Ah Tat.'

'It's a lot of money. We could buy back that house in Kenny Hills. Get back to where we ought to be. What do you think?'

'I don't know.'

'Then there's the children to think about. We'd be able to send them to international school. I hate the bloody local curriculums now. What the hell do I want my children learning Bahasa for?'

June lay quietly in the dark, staring up at the walls of the room, streaked with bars of moonlight patterned by the thin embroidered curtains.

'Tell me what to do,' I said.

'I don't know what to do, Ah Tat. Don't ask me.'

'What do you want?'

'Nothing. Anything. I don't know anymore. What do you want?'

I turned on my side so that my back was to her. 'We've been doing better, haven't we? I thought we had.'

She shifted closer, pushing her face into my neck. I could feel her tears on my skin.

'Hush,' she murmured.

'Haven't we?'

'Yes, we been doing better.'

'You're happy now, aren't you? June?'

'I don't know, Ah Tat. Are you?'

'Who knows.'

'Do you think I am a good wife?' she said.

I turned to face her. 'Why do you ask that?'

'Am I a good mother? You think Rosie and Kieran think I am a good mother?'

'You're having those thoughts again,' I said.

'No.'

'You still have them. Don't you?'

'Hush, Ah Tat, there's no more bad thoughts. I am better now, it's better. Go back to sleep.'

In the morning I washed my face and dressed quietly before the sun came out. I packed the proposal into my small suitcase along with a few other items: the camera and rolls of film, my clothes and toiletries and the souvenirs I'd bought for the children. I put the suitcase by the room door and stood over June and watched her sleep. She stirred a little.

'June.'

Suddenly she sat bolt upright, looking about the room with a panicked expression. After a moment, she settled and peered at me from the bed in the eerie dawn light, as if unable to recognize me.

'It's you,' she croaked, slumping back onto the mattress.

'Did I wake you?'

'It's cold,' she said. 'Where's my robe?'

She groped around the bedclothes and pulled the bathrobe out from under the sheets and shrugged it on, cinching it in tightly at the waist. Then she reached over and turned on the bedside lamp and rubbed her eyes. She stared at me.

'What's the matter?' she said. 'Why are you dressed?'

'I decided to drive back to KL today.'

'Right this minute?'

'I have to see what Terrence and Dieter think about this whole takeover business.'

'We're not staying the rest of the week?'

'You stay. I paid for the room already. You stay and enjoy yourself. I'm sorry but I got to get back to KL. I must talk to the others, soon as I can.'

June squinted over at the curtains. At its edges, the morning light was slowly turning white.

'Your mother will want to know why I didn't come home with you,' she sighed. 'It's better if I come back too. Give me a few minutes to pack.'

'Don't worry so much about what Ma Ma thinks all the time.' I went over to the bed and kissed her quickly. 'Go back to sleep. Aren't you always complaining about how you never got any time for yourself? Take the rest of the week and relax.'

'But how will I get home?'

'Kin Chew can drive you back Monday. He won't mind. The two of you can go around and see Genting together. I'm sorry but I have to go now.'

She frowned. 'Are you sure, Ah Tat?'

'Go back to sleep, darling. No sense in letting the room go to waste.'

1987

Twenty

By October it seemed the country would once again erupt in race-fuelled violence, as it had done in '69. Tensions had already been running high between Chinese and Malays since the beginning of the year, but with the latest protests staged by Chinese educationists at the Hainanese Association Building, the situation became outright explosive. The Dong Jiao Zong, outraged by the Education Minister's decision to appoint teachers in their schools whom they had not endorsed, signalled their intent to boycott the school system for three days. The Chinese lobby was aggrieved that the teachers had not been formally educated in Mandarin—*our mother-tongue* they'd called it—and interpreted the move as yet another ploy by the government aimed at eroding the foundations of their identity, this time against that most fiercely guarded of institutions, the Chinese language school.

'We may not be *Sons of the Soil*, so be it. We are Chinese first, in any case. And so will our children be, Chinese first, Chinese always. They will speak the mother-tongue. Malays have not the power to control the words out of our own mouths!'

The educationist protests had been organized, infuriatingly to the Malays, in collusion with some of the government's own Malaysian Chinese ministers. UMNO Youth responded by organizing a rally of their own. Thousands of Malays gathered in Kampong Baru—ground zero for the May Thirteen riots almost two decades earlier—in a thinly veiled warning to the Chinese.

I'd been cleaning my car when I first heard news of that UMNO rally, crawling about the leather cabin of the Mercedes with a cloth and bottle of upholstery spray. The bulletin had come over the radio quite suddenly, cutting off one of the songs, and I stopped what I was doing and sat very still in the car. An attendee of the rally was being interviewed:

'Mother-tongue education, they call it. Tell me, which is their motherland? Is it China or Malaysia? Are they Chinese, or Malaysians? *Bahasa Jiwa Bangsa*! These educationists do nothing but sow seeds of disunity here, raising children who will read and think in Chinese, who will congregate and worship and trade and become politicised in Chinese. Like wasps laying eggs in the belly of our nation. These protests are proof they do not seek to assimilate. In their hearts, they look to displace us. Very well, if we must make a stand then so be it. If they will have a fight, we will give it to them.'

Once the segment was over, I scrolled across the radio dial searching for further updates but could find nothing more. I got out and went straight into the house to call Terrence. His voice was low, grave:

'You're only just now hearing about it, are you? UMNO Youth. Thousands of them apparently.'

'Should we be worried?'

There was silence on the other end of the line.

'Terrence,' I said. 'Terrence, should we be worried?'

'I heard rumours they are parading banners calling for May Thirteen again. Soaking the *kris* in Chinese blood, all that old madness.' His voice became muffled over the line. 'It was those damn Dong Jiao Zong protests lah. The whole thing really stirred them up. There is talk now of UMNO massing an even bigger show of force soon. They say half a million Malays are expected to attend the next rally.'

'Half a million? That cannot be true.'

'They're supposed to be coming into KL from all over.'

'When?'

'November first. In Kampong Baru, no less.'

'November first?' I flipped the page of the calendar on the kitchen wall. 'That's only a couple of weeks away.'

Terrence laughed humourlessly. 'I'll say this for them. If something really does happen, cannot say they didn't warn us this time.'

The following morning, I took the station wagon on a special trip out to the Jaya Jusco Supermart in Damansara Utama. I filled one trolley-load, then a second, with various canned foods and tubs of distilled water, rice and flour and eggs, batteries, cigarettes, two-way radio, and a fully stocked first-aid kit. While waiting for the cashier to ring up my goods, I noticed the front page of *The Star* on the rack by the checkout; a Malay army private had gone on a shooting spree in Chow Kit. I leafed through the paper. Page after page of urgent black block print looked back at me:

SECURITY CONCERNS AMID PLANS FOR MAMMOTH
UMNO RALLY
MCA DEPUTY PRESDIENT POSITION UNTENABLE,
DECLARES MINISTER
DETAINEES PLAYING UP FEARS OF MUSLIM APOSTASY
RECESSION: NO END IN SIGHT

On the way home, I stopped by the service station and filled the tank of the Mitsubishi and two more jerrycans, and loaded them into the boot. I topped up the water in the radiator and pumped the tyres. Then I drove to the local hardware store. I picked up a chain with solid iron links and a steel padlock. The owner of the store, a Chinese man around the same age as me, looked at the chain and padlock when I placed them on the counter.

'Preparing for the worst,' he said.

I nodded, opening my wallet. 'And you? Will you stay open come the day of the rally?'

'I got Chinese characters all over my signboard, what do you think? No lah, I don't tempt fate.' The man leaned in and then switched to Cantonese conspiratorially, 'I got parang for sale in the gardening aisle. If you need, that is.'

Once at home, I left a can of fuel in the boot of each of the cars while my mother stashed the extra supplies in the kitchen. I brought the new chain out, wrapping it tightly around the front gate several times before locking it. I stood back and drove my foot into the gate, kicking it repeatedly, putting all my weight behind each lunge. The iron bars jangled nastily, grating against the driveway. The neighbours' dogs howled and bayed up and down the street. June was watching me from the front door.

'Let's see those babis try and get in here,' I said.

Twenty-one

Amid all this, I was invited to a ceremony for the presentation of Hasan's new-born son. I wondered whether I should accept, as it was certain the event would be overwhelmingly attended by Malays, and I recall going back and forth about it right up until the very last minute. Finally, June said:

'Forget all that nonsense on the news. Is he your friend or not?'

So, the following day, I drove to the Masjid Wakaf Baru Mosque in Kampong Pasir, parking the Mercedes under the cover of a massive angsana tree that cast its shade over the entire parking lot. Stapled to the tree trunk was a colourful hand-drawn poster:

Family and Friends,
Selamat Datang!
Cukur Jambul for Ahmad Azmin bin Hasan
10 a.m. in the Main Function Hall

I followed a trickle of smartly-attired guests across the parking lot to the community hall. The hall shared a common area with the mosque and out in the courtyard, a pink lamb carcass was turning on a spit, suspended over a large steel barrel that had been shorn in half and filled with hot coals. Guests were milling around the smoking brazier making small talk, while children chased each other across the yard. Inside the hall itself, balloons and streamers festooned the cornices and high-arched doorways. Several large tables were laden with food; steaming bain maries filled with *biryani* and *rendang*, yellow rice with nuts and raisins, roti, *satay*, fried noodles and *dim sum*. A long procession was filing past Hasan's young family at the head of the hall, and groups of people were continually circling the baby. When my turn came, I greeted Hasan and his wife with an *ang pao* and they smiled and accepted it with two hands and presented little Ahmad Azmin, swaddled in white muslin, dozing in a bassinet adorned with *pandan* and turmeric leaves.

Later that morning, after much of the guest greeting had been done, I went out front for a cigarette and found Hasan leaning against his Datsun in the parking lot.

'Ai? What are you doing out here so long-faced one? Supposed to be a celebration, what.'

He looked at me with bags under his eyes.

'Got a cigarette on you?' he said.

'Sorry, my last one.'

'Shit. I left mine inside.'

'So, go fetch. I'll wait for you.'

He smiled wearily. 'I only just managed to fight my way out here. I'm not heading back inside until I am forced to.'

'Aw, like that, is it?' I laughed. 'Never mind. Here, smoke the rest of mine.'

I looked at him as I handed over the cigarette. He had unfastened the high collar of his *baju* shirt and his songkok was overturned on the roof of his car, headband damp with a darkened ring of sweat.

'What's the matter?' I said.

'It's my parents,' he sighed. 'They're sulking. They wanted to hold the *kenduri* back in the village.'

'You mean back home? Home, home?'

'Home, home. Mimpi. They were planning to invite their whole kampong along.'

I glanced back at the mosque. 'What's wrong with this place? Seems as good a venue as any.'

'No lah, not for the first grandson. A rent-hall in the big city don't feel proper to the old folks. But then Wadida insisted on having it here. She says Kuala Lumpur is my home now, it will be little Azmin's home, so for better or worse, we must hold the ceremony here. Cannot keep running back to the village kampong forever, she says. Those days are gone.'

'Maybe she got a point.'

Hasan looked at me and sighed. 'Point or not, my mother's not happy.'

'Mothers quarrelling with wives,' I laughed. 'Tell me about it.'

He dropped the cigarette at his feet and stepped on it. Smoothing down his hair, he placed the songkok on his head and did up the collar of his shirt.

'I better get back. The *Merhaban* is starting up already. How do I look?'
I smiled. 'Like a man.'

After prayers, a pair of scissors was passed around between the family members at the front of the hall. Each of them took turns cutting off a snippet of the baby's hair. When the scissors came to him, Hasan's father-in-law doffed his songkok to reveal a balding pate and declared:

'Lend your old *Atuk* a few humble strands, won't you?'

The gathering laughed and took photos, and the old man carefully placed the boy's fine black hairs into a hollowed-out green coconut. After the ceremony, the imam was invited to speak. A spectacled man dressed in a white *kaftan* and *taqiyah* made his way to the front of the hall.

* * *

Once the imam had finished speaking, most of the guests began wandering out to the courtyard for the spit-roasted lamb. I remained seated, watching a small group of men hurry over to the imam. They surrounded him, bowing obsequiously and talking all at once, as though he was a celebrity. The man was smiling and nodding and when he said something, they all fell silent, hanging on his every word. I stood up, shaking my head quietly, and left the hall. My hands were shaking uncontrollably. I spotted Hasan across the crowded courtyard, making the rounds with his wife and daughters and the newborn. I went straight over to him and pulled him aside.

'Can you believe that joker back there?' I said.

'Who?'

'The fellow that made the speech just now. Dressed like an Arab.'

Hasan glanced back at the community hall. 'Imam Musa?'

'Whatever you call him.'

Hasan looked at me carefully. 'He's an important man, Ah Tat. A true *ustaz*.'

'Didn't you hear the things he was saying? This is a kenduri for God's sake, not some bloody UMNO pep rally. I can't believe he got the nerve to say such things with all the tensions in KL right now. *Pendatang*, he called us. I heard it with my own ears. How dare he? I am no more an immigrant than you or him. Did you hear that?'

'I heard.'

'And you agree with all that rubbish?'

Hasan sighed. 'I don't disagree.'

I stopped and looked at him. 'What?'

'He's a good man, Ah Tat. Imam Musa was the one who helped me quit drinking all those years ago. And my uncle too. He got Zainuddin enrolled in the drug-rehab program over in Cheras.'

'I am not talking about that. Didn't you hear what he was saying?'

'Calm down, Ah Tat. Lower your voice already.'

'Don't worry about my voice,' I snapped. 'I'll worry about my own voice.'

Around us, guests were laughing and eating and chatting in the sun. Children were dancing excitedly before a couple of foldaway tables on which chocolate cakes and halwa and sticky balls of *ladoo* were arranged in colourful rows of fluted paper cups. Waves of heat emanated from the *kambing guling* brazier, giving the air around the coals a molten viscid quality, and guests were gleefully hacking off great chunks of the roasting meat.

'Go home? Go home and eat pigs over there? Tell me, Hasan. What home is it that I'm supposed to go to? Don't tell me you're going to stand there and defend that.'

'Be careful, Ah Tat.'

'But then I must always be careful, mustn't I? Even when the two of us are speaking privately, I must be careful. I am tired of being careful. You should be ashamed to follow an imam who says such things.'

The women nearest to us, dressed in *hijabs* and *jubah* and *kebaya*, seated on the plastic chairs arranged around the perimeter of the yard, paused as they were eating and glanced over. Hasan stared at me.

'Calm down, Ah Tat.'

'You should be ashamed,' I went on. 'Are you not ashamed?'

'Ashamed?'

He took my arm and pulled me aside, glancing back at his wife and children. His eldest daughter had taken few steps in our direction and was now observing us closely. Hasan smiled at the girl before turning to me once more. His words were hissed:

'What right do you have to talk of shame? Your own associations are not exactly the most honourable.'

I looked at him.

'I read the papers, Ah Tat. I am not as ignorant as you might think. What of this Yeung Yau Yu you work for? Corruption charges. Fraud and embezzlement. Nothing but a regular thug in an expensive suit, is he not? Do you deny it?'

'You don't know what you're talking about.'

'Do you deny it?'

I tore my arm from him and started to walk away. 'You're talking rubbish.'

Following me, he grabbed hold of my elbow and pulled me in close. I snatched my arm back and he followed and took hold of me again and looked me in the eyes.

'And what about these rumours your company is engaged in *Ali-Baba* practice? Getting rich by exploiting Malays. You should be the one who is ashamed.'

I pushed him away. 'Exploiting? They come to us, smiling through their teeth, hands in our pockets and it is we who are exploiting them? Don't make me laugh. What do you know anyway?'

'So you do not deny it.'

'I don't deny we been forced to survive. This bloody government you love so much is making sure of that.'

'Survive? Are you talking about this multi-million *ringgit* deal you keep bragging about? All about survival, is it? What do you know about surviving? I left my family home when I was twelve, Ah Tat. You got any idea what it's like to leave your family behind at twelve years old and try and make it in this city? I had never even seen a traffic light before then.'

'My God, cry me a river. You think I grew up in a palace? My house was made of attap, same as yours,'

'You cannot excuse your behaviour, Ah Tat. Companies like yours, men like you and Yeung Yau Yu. You're all undermining the NEP, undermining this country.'

'NEP? I spit on the NEP.'

'How can you say that, Ah Tat? How many people has the NEP helped? How many Malays were lifted out of poverty?'

'Who does the NEP help? Who?' I laughed incredulously. 'You said it yourself. The only people it ever helped are your own people.'

'Damn right, my people. My people who can somehow come out with less, even in our own damn country. My people, my people. Good proud humble Muslims, Bumiputra, damn you, cannot even protect ourselves, is it? What should we let you do? Run all over us, like the British? Like the Dutch, the Portuguese? Smile and bow and say, thank you sir, thank you towkay, while you get rich telling us how to run our own country? No lah, you won't run over us anymore. No one will run over us ever again.'

Suddenly, I became aware that the entire yard had fallen silent. People were no longer laughing or chatting, and the only sound that could be heard was the occasional snapping of fat globules from over by the lamb spit. Hasan too, at that moment, seemed to recall himself and looked around sheepishly. He had been shouting and tripping over his words and his entire body was trembling, as if he'd just been drenched in freezing water. His face was streaming with tears. Most of his family and friends were looking down at their feet, or off into the distance. A few were shaking their heads quietly amongst themselves. Hasan's wife was standing over their eldest daughter, hands wrapped around the girl's tudong, covering her ears. The girl had an unknowable expression written on her face. Wadida turned to her guests and laughed:

'Seems like every conversation now must turn to politics.'

Her face was bright red. She shot Hasan a dark look and quickly led the girls back inside the hall. Several people followed suit.

Afterwards, the other guests avoided me. Everywhere I went, they would smile and nod politely before finding a way to remove themselves from my presence. One or two did not bother to conceal their hostility.

'If you don't like it here, can go back to your own country.'

'This is my country, you bastard.'

'Get out already. Who invited you, anyhow?'

'That's just what you'd like, isn't it? Well, let me tell you something, I am not going anywhere. We're here to stay!'

Later, I watched from the back doors as Hasan and Wadida took their newborn son to the front of the community hall. The little boy looked up, blinking sleepily with eyes fresh to the world, surrounded by his two older sisters and his parents, his parents who in turn were encircled by their parents; their in-laws, their uncles and cousins and kin, their neighbours, colleagues, classmates, their good friends and old friends, the Merhaban and the well-wishers and the plus-ones, all gathered round the little family, enveloping them in a great formless huddle while the Imam Musa stood before the assembled gathering and recited a solemn passage from the Quran, looking down on the child; Ahmad Azmin, son of Hasan, son of Muhammad Yahaya bin Budiarto, a line of sons unbroken.

I watched from the back of the hall, ready to stare down any who would dare challenge my presence, but nobody bothered to look back, there were none who cared enough to, and before the ceremony ended, I snuck out to my car and got in and drove away.

Twenty-two

I sat hunched over my desk in the study upstairs. The latest proposal sat before me, the document's orderly rows of neat type-faced print now overrun with frantic red annotations. I took off my reading glasses and rubbed my eyes. My mother knocked on the door, entering with a bowl of rice and salted fish.

'You missed dinner again, boy.'

'I am working, Ma. There's always work to do. Too much.'

'Well, we can be thankful for that.' She nodded at the food. 'There's broth downstairs too, if you want.'

I cleared some space on the desk and began to eat. Looking up, I said:

'The children been fed?'

'They're fine. They've been fed.'

I pushed a warm mound of rice into my mouth and continued pouring over the documents. After a moment, I glanced across at my mother. She was sitting on a corner of the desk, watching me silently.

'What's the matter?' I said.

'Nothing. I'm simply sitting.'

'I'm busy right now, Ma Ma. I have deadlines. On top of everything else, there's this new government tender Mr Yeung wants me to look over. It's never-ending.'

'If you have to work, then work. Who's stopping you?'

I went back to my files, continuing to eat while going over the document, alternating between the chopsticks and the pen. Outside, the sun was already sinking beyond the horizon, but the last traces of evening light reached the into room so that my mother's shadow fell across the pages before me.

'What?' I sighed. 'What is it? Who can concentrate with someone lurking over their shoulder this way?'

'If you must know,' she muttered. 'It's about your wife.'

I scribbled out a hasty note in the margins of the document, nodding absently.

'Look at me when I talk to you, boy. Did you hear me? It's time you did something about that wife of yours.'

'Not this again lah, please. Did you really come up here to bother me about this again? You two cannot just get along?'

'Do you have any idea what she gets up to when you're at the office? Once Rosalind's at school, she simply disappears for the rest of the day. Just like that, without a second thought. The little one used to cry and cry when she left the house, but it's gotten so bad the boy hardly even notices when she's gone now. What kind of a mother is that?'

I rubbed my temple. 'I'll talk to her.'

'Don't you ask yourself where she goes all day?'

'I'll talk to her about it, Ma Ma. First thing in the morning.'

My mother got up from the desk and glared at me. She strode over to where I was working and reached over and, one by one snatched all the files and folders out from under me. She tossed the papers aside and then looked at me for a long moment. When she finally spoke, it was in a subdued manner:

'It's not your fault. You've been too busy to notice.'

'Notice what?'

'You leave her alone too often. She's still a young woman.'

I looked at her. 'What's that supposed to mean?'

She pursed her lips, on the verge of saying something, then paused. She frowned at me.

'What? What are you trying to say?'

'She's been going to see your cousin. Two, sometimes three times a week. When you are at work.'

I laughed. 'She's been going to see Kin Chew?'

'You think I am lying?'

'I think you let your imagination run away with you.'

'I want to show you something.' She went over to the window behind the desk and beckoned to me. 'Come. See for yourself.'

From the second-storey study window, I could see into the little park across the street. Two distant figures were just about visible in the evening gloom, seated beside each other on a bench beneath the tamarind tree.

'Who's that?' I said. 'Is that June?'

'And your Sam Ji,' she said, shaking her head. 'They've been out there almost an hour now.'

'So what?'

'Every other night, the pair of them have been sneaking out after dinner. For nice long walks together. You haven't been paying close enough attention.'

I turned to her, confused. 'What does that have to do with anything?'

'Are you blind, Ah Tat? It doesn't occur to you what those two would have to say to each other in private? The kind of secrets they would share? There's only one person they could be discussing.'

I looked out across the park. The figures of the two women had become indistinguishable from the greater silhouette of the tamarind tree, subsumed in its great shadow in the dwindling light.

'Open your eyes, boy. They're talking about Kin Chew. Your wife's been going off to see him and your Sam Ji knows all about it.'

'Nonsense.'

'You don't know your aunt like I do. You think of her as this harmless, doddering old fool. But her manoeuvring is almost invisible, like a snake in the grass. She may be fond of you, it's true, but she will never take your side where her own son is concerned. Don't you know what people are like? They protect their own, first and always.'

'Enough, Ma. Stop it.'

'Listen to me,' she insisted. 'You worry about some war brewing in the rest of the country, checking the newspapers and TV programs every day? Let me tell you, there's a war in your own family you can't even see.'

I tried to brush her aside, but she slapped me across the face and took my hands into hers and pressed the tangle of fists and fingers to her breast, glaring at me ferociously:

'And to think. You took her into your own household all these years, when her own son neglected to care for her. Who can conceive of such treachery? No wonder you don't see what's before your very eyes.'

* * *

The following day I told June I'd been called away to oversee the work on some new machinery at a site out in Puchong and would not be getting home until late that night. Then I got in the Mercedes and drove out to Bangsar, to the top of Bukit Bandaraya where all the new condominiums were, and parked the car in an adjacent block, continuing the rest of the way on foot. I found the perfect spot right across the street: inconspicuous, but with a clear view into the back of Kin Chew's apartment building.

I waited.

At around ten o'clock, our Mitsubishi pulled into the lot. I watched the station wagon reverse into the space behind Kin Chew's black Jeep and a sick feeling seized me in the gut. June got out and stopped to talk to a group of children who were playing in the courtyard. She was smiling and laughing and wearing a bright yellow dress I'd never seen before. Then she disappeared into the stairwell, emerging a moment later on the fourth floor. She knocked at Kin Chew's door. The door opened, she smiled and stepped inside. Then the door closed behind her.

I stood there, paralyzed.

I watched people wander in and out of the building all morning: an elderly couple carrying up some groceries, a postman feeding the bank of letterboxes; moving trucks and cleaners and young mothers with their babies. I stood across the street the whole time, pacing up and down the sidewalk, an entire pack of cigarettes smoked into ash, my throat afire.

Kin Chew and June emerged from his apartment later that afternoon. Despite everything, I ran and hid behind a large skip bin parked by the kerb. He was carrying her handbag and the two of them went down to their vehicles together and kissed and got into separate cars: KC in his black Jeep, June in the Mitsubishi. Just as I thought he was going to drive away, Kin Chew flung his car door open and ran laughing to the window of the station wagon, holding out June's handbag. He passed it to her through the window and they kissed again. Then they each took off.

June happened to drive right past me as she left. I stood in the street like a fool, watching her disappear into the traffic on the main road. She'd been singing and her hair was wet.

* * *

The following week, I went to see Kin Chew.

On the way over, passing through the suburbs of New Bangsar and Pantai Hills, I noticed rows and rows of old-style shophouses had been cordoned off in the main district, marked for demolition, with massive billboards depicting a modern-looking plaza looming over the site. Above roared the Bangsar Bypass, vehicles pouring along the overpass in a steady stream of headlamps that arced across the city night like a relentless meteor shower. I felt in that moment that I no longer recognized Kuala Lumpur.

Following the road up to Bukit Bandaraya, the surroundings once more slipped into darkness, and I turned into Kin Chew's block at the top of the hill. As I drove into the courtyard, I could see the light on in his flat. I parked behind the Jeep and went upstairs and knocked at the door. He answered in his underwear.

'Ah Tat?' he said, peering out into the night behind me. 'What are you doing here?'

'Expecting someone else?'

'What? No,' he looked at me for a moment. 'Come, come in. It's been a long time since you dropped by, that's all.'

I stepped inside, removed my shoes and followed Kin Chew into the apartment. Straight away, it struck me that the place looked different. Gone were the taped-up boxes in the corridor, the overfull ashtrays, and loads of unironed business shirts piled on the couch. The sitting room was now neat and well-ordered. Kin Chew told me to sit and went down the hallway to put on some clothes. As I looked around it occurred to me that, in fact, the apartment seemed a little too tidy; a little too tastefully decorated. I began noticing small details that had escaped my attention at first: the embroidered curtains and batik slipcovers on the cushions; a decorative throw blanket draped over the couch. Pewter antique figurines on the bookshelf. There were even flowers on the mantel and in the kitchen. Kin Chew shouted at me from his bedroom:

'Actually, I am glad you stopped by, Ah Tat. I have been meaning to talk to you for a while now.' He reappeared in the sitting room a moment later, dressed in a robe. Turning off the television, he sat down next to me and lit a cigarette. 'There's something important we need to discuss.'

'Your flowers,' I said. 'They're fresh.'

'What?'

'The flowers. Up on the mantelpiece. I just noticed they're fresh, not fake ones.'

He looked at the mantel and then turned around and looked back at me. 'Right, I guess they are. Why?'

'You got them in the kitchen too. Fresh ones. Somehow, I just can't picture you buying flowers. Taking care of them. Changing the water, all that.'

'Is everything alright with you, Ah Tat? You seem a bit strange.'

'Me? I'm fine.'

'Good. Listen, we need to talk. Our situation is getting critical here. Where did I put that file?'

There was a large stack of documents heaped haphazardly on the coffee table in front of him and he started going through the pile, sorting through the binders one by one. Finally, he pulled out a thick sheaf of papers.

'Ah,' he said. 'Here it is.'

He handed the file to me.

'Have you had a chance to finalize this transfer of ownership? Mr Yeung needs you to sign the papers right away so we can get the ball rolling. He's getting impatient.'

I casually flipped through the document. 'The old man's waiting, is he?'

'It's been close to two years now you've been delaying. I know it's no easy thing, signing over your company. But it's time to move forward now, Ah Tat. Mr Yeung told me he talked to you and it's all been agreed. You just need to sign the papers.'

I put the document on the armrest beside me.

'No problem,' I said. 'First thing tomorrow I'll get Terrence to come with me to the lawyers. We'll get them to finalize the details. You can tell Mr Yeung he'll have the agreement by the end of the month. I'll sign it.'

Kin Chew looked at me for a moment. 'You will? You'll sign?'

'I'll sign.'

'By the end of the month?'

'That's what I said.'

KC continued to watch me.

'You are certain, Ah Tat, that you'll sign? If I tell Mr Yeung to expect the documents by the end of the month, then that's exactly when he'll expect them. End of the month.'

'Tell him the twenty-eighth.' I drummed my fingers on the cover of the document. 'What's the matter Kin Chew? You look surprised.'

KC sat back on the sofa and let out a long sigh. 'That's fantastic news, Ah Tat. I am so relieved. You're doing the right thing.'

'You got anything to drink back there?' I said.

'Yes, of course.' Kin Chew leapt to his feet and hurried off to the kitchen. 'What am I thinking? We should celebrate.'

I could hear him rummaging through his cupboards, the doors opening and closing as he continued talking across the room:

'It's perfect timing as well. There's some new land the government recently cleared for logging next year. Mr Yeung got connections with the company putting in one of the tenders, some up-and-coming outfit based in Johor Bahru. Where did I put those damn brandy glasses? He thinks we got a good chance of landing a contract to equip those fellows with the new machinery. It's looking good.'

Kin Chew reappeared holding two glasses and a bottle of Cuseniers'. He set them aside and then started clearing away the files and documents that were heaped on the coffee table, making space for the drinks. As he was shifting things around, one of the piles of paper toppled off the edge of the table, splaying loose leaves across the floor, and he swore and crawled over on all fours, trying to reorder the pages. Kin Chew's pistol had been lying underneath some of the documents and now sat in plain sight before me. I leaned across and picked it up.

'You leave this thing just lying around?' I said.

KC looked up from the floor, his hands full of sheets.

'Oh, that. Careful with that, Ah Tat. It might be loaded still. Old habits, you know.'

I turned the pistol over in my hands, feeling its weight, and then held it up and pointed the gun at Kin Chew. He had his back to me and was ferrying the documents over to a bookshelf in the corner of the room, saying:

'I got to say, Ah Tat, I am a little relieved to hear you finally agree to this whole deal. The only reason Mr Yeung let you delay so long was because I am your cousin. I kept assuring him, don't worry Mr Yeung, don't worry. He'll sign over in the end. Ah Tat will sign.'

KC gathered up the drink glasses in one hand and the bottle of brandy in the other, still chatting away:

'But all the while, in the back of my mind, I was starting to get the feeling you were going to back out for some reason.'

He stopped when he saw that I was pointing the gun at him.

'What are you doing?' he said.

'Nothing.'

'Careful you don't slip, Ah Tat.'

'Slip? No. I won't slip.'

We looked at each other for a moment.

I lowered the barrel and placed the pistol back onto the table. Kin Chew smiled and held out one of the brandy glasses. I took the glass, and he filled it with an inch of the dark liquor.

'I'm not sure why I thought you would renege on the deal,' he went on. 'Must have been nerves lah, on my part. I don't have to tell you what kind of disaster that would have been. For the both of us.'

'Yes, well. You can tell the old man he'll have his company soon enough.'

Kin Chew poured his own glass and sat back against the couch.

'This is really going to make us,' he grinned. 'Who would have thought? Me, chairman. I only wish Ba Ba was still around to see it.'

'You've come a long way.'

'We both have.'

I took a sip of the brandy and looked at Kin Chew. I couldn't recall the last time I had seen him so chatty; he looked like his old childish self, brimming with happy mischief. I said:

'You're probably wondering why I showed up out of the blue tonight.'

'What is it, Ah Tat?'

'I been thinking more and more about the old days lately. Back when we were seventeen, when you were running around with the Hokkien Society Boys on Foch Avenue. Remember that little dosshouse in Chow Kit?'

Kin Chew looked away thoughtfully. 'In Chow Kit? There were so many places.'

'It was around the time the police wanted to pull you in over that incident. Beating the fourteen-year-old in the eye with a brick.'

'That was over the line,' he sighed. 'I was too young lah, too angry. I regret that.'

'The police almost caught you too, remember? But you got away, like you always do. By the skin of your teeth. The inspector showed up at the dosshouse one day after you cabut.'

'Where is this going, Ah Tat?'

I got up from the sofa and went to the window, pulling aside the curtain and staring out on the darkened courtyard below. I turned back and looked at Kin Chew. He was watching me.

'I never told you,' I said. 'But it was me.'

'What was you?'

'I was the one who told the police where you were hiding.'

Kin Chew looked at me for a moment and frowned. 'That was a long time ago, Ah Tat. I'm sure you had your reasons. To tell you the truth, I barely remember anything from that time, so it's all water under the bridge as far as I'm concerned.'

'The thing of it is. It never occurred to me to ask myself how you knew to get away. In the nick of time too. I always assumed it was plain coincidence. But it wasn't, was it? Somebody tipped you off.'

'Are you sure you're alright, Ah Tat? You been acting strange all night.'

'There was only one person I ever told about sending the police in after you. She must have come to you, even after we were together. I know now. You can say it.'

'Say what, Ah Tat? I'm not sure what you're talking about. Honestly, the old days are a blur to me now. What's this all about?'

I finished the rest of my brandy in one go and went over to the coffee table and set down the empty glass.

'I just thought you should know,' I said. 'It was me all along.'

'I hardly even remember it, Ah Tat.'

'Probably for the best,' I checked my watch and picked up the document on the armrest. 'I better be going, it's late. I'll have the lawyers finalize the proposal in the morning. Thanks for the drink.'

'You're going already? Stay and have one more. Come, Ah Tat. It's not often in life you can just sit back and savour the moment. Stay lah.'

'No,' I said, moving quickly towards the hallway. 'I am off. Things to do in the morning. Many, many things.'

Twenty-three

By the end of the month, there was no turning back. I'd spent the previous two weeks placing phone calls to various associates of mine, ensuring that my instructions were clear and that the plan would be executed to the letter. It was vital that no misunderstandings occur at the eleventh hour. Once the wheels had been set in motion, I was able to sit back and allow events to unfold at their own pace. Strangely enough, it all seemed to be coming off without a hitch. Finally, the week before Christmas, I told June I was flying out to Johor Bahru in order to finalize my dealings with Yeung Yau Yu.

'How long are you gone?' she said.

'A few days, a week at most. The old man wants me to meet some potential clients over there.'

'Alright, if you must. Will you be back for Christmas?'

'Donno. Depends on how things go.'

'Try to make it back in time, Ah Tat. The children should see their father at Christmas, at least. Where did you say you're going again? Johor Bahru?'

'That's right. Johor.'

The next day I caught a taxi outside the house and told the driver to take me to the airport.

'Where to, boss?'

'Subang, please. International terminal.'

'Aw, aw. International, no problem encik. Where you flying to?'

'Sydney,' I said. 'Australia.'

* * *

A balding, middle-aged man I barely recognized was waiting for me as I came out of Arrivals at Kingsford-Smith Airport.

'Ah Tat,' he waved. 'Lim Kin Tat. Over here.'

I laughed, making my way down the ramp through the slowly dispersing crowd. He looked about thirty kilos heavier than I remembered.

'Sonny, my old friend. Sonny Tong. How long has it been? I almost didn't recognize you after all these years. You look so different.'

'Ayah, no need to shout it out loud for the whole world to hear. I know, I know. I got fat and bald.' He wrested the suitcase from me and started wheeling it out towards the exit. 'You on the other hand, you look the same. As trim as you were back in Boy's Brigade days. How was your flight?'

As soon as we drove out from under the tremendous shadow of the terminal, the white sun shone down bright and warm on my face. Overhead, planes were continually taking off and coming in to land, their silver underbellies glinting briefly in the light, and we passed under green signboards pointing off left and right at the pleasant-sounding suburbs: Kingsgrove and Rockdale and Earlwood, then later Enfield and Croydon, the kind of British place names that had once looked over the streets of Kuala Lumpur from similar signboards, like Mountbatten, Cecil and Birch, names that Malaysians had abandoned since Independence. Sonny came off the main road and took us through the deserted backstreets. For much of the drive, we laughed and talked over one another.

'I left London, let me see, in seventy-four. Liz wanted a change of scenery after her folks passed. They were practically begging British to come over back then and she got family in Wollongong, so it was only natural. Anyway, there's more sun down here.'

'I see you never lost your accent.'

'Sure, what. Once a Malaysian, always one, isn't it?' He looked at me after a moment. 'June and the kids alright?'

'They're fine.'

'On your own for this trip, are you?'

I nodded. 'On my own.'

We continued driving through several neighbourhoods. People were in their yards, washing cars and watering gardens. Clear pristine light dappled the windshield as we passed flickering under tree-lined streets. The roads were everywhere quiet and clean. Sonny stopped at an intersection and turned to me.

'You still stay in Batu Road?'

I laughed. 'Batu Road? No lah, many years removed from there already. It's not even called Batu Road anymore. That area is all hotels and restaurants and mega malls now. KL no more got any humble little kampongs, my friend.'

'Of course, of course. I always forget how long it's been.'

'And how long is that?'

He squinted. 'Since I been back? Wah, since my father's funeral.'

'I was sorry to hear about it. I always admired your father very much. I still shop for groceries at Tong Hing Soon & Son.'

'My mother still lives in KL, with my uncles and all the *kuchehs*. She will never leave Malaysia. That whole generation will never leave. The rest of us young ones have packed up and shipped out already. Fast as we can.'

'Who can blame you?'

We drove by a series of large green fields swarming with children playing rugby on the manicured grass, the brightly coloured stria clashing up and down the park. Spectators mingled on the sidelines and a barbeque was smoking from the clubhouse.

'So, how?' Sonny said. 'What news from the mother country?'

'Don't get me started.'

'What's all this I hear about some emergency crackdown? The papers here don't give much detail. A few lines in the foreign news only.'

I sighed. 'It's true. The crackdown started last month.'

'Why? All because of that big UMNO rally, was it?'

'That's the story they keep telling us. At the time, everybody was frightened the demonstrations would spark another May Thirteen. I myself barricaded my house in Happy Garden. Got a big chain and lock for the gate. I bought a parang even.'

'That bad?'

'It could have been. In the end, Mahathir called off the UMNO rally. For the sake of public safety.'

'Sure, sure.'

'Of course, nobody expected what happened next.'

'You mean the arrests?'

'More than a hundred Malaysian citizens detained without trial.'

'Jesus, one hundred. Who? Chinese?'

'Chinese. But Malays also, and Indians. Anti-government persons loh. Anybody making too much noise. Educationists, activists. Even some UMNO members themselves were locked up. All behind bars, indefinitely.

Mahathir says it's to prevent another race riot, but anybody with eyes can see lah, it's all his political enemies behind bars.'

'Mahathir, you say?'

'He's gone power mad. Nobody will dare stand up to him after this. He even shut down a few newspapers. *The Star* is gone.'

'*The Star* newspaper is shut down?'

'Gone.'

'My God.'

I nodded soberly. 'Malaysia got itself a real dictator now. You watch. This is only the beginning.'

'Can he even do that?'

I laughed. 'You been living too long with white people, my friend.'

Sonny's home was in a quiet suburb west of Sydney; a low brown brick bungalow with a garden and a porch, one of a long row of similarly styled houses facing onto the public school opposite. The jacaranda trees that lined the street out front were in full bloom, their blossoms carpeting the sidewalk and car tops in a thin mantle of lavender rime. Sonny led me into his house, wheeling my suitcase into the guestroom, and then we went and sat on the back porch on water-stained deckchairs. His yard was overrun with dandelions and tall reedy grass, and I could feel the grass-mites hopping on and off my ankles as we talked. His wife brought out coffee and lamington cakes as we reminisced. I said:

'It hasn't been that long, has it?'

'More than fifteen years now since I last saw your face.'

'Is it truly that long?'

Sonny sighed. 'The last time I saw you was for your wedding, remember? At the Federal Hotel in Bukit Bintang. June was wearing that old-style red cheongsam, the most beautiful bride I have ever seen. How is she, by the way?'

I gazed out on his yard for a moment.

'It's still there,' I said.

'What is?'

'The Federal Hotel. Still standing. Everything else seems to have changed around it but the Federal Hotel is still there.' I sat up on the deckchair, scratching absently at my ankles now reddened with insect bites. 'Sometimes, I can look out at KL and suddenly feel like I don't recognize it anymore. But the Federal Hotel is still there.'

'MBS is still there too, isn't it?'

'Right. Methodist Boys is still there.'

He sighed. 'MBS days.'

'MBS days,' I said, nodding quietly.

Sonny laughed. 'You remember? Back then? Loitering outside that coffee shop on Foch Avenue after school. It was always the three of us: you, me and that Malay fellow.'

'Hasan.'

'Hasan, right. You remember, Ah Tat? Waiting for the afternoon bus to come in from Bukit Nanas every day. The girls from the Catholic school. My God, Ah Tat. What I wouldn't give to be sixteen again.' Sonny laughed and slapped his thigh. 'Talk about memory lane.'

I smiled and nodded, looking off into the distance. We were silent for a while. Eventually, Sonny turned to me:

'I know that look,' he said. 'You're gazing back in time right now.'

'I guess I am.'

'What do you see?'

'June. I see June.' I turned to Sonny and smiled sadly, before going on, 'And I see the headmaster, standing me up in front of the school assembly that one time.'

'Headmaster Liew.'

'To this day, I still remember what he said. He made me stand up in front of the school assembly, the whole assembly mind you, and declared in front of everyone: the future is bright. I still remember it like it was yesterday, Sonny. The future is bright, he said.'

'Good memories.'

'We have so much promise back then, isn't it?'

Sonny chuckled. 'Now look at us.'

The next day, Sonny and his wife took me on a tour of the city. We had lunch at the Royal Botanic Gardens and then strolled down to the harbour, emerging in a sunny open plaza. The famous white wedged sails of the Opera House loomed before us, each encasing a carpal of spotless black glass, and tourists were streaming up and down the marina, eating ice cream and drinking soda. The white ball of the sun blasted everything underneath it with an atomic brilliance and people meandering across the plaza were transformed into featureless black figures against the light, figures who in turn cast their own long black doppelgangers against the hot pavement so that the plaza was crisscrossed with these peculiar double-shadows, like paired clock-hands.

I took off my sunglasses and looked straight up. The sky seemed endless in Australia: a pale pellucid blue, unblemished from horizon to horizon, but for a lone lightplane weaving thin cottony lines in the sky. I peered up at the skywriting. It seemed to be spelling out

BOYCOTT

We walked along the seawall, past a small crowd gathered around a street-performer juggling barstools, past the trains coming in over the quay. It was dry and hot, but a strong breeze swept in from the harbour. I looked out on the glittering water, leaning on the sandstone blocks of the seawall. It was lovelier than even the postcards could make out.

That night we had dinner at Sonny's house. After we'd eaten, I had a shower and lay down on the bed in his spare room, turning on the evening news: their Prime Minister was riding around on the back of a utility truck with a pair of sheepdogs. I fell asleep for a few hours and woke up crying out in the middle of the night.

The room was dry and chilly and dark.

* * *

Sonny took me to the airport at the end of the week. On the drive over, we passed by a local shopping village. The milk bar and the barber were open and there was a little Lebanese grocer at the top of the road. I could hear bicycle bells ringing in the air.

'It's good here,' I said.

Sonny smiled. 'Too much tax. But yeah lah, it's good.'

We arrived at the international terminal at Kingsford-Smith airport, behind a long queue of vehicles letting out passengers. People were embracing by their cars and wheeling their suitcases up the sidewalk. A giant billboard overlooked the departures ramp,

BICENTENARY 1988 LIVING TOGETHER,

over which BOYCOTT had been scrawled in dripping crimson spray paint. I turned to Sonny.

'That's the second time I seen that already. Boycott. What does it mean?'

Sonny looked up at the billboard and shrugged. 'It's their blacks.'

'Blacks?'

'The Aborigines lah, the natives. You think Malaysia is the only place in the world got problems with race, is it?'

Sonny pulled over to the side of the road and helped me unload my luggage from the back of his car. We stood outside the terminal and embraced briefly.

'Bring June next time,' he said. 'And the kids. I want to meet the kids.'

'I know. I will.'

'And listen. Don't be a stranger. Better not wait another fifteen years before I see you next, Ah Tat.'

I picked up my suitcase and turned to leave, smiling back at him.

'I got a feeling you'll be seeing me sooner than you think.'

* * *

I touched down in Kuala Lumpur late on Christmas eve and hailed a taxi back to the house in the familiar sticky heat. As the cab sped down the highway, long dark belts of jungle-land watched our passage back towards town, but across the night-time terrain I could make out sections of Petaling Jaya, illuminated from afar by the decorations of several shopping malls, still carrying on with their holiday trading. The hot wild tropics had somehow managed to spawn a terrifying electrical forest in this little corner of the world, and I was suddenly nostalgic for the little kampong off Batu Road I had grown up in.

Closer to home, many of the houses in the Chinese and Indian neighbourhoods had their doors hung with wreaths, their balconies draped with red and green fairy lights, and throughout the drive, the presenter on the car radio was jabbering happily:

'Selamat Malam Natal! Merry Christmas to our Christian brothers and sisters out there!'

The next morning, I attended Mass with the family and afterward we all went back to the house and watched the children open their presents. June looked on with a big smile on her face.

'Look at them. Look how happy they are.' She turned to me, squeezing my arm, 'I'm glad you made it home in time for Christmas, darling.'

'Why don't we go out for lunch,' I said. 'It's such a nice day.'

'Now? We can't go out now. The kids are too excited to eat. Look at them.'

'Leave the kids to play. The two of us will go out to eat, husband and wife. What do you say?'

She turned to me, a little surprised.

'That sounds nice actually,' she smiled. 'Lunch. Husband and wife.'

The only thing open was a little coffee shop in Kuchai Lama that was stuffy and overcrowded. Tables had to be set up on the sidewalk to accommodate all the customers, and people were shuffling into the eatery, pressing up against each other behind the various food stalls. Waiters were shouting across the smoky room at the cooks, signalling with their hands over the noisy din. We sat down at one of the corner tables as soon as it became free, and I ordered two bowls of wanton noodles.

'So,' I said. 'What did you get up to while I was away?'

'Nothing special really,' she shrugged. 'This and that.'

'Is that right? Ma Ma told me you went to visit Kin Chew.'

I was watching June closely and she gave a little frown, looking away for a moment. She cleared her throat and said matter-of-factly:

'Sure, with Christmas coming I thought he might be lonely in that little condo of his. I went over to keep him company.'

'Ma Ma said you went over there more than once. She said you visited him quite a few times.'

'A few times?' She furrowed her brow as if trying to remember. 'I suppose I did go over a couple of times. You know what it's like for me, cooped up in the house with your mother all day. Sometimes I just need to clear my head.'

'I see.'

'Kin Chew humours me. He lets me complain. I probably shouldn't bother him so much. Anyhow, what about you? How was Johor?'

'I didn't go to Johor.'

'You didn't?'

'No. I went to Sydney.'

June paused for a moment and looked at me. 'Sydney?'

'That's right. Australia.'

'Australia? You went to Australia?'

The waitress brought over a serving of clear fishball broth and a short stack of plastic bowls. I rinsed the bowls out with hot water from the tea kettle and slung the excess water out onto the grimy shophouse floor before spooning some soup and fishballs into June's bowl. The waitress returned with extra servings of wantons and mee and placed my change on the table.

'I don't understand, Ah Tat. You told me you were going to Johor Bahru. What on earth were you doing in Sydney?'

'I went over to have a look. It's nice there. You would've liked it.'

I cleared some space on the table and dribbled a little soy sauce into a tiny saucer filled with cut-up chilies. I soaked a fishball in it.

'I stayed with my old classmate, Sonny Tong. You met him a few times back in school days, maybe you don't remember him. He was at our wedding. Anyway, Sonny showed me around town. It's nice over there. A nice place to live.'

I started eating.

'How come you didn't tell me you were going to Australia, Ah Tat?'

'I don't tell you everything,' I said, looking up from my bowl of noodles. 'But then again, neither do you.'

'What's that supposed to mean?'

I shrugged. 'It means you don't tell me everything.'

All across the floor, patrons were hunched over their steaming meals, dabbing perspiration from their faces and fanning out their shirts while chattering loudly. A hot wind swept into the coffeeshop and I continued eating, sweating over my bowl of noodles. I went on:

'To tell you the truth, I've been thinking of a change for a while now. I went down there to have a look for myself, to see how it would all work. I have to say, June, I came home with my mind made up.'

'Made up about what? What are you talking about, Ah Tat?'

'They need engineers over there, especially in the agricultural sector. You remember Ramesh, my old boss at Briggs? He still has some contacts in Sydney, and he recommended me for one of their projects. I went to interview for a position. They offered me the job straight away, starting early next year. They'll even sponsor my visa.'

'Wait a minute, Ah Tat. You're thinking about moving?'

'More than just thinking. Like I said, I've made up my mind already.'

'You're going to live in Sydney?'

The electric fans mounted high on the tiled walls of the coffeeshop buzzed in a slow-moving arc and one of the waiters went around misting cold water from a spray bottle at each of them.

'We,' I said.

June narrowed her eyes at me. 'What do you mean, we?'

'We. We're all moving there. The whole family.'

'The whole family? You want the whole family to move to Sydney? All of us?'

'That's right.'

A large group of people came into the coffeeshop at that point and a couple of waiters set about hurriedly clearing the bowls and empty soda bottles from the table beside us. June watched them go about their work with a vacant expression on her face, looking baffled by what I'd said. Finally, she turned to me:

'But I don't want to move to Sydney.'

'I hardly care what you want anymore.'

'What?'

'You heard me.'

I finished my noodles and pushed the bowl away. June started to say something and then paused for a moment to compose herself. She had hardly touched her food.

'Wait a minute, Ah Tat, you're being ridiculous. We cannot simply leave Kuala Lumpur. You've got a business here. That big merger with Mr Yeung, what about that? You won't leave all that behind, surely not.'

'I am not going through with the merger. I only strung Yeung Yau Yu along to strengthen my bargaining position. I decided to sell the company to someone else. Some outfit in Shah Alam. Bumiputra Agricultural Corporation, they call themselves. Bumicorp. The lawyers are finalizing the details as we speak.'

'You sold out from under Mr Yeung?'

'I never liked the idea of handing everything over to the old man. I much prefer the fellows over at Bumicorp. I expect they will be announcing any day now, or maybe early next year. It hardly matters. It's nothing to do with me anymore.'

'You sold the company?'

'I did.'

'How could you make a decision like that without discussing with me first? I am your wife.'

I laughed. 'My wife? You're my wife now, are you?'

'What's the matter with you, Ah Tat?'

I sat back and lit a cigarette, tapping the ash into the left-over soup in my bowl. June leaned over the table and snatched the cigarette right out of my hand, stubbing it out irritably on the table before tossing it away. She looked at me.

'You haven't thought any of this through.'

I reached into my pack of Pall Malls and pulled out another cigarette. I lit it.

'Actually, I've done nothing but think things through. It's all taken care of. We should be settled in Sydney sometime early next year. Everything will go smoothly, believe me. There's no need to panic.'

'I'm not panicked.'

'Good for you.'

'Why are you acting this way, Ah Tat?'

'I don't know what you mean.'

'What about Kin Chew then?' she said. 'Did you think about how all of this will affect him?'

'What about him?'

'If you sell off LKT Holdings, Kin Chew will be left out in the cold. Your cousin was depending on you, Ah Tat. He made assurances to Yeung Yau Yu. If this deal doesn't go through, it will be a disaster for Kin Chew. Did you think about any of that?'

I frowned. 'You seem to know a lot about Kin Chew's affairs.'

She paused, seeming to falter for a moment.

'Yeah lah, well. Of course, I know. We've been talking more lately.'

'Talking?'

'Yes, talking. I told you, I go over there sometimes. And we talk.'

'Is that right?' I said, raising my voice. 'You talk.'

June looked back at me for a moment. Slowly, her face started to change, her features taken over by a peculiar expression. Finally, she turned away, covering her mouth.

'How long have you known?' she stammered.

'Long enough.'

We were silent for a while. People on the next table were pretending to mind their own business, but I could tell they were eavesdropping, aware that we were quarrelling. I sat back, watching June as I finished off the last of my cigarette. Finally, she said quietly:

'So that's what this is all about.'

I laughed, shaking my head. 'Despite what you may think, June, I don't make any of my decisions because of Kin Chew. As far as I am concerned, he was never anything to me. We go about our separate lives; he does what he wants and so do I. No, I decided to sell up and leave because this country is going to hell. The children deserve to grow up in a place better than Malaysia.'

June looked at me. 'The children? You're doing this for Rosie and Kieran's sake, are you? Come, Ah Tat. I know you better than that. Who are you trying to fool?'

I went on talking over the top of her:

'Over there, they won't have to walk around with an IC card that tells them they are second-class citizens in their own country. They won't have to worry about race riots, and Bumiputra quotas at university or job interviews. When they buy a house, it will be the same price for everyone, whether they are Bumiputra or Chinese or Baba or Orang Asli or bloody Martians from space.'

June picked up a serviette and turned away, pressing the tissue discreetly to her eyes. When she looked back at me, her face had become the expressionless mask that I had so often seen in her dealings with my mother.

'Are you done?' she said flatly.

'I got plenty more to say about it, actually.'

'No, I mean are you done with your food? Can we go?'

I looked down at the empty bowl in front of me. I frowned.

'You're not going to argue with me?' I said.

'It looks like you made up your mind. Are you ready to go?'

'I guess I'm ready.'

'Good. I'll meet you at the car.'

She stood up and marched to the door.

'There's no point in arguing about it, June,' I called out to her. 'We're going whether you like it or not. You hear me? June?'

1988

Twenty-four

Of the final errands I needed to tick off my list before leaving the country, the one I was least looking forward to was selling off the Mercedes-Benz. Terrence Tan knew a lot about cars and had always been very good at all those kinds of negotiations and so I arranged to meet him at a used-car dealership in Salak South. We stood in the crowded lot under strings of pennants fluttering gently in the wind and smoked cigarettes looking out over the colourful sea of steel cartops, each with a bright banner pasted to its windshield.

'I been to Sydney once,' Terrence was saying. 'Back when May Chin and I were still together. We visited the Harbour and the Bridge. The zoo.' He shrugged.

'Not impressed ah, you?'

'No, it's nice. I like it down there. But the food's terrible. You'll miss the food.'

I nodded and flicked my cigarette butt away.

'I suppose that's true. I'll miss the food.'

A man emerged from the building at the back of the lot and came over to greet us. He was wearing a short-sleeved shirt with a brown tie, and he wiped his palm onto his trouser leg before shaking our hands. He walked slowly around the Mercedes.

'Looks in good shape,' he said. 'Let me take it for a test around the block. Then I'll come back and look under the hood. I'll give you a fair offer.'

'You said twenty-two on the phone.'

The salesman grinned. 'If it's in good condition. Maybe twenty-two.'

I grunted and handed him the keys. We watched the Mercedes roll down the ramp and turn out of the dealership, disappearing around the corner. Terrence smiled at me, shaking his head.

'You won't get twenty-two.'

We started walking idly through the dealership, passing the time by looking at some of the nicer vehicles up for sale at the front of the lot. Terrence got behind the wheel of a silver Ford, fiddling with the seat adjustment and console, and I sat in the passenger seat beside him.

'How are June and the kids?' he said. 'Prepared?'

I shrugged. 'Kids are kids.'

'And June?'

I frowned, staring out the windshield at the customers strolling around the dealership. After a moment, Terrence looked across the dash at me.

'Ah Tat? How's June?'

'June's never been happier,' I said. 'She cannot wait to leave.'

Terrence sighed. 'I suppose if you must cabut then there's no better time to leave than now. Did you read the paper? It's official. The Lord President of the Supreme Court was dismissed, plus two other judges. Mahathir's lost his marbles.'

'The country's gone to hell, Terrence. I cannot get out fast enough.'

As we sat in the cabin of the Ford, I noticed a group of Malay men appear on the far side of the dealership. All four men had long full beards and one of them was dressed in a spotless white jubah. The man wearing the jubah was leading the others along a row of vehicles lined up on the other side of the lot. I nudged Terrence.

'Look at these jokers. Where do they think they are? Saudi?'

I watched as the men milled around the vans, casually inspecting several of the Japanese models. They began drifting over towards the Ford where Terrence and I were still seated. I opened the car door and was just starting to move away when the Malays passed in single file alongside us. I smiled and nodded politely at them, one after the other, until at the very end I caught the eye of the man who was bringing up the rear. I looked at him and he looked at me and we both stopped for the briefest of moments. Then, just as quickly, we each turned away and continued as if nothing had happened, moving hastily in opposite directions. He looked completely different, having grown his facial hair out in the traditional Muslim fashion, but there was no doubt in my mind that it was Hasan. When the

group of Malays was at the other end of the dealership, Terrence turned
to me and said:

'Who was that?'

'Who?'

'That fellow.'

'What fellow?'

'That fellow lah. The one that gave you a funny look just now. Do you
know him or something?'

I frowned.

'Never seen him before in my life.'

Twenty-five

After the program had finished, I got up and stretched and switched off the television. I turned out all the lights downstairs and checked the doors were locked and went up to the bedroom. Standing before the dresser, I took off my wristwatch and placed it in the top drawer. June was sitting up in bed, watching me. We caught one another's eyes in the dresser mirror for an instant and then each turned away. I got some clothes from the wardrobe and went out and closed the door.

I changed into my pyjamas in the study and lay on the portable fold-out. The room was unrecognizable now, stripped of its furniture and curtains and picture frames. I fell asleep staring at the bare walls. Later, I was woken by a gentle tapping on the study door.

'Ah Tat, it's me. Are you awake?'

June crept inside and stood against the window. Now that the curtains were gone the room seemed eerily bright and looking at her face in the moonglow I was momentarily reminded that she was still a rather beautiful woman. She said:

'It's all happening so fast.'

'What is it, June? I'm trying to sleep.'

She turned from the window and came over, kneeling before me in front of the fold-out bed.

'What if I stayed behind?' she said. 'You could take the children with you. Start over in Australia. I know your mother would take good care of them, my babies.'

'Don't be stupid, June. No more of your theatrics, please.'

'She's more their mother than I'll ever be.'

'How much of this nonsense do I have to stomach?'

'I know, I'm sorry.' She started to cry. 'Why am I so weak?'

I rolled over in the fold-out, turning my back on June, and stared at the wall. Eventually her sobbing died down and all I could hear was her occasional ragged breath.

'He called the other day,' I muttered.

'Who called?'

'Who do you think? Kin Chew.'

June didn't say anything for a long time. Finally, she asked in a small voice:

'What did he say?'

'He said what I expected he would say.'

'What was that?'

'You want me to pass messages between you two now, is it?'

'No, you're right. Never mind. What about you?'

'What about me?'

'What did you say?'

I continued staring at the wall.

'It's you,' I said.

'Yes. Hello, Ah Tat. It's me. Don't hang up.'

'I been waiting to hear from you. I wondered if you'd have the nerve to call. I had a dream not so long ago that you telephoned. To stake your claim.'

'No. I didn't call for June.'

'No?'

'No, Ah Tat.'

'What then? What do you have to say?'

He cleared his throat. 'Truth be told, I got no idea what I want to say.'

I could hear traffic over the line. He was outside, calling from a telephone booth somewhere. The whip of wind ripped and flagged against his mouthpiece. Finally, he pressed on:

'I heard you are leaving Kuala Lumpur for good.'

'You know very well that I am. We both are.'

'Both of you?'

'Yes, both of us. Why? Did she tell you she was staying?'

'She's told me nothing, Ah Tat.'

'Don't treat me like a fool, Kin Chew. You think I don't know the two of you are still carrying on? Even now.'

He sighed and the blare of a horn sounded off, obliterating his next words. I realized then that he was at a dock somewhere and what I took to be the distant roar of traffic was actually the steady wash of seawater. The foghorn went off again.

'Where are you calling from?' I said.

'Port Dickson.'

'Port Dickson? What are you doing all the way out there?'

'Trying to get away.'

'After all these years, you still haven't changed. You ran away from your troubles when we were thirteen and you're running away now. What do you imagine, Kin Chew? Do you imagine she will came chasing after you, run off to Port Dickson to be with you? Abandon her children? Is that what you think?'

'Of course not.'

'What kind of life do you think you can provide for her? She got children lah. We have a family for God's sake. What do you have?'

'You're right. I have nothing.'

'She won't stay for you.'

'I know. She told me she can never leave you, Ah Tat. Or the children.'

'She said that?'

'That's what she said. We've broken up for good now. You don't have to worry about me interfering again. I promise. When are you flying out?'

'The eighteenth.'

'So soon.'

'Don't come looking for us, Kin Chew. Even to visit. I don't want you anywhere near her from now on. And as for Malaysia, well. I don't want to see this country ever again. So . . .'

'So?'

'So, that's it between us. I'll see you in the next life.'

His voice come out, quivering, 'How did it come to this?'

'I don't know. Search your own conscience.'

'Too many wrong turns. Too many blind alleys. Now everywhere I look there are only dead ends. Do you think it was fated from the very beginning?'

'Ha?'

'Is it that we have some say, or do you think everything just happens to us? From forces above? I used to think I was the master of my own destiny. A young man's conceit lah, maybe. Now I prefer to think somebody up there is playing chess with us. It's too painful to face up to otherwise.'

'Are you drunk?'

'I'm scared.'

'You're drunk, Kin Chew. Pull yourself together.'

'Can we say a proper farewell at least? Face to face?'

'No.'

'Meet me for dinner, Ah Tat. One last time. Just me and you. I need to say goodbye properly.'

'I told you already. I don't want to see you again.'

'There's a nice seafood restaurant out here. It's called Ah Beng's. On the waterfront.'

'Port Dickson? You're joking, right? I am not driving all the way out to some restaurant in Port Dickson. Not for you.'

'I would come to you myself but I cannot show my face in KL right now. Come to Port Dickson. We shouldn't leave things like this.'

'What's the point? There's no point.'

'Meet me, Ah Tat. Tuesday night. Will you? There are things to say.'

June was watching me quietly on the fold-out bed. She seemed to be aware that I was listening to the voices in my head. I shifted my weight, the springs underneath the old mattress groaning, and turned to my wife.

'I said I'd meet him for dinner Tuesday night. One last time. And then I never want to see him again.'

June stared out the window of the study, her face obscured. After a moment, she said:

'Will you tell him I said goodbye?'

* * *

I stood on the wharf, looking back at the strip of restaurants facing out onto the waterfront. Overhead, the night sky was clear. It was low season and the rain had come down hard earlier, sweeping through the little port town and driving what few tourists there'd been away. It was now dark and serene. I walked along the pier and then stopped to smoke a cigarette beneath the neon signage of AH BENG'S FAMILY SEAFOOD RESTAURANT PORT DICKSON, its traffic-light green reflection shimmying in the inky puddles of water that streaked the wooden boardwalk.

Ah Beng's was almost entirely empty. The only patrons in the restaurant were a party of six, all elderly, seated in a circle by the fish tanks. A wide mirror, whose purpose may have been to exaggerate the numbers in the establishment, ran the length of the room. Presently, it served only to underscore its emptiness. I sat down at one of the small side tables. Plastic models of crabs and starfish adorned the walls. The waiter came by and filled my cup with hot tea and set the kettle down on the table and waited while I flipped through the menu.

'This chili crab looks good. I heard you make it special in these parts.'

'The crab takes a little while to cook,' the waiter said.

'That's fine. I'm waiting for someone anyhow. I'll have two, one for each of us.' I handed him the menu.

The young man signalled someone at the back of the restaurant. The manager, an elegant-looking middle-aged woman who was going over some paperwork behind the bar, stopped what she was doing and came over to the table. She nodded to the waiter and the young man bowed and went away.

'You want crab?' she said.

'Is it too late? You're not planning to close soon, are you?'

'Can still make, if you want. Are you waiting for somebody?'

'Yes. He'll be here soon.'

'He?'

'Yes, he. Is there a problem?'

'No, no problem. I thought maybe you are waiting for your wife. Or a sweetheart.'

'Well, I'm not.'

She nodded. 'So, two then? Two chili crabs?'

'Yes, two.'

The manager looked at me for another moment and then nodded and left. I watched her disappear into the back of the establishment. I frowned and sat back.

Over by the register, the young male waiter was ringing up the bill for the other table. He brought the bill over to the small party on a metal plate and after they'd settled up, the old people pottered about the table for a while, gathering up jackets and purses and umbrellas, making comments about the décor and the weather and the food, before beginning their slow shuffle toward the door. When the group had finally gone, the waiter set about clearing their table. The manager came back out onto the restaurant floor. She went directly over to the young waiter and stopped him in the middle of his task. The two had a brief exchange and the waiter was sent out to the back. He re-emerged a moment later, wearing a leather jacket and motorcycle helmet. The manager walked him to the door and let him out of the restaurant, flipping the OPEN sign around so that it faced inwards, then locked the door behind him. She walked back across the floor and went behind the bar.

'Do you drink?' she called out.

I looked around. 'Who? Me?'

'No one else here but you.'

'I'm waiting for someone actually. I don't want him to think you're closed already, auntie.'

'Auntie? How old do you think I am? What do you drink?'

I turned around and looked at the front door.

'He should be here any minute,' I said.

'Don't worry lah, I'll let him in when he gets here. What do you want? Whiskey? Port?'

'Brandy.'

'Brandy?'

'Aw.'

She set two short glasses on the bar and reached for a bottle on the high shelf and poured the glasses out. Then she came over to my table and set them down and sat opposite me. She held out her glass.

'Health and prosperity.' She drank quickly.

I watched her for a moment.

'You drink with all your customers like this?'

She winked. 'Only the special ones.'

I swilled the liquor around and held the glass up to the low light and sat back and took a sip. I looked at it and then looked at her. I took another mouthful.

'This is very good,' I said.

'I know. I keep the best for the end of the day. Enjoy it, please.'

We sat in silence for a while, and she watched as I drank.

'You visiting from somewhere?' she said.

'KL.'

'I thought so. All you city folk got the same look.'

I chuckled. 'And what look is that?'

'Tired.'

'Tired?'

'Yeah, what. Can see how tired you are, soon as you walk inside. All you all, running around all-day, every-day. Then drive out here to unwind when you cannot stand it any longer. I am not complaining of course. Good for business, you lot.'

'I guess I am tired.'

'Sit back then. Enjoy the drink. Do you like it?'

'Yes. Very much.'

'I am glad.'

When I'd finished the brandy, the woman took the empty glass and went back around to the bar. She poured another glass and brought it back to my table and looked at me.

'Have another one.'

'Not right now. But thank you.'

'Trust me. You should have one more.'

I looked at it and then looked at her.

'Is something wrong?' I said.

'There's nothing wrong. Just take another drink. You don't have to pay for it.'

'I don't want it.'

She sighed and went back around to the bar.

'He's waiting for you,' she said.

'Who is?'

'Your cousin. He's waiting out the back in the kitchen.'

'He's here already?' I glanced at my watch. 'Why didn't you say sooner?'

The woman stared at me from across the room. She frowned and gave a slight shake of her head and looked down.

'There's no rush,' she said. 'Take my advice and have another drink. Smoke a cigarette if you got. When you're ready, you can go out back.'

I got up from the table. 'Why doesn't he just come out here?'

'There's no rush,' she called after me.

I went on through the dark narrow corridor at the rear of the restaurant, made narrower still by crates of dusty soft drink stacked against the wall, and carefully went down a few wooden steps that were slick with cold grease.

I emerged in a brightly lit kitchen.

Two big men were standing in the back, peering down at a very deep trough-like basin made of concrete. Water was gushing into it from an open faucet and the concrete basin was close to overflowing. The two men looked up and turned to stare at me as I came in. I called out to them, shouting over the sound of the water, splashing noisily from the tap:

'Excuse me, the woman said my cousin is waiting for me back here. Have you seen him? My cousin?'

The men ignored me. I looked around the kitchen. All the cooking equipment had been cleaned and pushed to the corners and a little table with two folding chairs had been set up in the centre of the room. Playing cards were scattered over the table.

'Sorry ah,' I shouted. 'But could you turn that racket off for a minute?'

One of the men twisted the tap closed over the basin. He turned around to look at me. Without the sound of rushing water, it had suddenly become very quiet in the kitchen.

'I'm looking for my cousin,' I said. 'Looks like me. A bit taller, one. I was supposed to meet him here tonight. You fellows seen him around?'

Both men stared back at me in silence. I was about to apologize for interrupting them and head back up to the dining area when I noticed their eyes shifting slightly. They were looking behind me. I turned around.

Piggy was standing there.

'You,' I said. 'What are you doing here?'

He was dressed in business attire, complete with suit jacket and tie, though oddly enough, the bottoms of his trousers had been folded up to his knees and he was wearing a pair of rubber flip-flops. The kitchen floor was soaking wet. Under his arm, he had a folder containing several documents and he went across to the little table in the middle of the room and set the folder down.

'Sit, Ah Tat. I've been waiting for you.'

'Why is it lah, every time I try to meet up with my cousin, you somehow got to show your face? Where's Kin Chew?'

'Late,' he said. 'You know what he's like. Always late.'

I looked at my watch.

'Well, how much longer will he be? Half an hour I've been waiting around. Bad enough he made me drive all the way out here, I got to run into you now. It was only supposed to be me and him.'

Piggy removed his jacket and draped it over one of the chairs and sat down. He acknowledged the two burly men standing behind me, giving them a curt nod, and then pointed to the other chair.

'Sit, Ah Tat. We have to talk before KC arrives.'

'What's all this about?' I said, sitting down. 'I thought I was done with you people weeks ago. As far as I'm concerned, we don't have any reason to see each other anymore.'

He forced a smile and looked at me across the table:

'There's still some business to conclude, Ah Tat. I been sent here to settle negotiations for LKT Holdings with you. It looks like there are some misunderstandings between our two parties.'

'LKT Holdings? You came all the way out here to talk about LKT Holdings? You're wasting your time. Like I told Kin Chew, the company's been sold to Bumicorp already. The paperwork has been filed.'

'But you haven't heard our final offer.'

'Final offer? It's too late for that. LKT is sold. It's gone.'

Piggy frowned and glanced over my shoulder at the men standing by the concrete basin. One of them had rolled up his sleeves and was now casually running his arm through the foot of water in the trough. He was looking at Piggy and something seemed to pass between them.

'Didn't you hear me?' I said. 'LKT is gone. It's done.'

Piggy shook his head. 'Nothing is done. Not until Mr Yeung says it's done.'

'This is going nowhere,' I sighed. 'Where is Kin Chew? Did he send you here to try and talk me out of the Bumicorp deal? I told him, just like I am telling you, the deal is done. I got nothing more to say about it.'

'You don't need to say anything, Ah Tat. Simply listen for once. We know you didn't like our previous proposal. We understand. In fact, Mr Yeung went so far as to go away and think about things for a while. He decided to redraw the agreement. He's giving you new terms.'

'It won't make a difference. No matter how good the terms.'

'Don't you even want to know what they are?'

Piggy opened his folder and picked out a tabbed document. He pushed the open page across the table at me.

I crossed my arms, turning away. 'You have my answer.'

'Very well. Let me save you the trouble of reading it then. Mr Yeung graciously decided lah, since you clearly got so much distaste for us as partners, he will let you leave the company altogether. You will now be paid out in one lump sum.'

'It's like talking to a brick wall. Can you not hear anything I am saying?'

Piggy continued, undeterred. 'You see this figure? This one here? That's Mr Yeung's final offer.'

I glanced down at the document despite myself. Leaning in closer, I looked at the page carefully, scrutinizing the print. Then I looked up at Piggy.

'What's the meaning of this?' I said.

'It's quite generous if you ask me.'

'Generous? That's less than half the amount I agreed to sell to Bumicorp for. Is this some kind of joke?'

Piggy levelled his eyes at me and very slowly shook his head.

'This is no joking matter, Ah Tat. Now listen carefully. Under the terms of the new arrangement, full control will pass to Mr Yeung. LKT Holdings will become a subsidiary of Yeung Yau Yu Multi-Purpose Enterprises. And since you will be leaving us, Mr Tan will take your place as managing director.'

I laughed. 'Terrence? Terrence will make a terrible director. This is a waste of my time. Where's Kin Chew? He put you up to this, didn't he? The bastard.'

'You still don't understand,' Piggy smiled. 'Two years we've been waiting for Kin Chew to sort this mess out. Two years, wasted. Delays and delays. I could have told Mr Yeung long ago that KC cannot be relied on to make this deal go through. No, Ah Tat. Thanks to you, KC is no longer in charge of anything. You deal with me now.'

'You?'

'Correct.'

'You are the last person I would ever deal with. Besides, why on earth would I sign anything so against my own interests? You don't seem to understand even that much about business.'

'It is you who do not understand, Ah Tat.'

'If you think I am signing that, you're even more stupid than you look, Piggy.'

'What?'

There was a brief pause in the conversation as Piggy looked over at the big men standing behind me. They stared back, sober, and expressionless. Both were standing very still.

'Did you hear what he just called me? He called me Piggy.'

I put my hands up slowly.

'I didn't mean to call you that. It just slipped out.'

Piggy closed his eyes and sat there for a moment, pinching the bridge of his nose. Then, quite abruptly, he brought his fist down onto the tabletop, striking the surface with tremendous ferocity and I half jumped out of my seat and stared at him. His face was bright red.

'Mr Yeung is always saying I got to control my temper. He says if I am to take over certain duties, then I must learn to control myself better. But you see, Ah Tat, we are business associates now. It's not appropriate for a business associate to call me by that name.'

'You're right,' I said. 'It's disrespectful. I won't call you that anymore.'

His eyes flashed at me.

'You know, Ah Tat. You say I don't know the first thing about business. And maybe you're right. Maybe I don't know how to charm people to get what I want. Maybe I am not so good with numbers. With management, all that nonsense. Okay lah, I admit it. But on the other hand, Mr Yeung says business is actually about knowing people. And that's one thing I do know. I know people.'

I stared at him as he went on:

'What they want, how much they will risk. What they're afraid of. You see, Ah Tat, if you know how to frighten people, you can get them to do many things. For instance, I look at you and I ask myself: what is it that you are afraid of?'

I swallowed.

'I am asking you, Ah Tat. What frightens you?'

'I don't know.'

'How strange. Something so simple, you don't even know about yourself. I got some ideas about it myself.'

I pushed my chair out from under the table and stood up.

'I think I want to go now.'

Piggy glanced beyond me.

As I took a step back, I bumped into one of the big men who was suddenly standing right behind me. He seized me by the arms, pinning my elbows to my sides, and forced me back down into the chair. I tried to squirm free, but he squeezed his arms together and they were like steel bars, and I felt my left shoulder pop out of its socket and I cried out but the cry only emerged as a weak little whimper. Someone had turned the faucet on again and I could hear the water being blasted into the deep trough, splashing over the lip of the basin and onto the floor. The second big man appeared at my side, stretching out a length of fishnet from both ends as if testing the nylon. He was on the verge of slipping it over my face when I said:

'No, please.'

Piggy held up a hand.

'Wait,' he said.

I started crying and the three men watched me and waited. I looked up at Piggy with tears running down my face.

'Don't do this. You can't.'

He said:

'You've never been very bright, have you, Ah Tat? Your type is always the most difficult to deal with. Too stubborn to bend. Too stupid to read between the lines, got to spell everything out for you. It's simple lah. Agree to Mr Yeung's terms or go headfirst in the trough.'

I struggled lamely against the steel arms holding me down.

'Whatever you want,' I said. 'I'll do whatever you want. Where are the papers? I'll sign, I'll sign.'

Piggy picked up the document and slapped it on the table before me. The large man released my arms and I fell to the kitchen floor, now overflowing with water, clutching my shoulder. Piggy threw a pen at me. I picked it up, shaking uncontrollably, and raised myself to my knees to sign the agreement.

'Careful now,' Piggy smiled. 'You're getting the pages wet.'

When it was done, the two big men packed up and let themselves out the back door, chatting between themselves as if nothing had happened. Piggy lingered behind, staring at me as I knelt on the floor and nursed my shoulder.

'One other thing I forgot to mention,' he said. 'Kin Chew drowned this morning. Out in the port.'

'What?'

'An accident, you understand. My colleagues, Frankie and Peter, they took him fishing out past the Yacht club at dawn. Somehow, he managed to get dragged underneath the boat, all tangled up in the fishnet. They tried to help him, but it was dark. There was nothing to be done.'

'Drowned?'

'Such a tragedy, really. This sort of thing is happening all the time out here. It's these damn unsecured nets lah, a real hazard. What can you do? It was a terrible accident.'

Piggy came over and crouched down so that he could look me in the eye.

'Now be very careful about how you answer this next question, Ah Tat. What was it again?'

I crawled away into a corner of the kitchen.

'I didn't hear you, Ah Tat. I want to hear you say it.'

'A terrible accident,' I howled. 'It was a terrible accident.'

1997

Twenty-six

After lunch I decided to take the long way home. Cruising past the old landfill site, I looked out the car window at the construction of the new modern-looking sports complex with its walls of green glass and modish architecture, rapidly displacing the great hills of trash that had once filled the area. Posters with COMMONWEALTH GAMES KUALA LUMPUR 1998 covered all the high boards that fenced off the lot and the driveway leading up to the work site was lined with Malaysian flags. As I continued through to Happy Garden, I could see the new expressway also taking shape. The district had been cleared of forty-foot palm trees and they now lay felled by the roadside, their ancient trunks chain-sawed into round sections, ready to be carted away.

When I got home, I parked in the driveway and brought the groceries with me into the house.

'I'm back,' I called out.

I went to the kitchen and filled the kettle and started unloading the groceries onto the counter. Then I opened the fridge and transferred the medicine from a shopping bag to the shelf on the fridge door. I took out one of the cold vials and shook it and went to the pantry to retrieve a fresh syringe.

'Are you awake? It's one in the afternoon. Time for your shot.'

I went out to the sitting room.

'Where are you?' I called out.

Sam Ji wandered slowly down the stairs at the sound of my voice.

'There you are,' I said. 'You should be careful going up and down the stairs with your hip. What were you doing up there anyway?'

'I was looking for my hair colour,' she frowned.

'You've run out, remember? I went to the shops just now to get you some more. Here, sit down, Sam Ji. It's time for your shot.'

The old woman smiled and patted me on the hand as she shuffled off to the sofa. I went to sit beside her and carefully drew out several units of insulin. She unbunched her blouse, lifting the thin material to expose her belly, and I leaned in to administer the dose.

'Have you eaten?' I said.

'Not yet.'

'Well, I've got some food for you. That hawker place you like in Kuchai Lama finally closed down. But there's a new place now. Golden Temple Sushi. It's Japanese.'

'Oh, Japanese. That's nice.'

'I had noodles there for lunch. Ramen, it's called. Like their version of mee. I brought some home for you to try.'

Sam Ji nodded and looked back at me vacantly.

'It's Japanese,' I said.

She smiled.

'Oh,' she said. 'Japanese.'

We sat at the dining table together and I brought her a cup of tea and unpacked the takeout for her, watching as she prodded the strange noodles with her chopsticks. After a couple of small mouthfuls, she seemed to lose interest and pushed the bowl away.

'What's the matter? Don't you like it?'

'It's fine. I'm just not very hungry at the moment.'

'Have a little more to eat,' I said, nudging the bowl of noodles towards her. 'You'll feel better afterwards. You know what happens if you don't eat enough after your shot.'

When she was finished with her lunch, I cleared the table and made another pot of tea. We sat there in the dining room together, sipping quietly at our drinks and listening to the sounds coming from the street: the birds, the rumble of a school bus pulling up to the stop at the bottom of our hill, laughing schoolchildren passing the house. Sam Ji was frowning at her cup of tea.

'It's so quiet here with just the two of us now.'

'Yes,' I said, glancing absently around the room. 'I suppose it is rather quiet these days.'

'You should think about marrying again, Ah Tat. Bring some life back into this big empty house. It's not too late to start again, you know.'

'Maybe,' I smiled. 'Something to think about.'

'Have some more children. You're still a young man.'

'I don't feel so young anymore, auntie.'

'Nonsense,' she said. 'There's still time.'

I smiled half-heartedly and shrugged, staring at the walls. Overhead, the roar of a jet plane momentarily filled the house before receding into the distance. The sound of birds gradually returned once more. Sam Ji sat back and let out a great sigh.

'I miss your mother,' she said.

'You do?'

'You sound surprised, Ah Tat. Of course I miss her. It feels like one half of me is gone, now that she's passed on.'

I sat up, looking at my aunt. 'I'm shocked. I always thought you hated each other. Constantly quarrelling and stepping on each other's toes. Even when I was small, I remember thinking the house was never big enough for the two of you.'

'I can't argue with that. We were very different people, your mother and me. But in the end, we were sisters.'

'Well. Almost.'

'Almost? Whatever do you mean, almost?'

'You weren't true sisters.'

Sam Ji frowned to herself, as if considering the comment.

'True enough,' she replied simply.

We sat for a while longer, glancing up at the wall clock every now and then and taking small sips from our cups of tea. Eventually, Sam Ji pushed herself out from the table and got to her feet.

'Look at us,' she laughed. 'Just wasting the day away. We must be careful not to get lost in our daydreams. Now, do your old aunt a favour and check the upstairs bathroom for me. I was planning to colour my hair today, but I can't seem to find any dye.'

'I got you more dye from the shops, remember? It's in the kitchen with the rest of the groceries.'

She looked at me and sighed, shaking her head.

'Oh yes, you told me that already.'

* * *

The telephone rang as I was coming out of the shower, and I answered in my towel.

'Hello?'

There was a brief pause on the other end of the line, like the sound of air slowly shifting in an empty tunnel, before someone replied in a faraway voice. It must have been a long-distance call.

'Hello, Ah Tat.'

'Who's that? Speak up a bit lah. I can't hear you so good over this line.'

'Ah Tat, it's me. It's June.'

I gathered the towel around my waist and sat down dripping next to the phone. I switched the receiver to my other ear.

'June,' I said. 'This is a surprise.'

'What time is it over there? I hope I haven't called too late.'

'No. No, it's fine. It's not late at all. Is everything alright?'

'Yes. Everything is fine. How are you, Ah Tat?'

'Oh, you know me. Same as always. How are the children?'

There was a slight delay over the connection and for a moment we kept interrupting each other.

'I wasn't expecting.'

'The children are fine. They're fine. What?'

'I said I wasn't expecting to hear from you until March.'

She paused for a moment, letting the conversation settle into its new, stilted rhythm:

'Yes, that's why I'm calling. There's been a change of plans, Ah Tat. I'm sorry but it can't be helped. I thought I'd better call you early to let you know.'

'Change of plans?'

'I'm sorry but we won't be able to come visit you this year. It's the kids, you see. Something's come up. A couple of things, actually. I thought I should call you early to let you know.'

'You're not coming?'

'Not this time, I'm afraid. Rosalind's going to be busy this year. She's planning a road trip with her friends during Easter break. They'll be away a couple of weeks early April.'

'A road trip? Can't she do that some other time?'

'Well, I told her you'd be alright with it if she went with her friends. It's the last chance she has to holiday with them before final semester starts. After that she'll be starting at the academy. You understand, Ah Tat. She's got her own life now.'

'I see.'

'You're disappointed.'

'No, no. It's fine.'

'I know how you look forward to seeing them.'

'But you and Kieran can still fly up to see me, can't you?'

'That's the thing. It's the start of the football season, you see. Gary promised he'd take the boy to the opening game. Kieran's very excited about it.'

'A football game?'

'You're disappointed.'

'Wait a minute, I don't understand. Kieran loves coming to KL. We had all that fun at the caves the last time he came. Don't you remember? With the monkeys. Put him on the phone, June. Let me speak to him.'

'Don't make this difficult, Ah Tat.'

'Did you ask him? Did you even ask him what he wanted to do? Put him on the line. I'll ask him myself.'

'I don't have to ask him. I know already. He wants to go to the game with Gary.'

I stared at the telephone cradle for a moment. I was still wet from my shower and a couple of droplets fell from my hair onto the plastic apparatus. I watched them land with a little tap, tap, and then sat back and closed my eyes.

'Ah Tat? Ah Tat, you still there?'

'Yeah lah, I am here. Still here.'

'I promised myself I wouldn't get into an argument with you. The last thing I wanted was to get into an argument. Look, I'm sorry.'

I cleared my throat.

'It's fine,' I said. 'You caught me off guard, that's all. Don't worry about it, June. Thanks for letting me know early.'

'You sure you'll be alright?'

'I'll be fine.'

'What will you do, Ah Tat?'

'You mean for Ching Ming? I don't know. I guess I'll just have to go on my own.'

'You'll hardly be on your own. You'll take your aunt. And Siew Mooi and her family always visits the cemetery with you, don't they? There are the twins as well.'

'The twins aren't coming this year.'

'What about your brother then?'

'Ah Di never shows up to these things. Look, I just got out of the shower. I'm dripping wet. Is there anything else?'

'Don't be like that,' she sighed. 'This was always going to happen. They won't be children forever. Time to start learning to let them go, don't you think?'

I laughed, shaking my head.

'Let them go? I feel like I never truly had them in the first place. And no, before you say anything, I am not blaming you. I'm not blaming anyone but myself. It's just that they're like strangers to me now. I keep having these dreams where Kieran doesn't recognise me anymore. And Rosie can't understand anything I'm saying. Like I'm speaking another language or something.'

'Oh, Ah Tat.'

'Listen to me go on. I guess I am a little disappointed, after all. Never mind. They got their lives over there. I understand.'

'I know how hard it is for you around April. I wish we could be there for you.'

'It's fine. I'll be fine.'

'I am sorry about this, Ah Tat. Maybe next year.'

'Yeah lah, you'll come next year. Better go now, June. This call must be costing you a fortune. Tell the kids I said hi. We'll talk again soon.'

I hung up before she could say anything else.

* * *

In April I took Sam Ji with me to the cemetery for Ching Ming. I parked the car near the entrance of the grounds, by the little temple that looked as though it was on fire, with smoke floating out the windows and off the red glazed-tile roof. Sam Ji and I waited in a fog of incense for the others to arrive. My sister soon showed up with her husband and two grown sons. After making our donation to the monks we all climbed the hill together, up the narrow rocky trail and past rows and rows of gravesites until we reached the family plot. The weeds had grown long in the last year and Siew Mooi and her boys immediately went to work cutting back the lalang while the rest of us brought out pork buns and mandarins, putting them on saucers to be placed before the portraits of my mother and father. We each took turns kneeling and bowing before the headstone with three thin reeds of incense held up to our foreheads. Then we built the pyre: a pile of imitation paper money and silver foil ingots, and standing back, set the stack of paper alight. We let it burn down in silence.

Afterwards, Sam Ji went off on her own, slowly making her way to a grave on the other side of the hill. I watched my aunt from afar, the small, crooked figure tidying up around the distant tombstone, feebly sweeping the slab around it. After a while I made my own way over. When I got there, Sam Ji was kneeling before Kin Chew's portrait with her rosary, talking quietly to her son:

'Now I don't want you worrying about me, boy. Don't you worry. Ah Tat is taking good care of me.'

I got down and started cleaning up around the gravesite. For a while I became lost in the work, sweating and grunting while fighting back the lalang grass, and when I looked up again, Sam Ji was still kneeling before the headstone:

'June sends you her prayers. She couldn't come visit you this year, but she sends her prayers. She hasn't forgotten you.'

I had to look away. On the far side of the hill, other families were wandering about the cemetery, burning incense and standing over the square stone plots. Siew Mooi and her husband were among them, making offerings at her in-laws' grave. My nephews ambled about in the sun, looking out on the sprawling city below and turning their faces up to the clear warm sky.

Before leaving for the day, Sam Ji said:

'Aren't you going to say something, Ah Tat?'

I looked down at the portrait of Kin Chew set in the stone. The photograph had been cropped from an old Hokkien Association staff book and he was very young in it, barely twenty years old. He looked handsome and cocky. I got down on my knees.

'Hello, Kin Chew.'

After a moment, I stood back up.

'This is stupid. I don't know what to say.'

I took a pack of Viceroys out from my pocket. I put two cigarettes into my mouth and lit them, sipping at the filters to get them burning, and then laid one on his headstone. I stood there smoking the other until it was gone.

* * *

A few months later Sam Ji was hospitalized with a brain haemorrhage. The surgeons told me there was nothing to be done but hope for the best and so I took some time off work to be with her. Most mornings I would go by the University Hospital with some breakfast, the kind of street fare that my aunt liked to eat, and if she was feeling up to it we would sit and eat a little and talk, but she was often too weak and disoriented to do much more than drift in and out of sleep. By eleven o'clock, visitors were ushered out of the IC ward and afterwards, I would drive aimlessly around the city with no destination or purpose in mind.

On one of those afternoons I remember going down a busy road towards Jalan Cheras, lost in my own thoughts, when I found myself trapped in a particularly heavy traffic jam. Billboards for Louis Vuitton and Honda motorcycles looked down on me from above and I sat in the car, crawling towards the Tesco and the mega-mall. The big Proton dealership was in the rearview, high-rise condominiums and service stations surrounding me on all sides. Trying to find a route out of the build-up, I turned into a side street and unwittingly discovered the cause of the jam. A crowd of spectators had spilled out onto the road, gathering around a platform upon which several dignitaries stood congratulating one another. They appeared to be unveiling a new street sign. When I finally inched past the obstruction, I looked up and was confronted with the words JALAN YEUNG YAU YU in gleaming silver, on a beautiful new street sign. I spotted Piggy standing with the officials amidst the banners and fanfare, shaking hands and waving to the crowd.

That night I called June.

It must have been late where they were, or very early, because it sounded as though she had just woken up:

'What's wrong, Ah Tat? It's not your aunt, is it? Did something happen?'

'It's not good news,' I said. 'She went into another coma today. The doctors think it's fifty-fifty if she ever wakes up again.'

'Oh no.'

'They won't say it but I don't think she has very long.'

June sighed into the receiver, 'Poor woman. I always felt sorry for her. One hardship after the next and then one day it's all over, just like that. What a miserable life.'

'Miserable? I'm sure she wasn't miserable.'

'You got no idea what it's like to be a woman, Ah Tat. Cooped up in the home for so many years, day after day, with nothing of your own. I can just imagine it; your whole life lah, slowly seeping away, bit by bit. Meanwhile, you men go off gallivanting about the world. Things to do. People to see. Never a thought about the women you leave behind.'

'Why do I get the feeling we're no longer talking about Sam Ji?' I said.

I could sense June smiling ruefully on the other end of the line.

'I suppose you caught me projecting a little bit,' she chuckled. 'You're right. That wasn't fair.'

'No, I hear you. At least you managed to escape the same fate.'

'It wasn't that bad with you, Ah Tat. We had some happy times. And you would have made a good husband to some other kind of woman. It's just we were never really suited.'

I picked up the telephone cradle and wandered down the hallway, trailing the cable behind me. None of the lights were on in the house and I went from door to door, looking in on the dark empty rooms.

'Do you think you were more suited to Kin Chew?' I said.

There was a long pause at the end of the line.

'June?'

'You've never asked me that question before, Ah Tat.'

'I am asking now.'

'If you really want to know the truth then, yes. Yes, I think we were suited. He was the love of my life.'

She paused again and I could hear her taking a choked breath, perhaps caught by some distant memory. She composed herself immediately.

'Is that hard for you to hear?' she said.

'No. I mean, yes and no. I don't know. All the anger's gone out of me these days.'

'You're not angry anymore?'

'I guess I'm just glad he had you. He had something.'

We stayed on the phone for a while longer, chatting quietly about the children and how they were doing. I kept walking up and down the hallway as we talked and by the end of our conversation, I found myself in the bedroom we'd once shared, looking out the blinds onto the street outside. Over the phone line, I could hear the sounds of activity.

'Is that the kids?'

'It's Gary. He's got an early start.'

'He doesn't mind you talking with me for so long?'

'No, he's good like that. Open-minded. Not like a Chinese lah. Not so rigid in his ways. It's nice.'

June stifled a yawn.

'Anyway,' she said. 'It's getting late. Or early I should say.'

'Look at that. Where did the time go?'

'It's been nice talking like this, Ah Tat. I didn't expect it.'

'June? Can I ask you one last thing? Before you go.'

'What is it?'

'Do you remember a few years ago? When you came back to KL to visit that time? My parents were still around, and they took the kids off to the cinema with them—and you and me, we had that night together?'

'Where is this going, Ah Tat?' she said in a low voice, slightly irritated for the first time. 'Gary is in the next room.'

'Why did you do it? Why get into bed with me? We were already divorced. I had no expectations.'

'I don't know. I guess I felt sorry for you.'

'Sorry for me?'

'Yes, I felt sorry for you. I feel sorry for you, even now.'

'You do? Why?'

'You know why. Having his mother in the house. Taking care of her. Seeing her day in, day out. Like his ghost is still around.'

I frowned, looking away for a moment.

'I never thought of it that way.'

'Nobody expects you to carry the burden on your own, Ah Tat. I am sure Siew Mooi would be happy to take your aunt for a little while. If she recovers, I mean. Let your sister care for her. Or one of the twins even.'

'No. I don't think so.'

'It can't be good for you. Being reminded all the time.'

'No lah. Sam Ji will stay with me. I owe him that much.'

June gave a sigh. 'It wasn't your fault, Ah Tat.'

'Wasn't it? I think about the way things happened sometimes. I go over and over it in my mind, again and again. We should have been brothers. But what did we choose instead? Look how we destroyed each other. Who wins? Me, in this house of ghosts. Him, in the ground. What was the point?'

'It's true.'

'There were so many things I could have done differently. There were so many mistakes.'

'It's true, Ah Tat. And yet what is left now but to go on living?'

* * *

The following night, the strangest thing happened.

For weeks the weather had been gradually getting warmer in KL, the humidity building up day after day and culminating in storms that lasted all afternoon and sometimes into the night. It was nothing unusual for that time of the year, being the monsoon season and all, but then quite unexpectedly, in the middle of this run of hot rainy days, I was woken one night by an intense, almost unnatural chill. It was so cold I was forced to find a cardigan. Pulling it on over my singlet, I went to turn off the air-conditioning unit but found that it wasn't on. Outside, the delicate patter of rain that had been falling continuously throughout the night seemed to falter and I went over to the bedroom window and pulled the curtain aside. A wafery crust of frost had spread along the outer surface of the glass. I stood there, staring at the window.

'What in the world?'

Reaching out, I tentatively put my palm against the glass. It was freezing cold. I yanked up the window frame to see what was going on and leaned out over the ledge, peering into the indigo dark. Rain was evaporating right out of the air before my very eyes. The droplets were being whittled down by their plummet to the earth so that the flecks of moisture became light enough to be taken up on feathery currents, tossed sideways and upward and round and round in whorls and spiralling drifts. The white flakes were everywhere falling from the sky.

'Is it ash?' I murmured to myself, but there was no burning in the air.

I laughed and thrust my hand out to catch the soft flakes and they danced away in a swirling puff only to have others replace them in a constant steady cascade from the firmament. I looked at my hand. The tiny crystals of ice dissolved in the heat of my palm.

It was snowing in Kuala Lumpur.

For a moment, my excitement overcame me and I saw myself dashing from room to room in the house, shouting, 'Look outside! It's snowing! It's snowing!' but then realized in the very same instant that there was no one else in the house, it was only me, and that I was listening in the night for some sound, any sound, that could tell me I wasn't dreaming, and that it wasn't a dream of being alone.

Twenty-seven

Not long after Sam Ji passed away, I was driving in circles round the streets of Kuala Lumpur—on another one of my listless excursions through the city—when I found myself heading in the direction of Kampong Pasir. It occurred to me that it had been many years since I'd last ventured into the little suburb and, as I drove past the Masjid Wakaf Baru mosque, memories of the past flooded my mind's eye and seemed to take over the steering wheel. Without realizing it, I was soon parked outside a familiar-looking house, wondering whether my old friend Hasan still lived there. The upper storey had a new extension and there were fully grown trees in the front yard where there had once only been little saplings in clay pots. If indeed Hasan still lived in the house, then he had finally gotten rid of the old Datsun, as a new Proton Saga was sitting in the car space. I crossed the street and let myself in through the gate. Climbing the steps to his front door, I could hear Dangdut pop-music coming from inside the house. I knocked tentatively and Hasan answered. Upon seeing me, he lost his smile and looked rather confused.

'Ah Tat,' he said. 'What are you doing here?'

'Hello, old friend.'

He stood there, taking in the sight of me.

'It's been years,' he said. The smile had still not returned to his face.

'I know. I was just driving past your neighbourhood and thought to myself: you know who I haven't seen in so long? My old classmate, Hasan. I wonder if he still lives in Kampong Pasir. I thought I would see if you were still around. And look, here you are.'

'Here I am,' he said.

'It's a shame we don't talk anymore.'

'Yeah lah. A shame.'

I cleared my throat and looked around.

'You know, I always regretted the way we lost touch. I seem to recall some argument between us. But who can even remember what it was all about? Really, it's a shame. We used to be so close.'

He nodded, glancing briefly into his house before turning back to face me. He looked much the same as I remembered, with one notable difference.

'You got rid of the beard,' I said.

Hasan's hand reflexively went to his mouth and he rubbed his clean-shaven cheek.

'It looks better now,' I went on. 'I never liked the beard on you.'

He looked at me and frowned. Then he stepped out onto the porch, standing in such a way as to block the front door. He said:

'You say you don't remember our falling out. Well in fact, I remember quite well what happened. And it seems to me now that you haven't changed all that much. If I want to grow a beard, Ah Tat, then that's just what I'll do. And if I want to shave it off, then I'll do that too. It's complicated. The point is lah, these things got nothing to do with you.'

I put my hands up quickly:

'No, no. You misunderstand me, brother. I just meant it's nice to see your face again.'

His expression softened momentarily, and he looked up and down the street, before turning to face me again.

'What do you want, Ah Tat?'

'I don't know. I thought I would pay you a visit, that's all. Can't two old friends visit together? I have known you my whole life.'

'Things were said, Ah Tat. You cannot simply take back all that was said. You think it's so easy?'

'Maybe you're right,' I sighed. 'I don't know what I'm doing here. I'll let you get back to your family. I shouldn't have come.'

At that moment, as I was turning to leave, Hasan's young son burst through the front door, flinging it wide open and pushing past his father to get to me. The little boy seized my hand and started tugging at me in a very insistent manner.

'Did you see the snow?' he shouted excitedly. 'Did you see it, pak cik? It was snowing!'

I stared at the boy as he continued repeating at the top of his voice:

'It was snowing! It was snowing! I saw the snow.'

Hasan immediately leapt on his son, prying him away from me. The boy protested loudly for a long time, becoming more and more agitated, until finally Hasan shouted at him to behave himself and shoved him back into the house. He slammed the door on the little boy. Then he looked at me with a slightly irritated air, shaking his head apologetically.

'I'm sorry about that,' he said. 'You remember Azmin, don't you? You were at his hair-cutting ceremony when he was a baby.'

'Of course I remember Azmin.'

'The boy's got no manners. Grabbing strangers and bringing them into his silly games. He's driving his mother up the wall.'

'What was he shouting about? Something to do with snow?'

'Don't pay any attention to him.'

'Wait a minute, Hasan. He said he saw snow, didn't he?'

'Just ignore it. He's at that age where he thinks it's fun to make up stories.'

'But he's not making up stories,' I said quickly. 'I saw it too. A few weeks ago, in the middle of the night. I woke up and saw snow falling outside my house. Your boy saw it as well?'

Hasan narrowed his eyes at me.

'What game are you playing at, Ah Tat?'

'No, I promise you, it's true. I been going around myself, asking everyone I meet if they saw it, but they all look at me as if I am mad. It was only for one night, weeks ago. For a few minutes there was real snow falling from the sky, and then it was gone. Disappeared, like it never happened. I thought I was losing my mind. There was nothing in the papers about it. I even called the Meteorology Bureau in PJ but they said I was mistaken. It was impossible, they said.'

Hasan stood on his porch eyeing me closely. He seemed to think I was mocking him in some outlandish way. All of a sudden, Azmin appeared out of nowhere, racing up behind me to take hold of my hand once again. The boy must have run out the back of the house, circling around in order to reach me. He cried out:

'I told you it was true, I told you! You see, *Bapa?* It's true! Uncle saw the snow too, he saw it as well. I wasn't making up stories. I saw it and he saw it and that means it must be true. It was snowing!'

Both Hasan and I stared at little Azmin, jumping up and down on the spot in a state of profound distress. The boy was beside himself with emotion and very soon, he was sobbing uncontrollably. When Hasan went to comfort him, Azmin pushed his father away and turned to me, wailing:

'Everyone said I was lying. They called me a liar, but I wasn't lying. You saw it too, didn't you, Uncle? You saw it too. Tell them! Tell them, Uncle!'

I looked at the little boy. Tears were streaming down his cheeks and he was pleading with me to agree with him. Hasan stood there with a shocked expression on his face, staring at his distraught son. I knelt down and gathered the boy in an awkward embrace, patting him on the back as he cried into my shoulder. I said:

'Yes, Azmin. I saw the snow. It was snowing. It truly was.'

After Azmin had settled down somewhat, Hasan gently dried the boy's face and whispered soothingly into his ear. He sent the boy back indoors to be with his mother and then stood in the doorway, watching him retreat to the kitchen. Then he turned around and looked at me.

'I've never seen him so worked up before,' he said quietly. 'What do you make of that?'

'I don't know. But he wasn't making stories.'

'No. I suppose he wasn't.'

'If I hadn't seen it with my own eyes then I'd think I was pulling your leg too. It was incredible. Unbelievable, really. But what can I say? It happened.'

Hasan stepped out from under the shelter of his porch and stared up into the clear cloudless sky.

'Imagine that,' he murmured. 'The world is a strange place indeed.'

'Isn't it?'

Turning back, he gestured at his door.

'You better come inside, Ah Tat. Come, come in. Wadida's making cakes. Stay for some coffee.'

'You want me to stay?'

'Yeah lah. Come inside.'

I smiled as Hasan led me into his house. Closing the door behind us, he said, 'Are you sure? Snow? Right here in KL?'

I could hardly believe it myself.

* * *